About the Author

Sheri Kunkle

Sheri is an Artist and Designer by trade. However, her true passion is caring for the forgotten generation, the elderly. For years she has used her talents and compassion to bring joy to their lives. ***Bundles*** is her debut novel, written with two close friends. The horrific story of one of the characters in ***Bundles*** is based on Sheri's own young adult life. She and her adopted daughter live with Sheri's father, close to Pittsburgh, Pennsylvania. The adoption of her daughter was the fulfillment of a life promise and provided much of the motivation to write ***Bundles***.

Mary Lynne Lorch

Mary Lynne is a recently retired Orientation and Mobility Instructor at a school for blind children in the Pittsburgh area. Her life's work has been dedicated to her desire to help other people. ***Bundles*** is her debut novel, written with two close friends. The journey of one of the three characters in ***Bundles*** is based on her own life experiences which moved from heartache to hope. Mary Lynne and her husband are the parents of a young adult son and daughter. The stories of their lives are the inspiration for Mary Lynne's journey in ***Bundles***.

Ruth Carosone

Ruth Carosone is a Human Resources professional in the Pittsburgh, Pennsylvania area. Her personal mission has always been to help others succeed in their careers. Though she has done extensive business writing in her corporate roles, ***Bundles*** is her debut novel, written with two close friends. It is the fulfillment of a lifelong goal. The tale of one of the characters in ***Bundles*** is based on her own life experiences. Ruth and her husband are the parents of two young adult daughters who were adopted as babies and provide much of the inspiration for ***Bundles***.

Dedication

We dedicate this book to all the wonderful and terrible people who taught us that life can be dark and overwhelming, but there can be a way to find the other side and a better life. We would also like to give hugs across time and eternity to Janet Janiro, Kelly Lorch, and Loretta Murray.

Sheri Kunkle, Mary Lynne Lorch and Ruth Carosone

BUNDLES

A Journey from Despair to Hope

AUSTIN MACAULEY PUBLISHERS™

LONDON • CAMBRIDGE • NEW YORK • SHARJAH

A CIP catalogue record for this title is available from the British Library.

ISBN 9781398406810 (Paperback)
ISBN 9781398406827 (ePub e-book)

www.austinmacauley.com

First Published (2021)
Austin Macauley Publishers Ltd
25 Canada Square
Canary Wharf
London
E14 5LQ

Acknowledgments

We would like to thank our family members and friends who listened to parts of our writing, and gave us feedback and suggestions. Your support and encouragement kept us moving towards our dream of publishing this book!

Our past walks with us every day, every step of our lives.

Beginnings

Prologue

Debbie knew more about the three coming tonight than she was officially expected to know. Somehow, she had crossed a line with them, and they had shared details of horrific stories. While she finalized their official documents, her mind turned to imaginings of rape, squeaky cries, and betrayal. The three stories crossed years, entwined with other faces, survived loss, terror, heartbreak, and despair. Debbie usually looked forward to these evenings and this was no exception. She was glad that she had helped them move towards joy, but she knew their feelings were still tempered by the roads they each had traveled to reach this day.

Debbie worked as a Social Worker for an adoption agency and had evaluated the women over the past 9 or 10 months. And tonight, finally, it was time for this special evening to celebrate the upcoming fulfilment of so many dreams! Last week each woman had received a photo, the first glimpse of the baby who would become her daughter. The photo didn't come until it was time to begin purchasing clothing and supplies for the baby and to start packing. The management team at the agency knew what happened when a woman received the photo. Somehow, the parent/child connection began at that moment. The woman's instinct to love and protect her daughter would be immediate and the wait would be agonizing if not filled with crazy days of preparation for travel.

Debbie would host a dinner tonight at her home. She had made life changing judgments about the women, their husbands, their homes, their occupations. She had undoubtedly also been influenced by the visions of horrific events they had shared with her. But there were other beginnings beyond the women's own stories, the stories of the bundles that were about to intersect with their lives. Debbie knew the true beginnings of the stories of the bundles were lost. She could only imagine what it could be like to be living in China and carrying a baby that could not be. She only knew what she had been told about life in China and the circumstances that led to such difficult decisions for so many women. What Debbie did know is that three women, in relatively close proximity considering the vastness of China, took actions that altered the course of many lives, including their own and three tiny female infants. In later years, the "forever families" of these three female infants, and in time the young ladies themselves, would imagine how it happened. In their imagination, the faces of young Chinese women emerge from the shadows carrying small bundles, wrapped warmly, and full of the last milk the women could provide. The bundles are left on the steps of a hospital, on the side of a busy market street, in front of a small home, wherever a crowd would gather when the bundle began to cry. The faceless women wait and watch until the crying begins and the crowd gathers. Perhaps they join the crowd themselves, anxious to be sure that the bundle is cared for and fed, taken to a safe place, a waiting place, where she could have a chance to survive. The faces fade from the story. The pain of the women is unknown, yet unimaginable, and the reasons for the leaving of the three will never be clear.

No matter the reasons, the love that would bring the bundles to the arms of strangers WAS love that surely must have defined much of the lives of the faceless women. Did they know that their daughters were taken to a waiting place? Would they know when they left that waiting place with strangers from another country? Would they track the years as they passed and visualize their daughters as they took their first steps, spoke their first words, started school, experienced their first kiss? Would they know which language those first words were spoken in? Did they whisper prayers for good health, wisdom, prosperity for their daughters as they closed their eyes each night? Did they wonder if their daughters looked like them? Would something in their biology react to their daughters should they ever come face to face? Was there any other love that could rival the love of these women for their bundles? Did the longing for the tiny bundles ever end?

In any event, the bundles would come soon. They would come to the United States and become part of "forever families." And another beginning of the stories was with the three women who would become the "forever mothers," the three women coming to dinner tonight. Their stories carried them to the moment when the tiny bundles became theirs, when they made the commitment to the faceless women to accept the honor and assume the role of mother. They would teach and tickle. They would clothe and comfort. They would hug and encourage. They would love the bundles as no one else could love them, other than the faceless women themselves. A few minutes later the doorbell began to ring. Smiles and hugs were exchanged as Shelly, Lynne, and Lora introduced themselves to each other.

Four weeks later the women were all seated on a plane heading to China to meet their daughters for the first time. As expected, it had been a frenzied time of shopping and packing based on the information they had received about the age and weight of their daughters. The women knew very little about each other, only that life circumstances had propelled each of them to turn to China to adopt a daughter.

It would be a very long trip. First the flight from Pittsburgh to Chicago and then the flight from Chicago to Hong Kong which would take them over Alaska, across the Bering Strait and then south. Overwhelming emotions of happiness, excitement, and anxiety enveloped each of them in different ways as they tried to rest and sleep in preparation for the busy days to come. Their thoughts looked forward with hope but also looked backwards, not forgetting their paths to this day.

"I can feel how this baby will fill the void in my arms. I can't wait to hold and snuggle with her!"

"It took days to get all the shards of glass out of my back and my arms."

"Lies, lies, lies! Who was he really?"

"This will be the fulfillment of my promise to God and myself! Your mom is coming, my daughter!"

"How did such dark days of despair lead to this moment of light? Could the man sitting next to me really be from another part of the universe?"

"Would there have been a different outcome if the batteries weren't dead?"

Chapter 1

Shelly's Story, August 1984
FIRST ATTEMPT

Shelly was in a cold sweat as she propped the door open with a rock and a log, just in case she had to get back in. Next, she grabbed a flashlight and a screwdriver she could use to try to get into another cabin. She would have to find a phone to call for help. She would never be able to walk out before dark. Somehow, she thought to pull on a jacket, just in case. Beyond a certain point she wouldn't be able to come back, no matter what. She also picked up a roll of masking tape to mark her way through the woods. She might have to backtrack. The woods beyond a few feet around the cabin were unfamiliar to her. She had learned the tape technique while a young girl, having fun hiking with the Girl Scouts. Who would have ever imagined it could be a potentially critical skill under these circumstances!

Shelly ran out the door and cut across the front of the cabin. Her heart pounded, she felt short of breath, and her legs shook but she was determined. There might never be another chance like this. She remembered that during the winter she had seen the roof of another cabin across and below the road. It was summer now and the forest was so dense that she couldn't see very far in front of her. She ran through trees and underbrush as quickly as she could, in what she believed, and hoped, was the most direct route, not feeling the scratches on her legs and face. She planned to stay in the wooded area until she was directly across from the other cabin. Then she would scurry quickly across the road.

After a few minutes, Shelly could see the cabin through the trees. It amazed her that other people could be so close. She always felt so isolated, so cut off from everyone. She darted across the road, like a frightened animal, moving quickly down the hill on the other side, towards the cabin. When she saw that there were no phone lines running to it, she turned and began to climb back up the hill toward the road and his cabin, their cabin, further above. The ascent was more difficult than the climb down had been. Her feet twisted on the uneven rocks and she could now feel the scratches on her legs and face.

When she reached the top of the hill, she saw another cabin and this time risked running down the road to get to it quickly. She didn't know how much time she had. There were no lights on in the cabin, but she did see phone lines. She ran onto the front porch and banged on the door.

"Hello, hello! Is anyone there?!! Please open up! Please help me! I need help!" She screamed hysterically and gasped for breath through her blinding tears, but no one came to the door.

As she turned to run away from the door, she saw that the window of a side room was cracked just a little. She tried, with shaking hands, to pull the window open. It was stuck and wouldn't budge.

"Please, God, just help me!" She took the screwdriver out of her pocket and tried prying it open. At that moment she heard a car in the distance, coming down the road. She recognized the rumble and knew it was Todd.

Panic swept over her as she thought, "He's going to kill me! He's going to kill me! I've got to get out of here. I've got to get back."

Shelly ran as fast as she could through the woods. She couldn't risk the road again for more than a brief moment. She couldn't use her flashlight for fear he would see it. It was a race between him and her. Who would get to the cabin first?

Shelly could see Todd's cabin at the same time that she saw the headlights entering the last stretch of road. The cabin was only a few steps away! She ran to the door, threw the rock off the porch, and pushed the log out. She threw her coat and the screwdriver into a closet, jumped onto the sofa, and picked up a magazine.

She sat on the sofa, tried to quiet her pounding heart, and tried to look absorbed in the magazine, till he came in the door. He walked in slowly, with a smile on his face and said, "Why do you look so flushed?"

"Nervous, I guess. Just waiting for you to get back. You know I'm afraid of the woods in the dark."

Todd began moving, from cupboard to cupboard, drawer to drawer, to be sure everything was where he thought it should be. She held her breath, waited and dared to hope that he wouldn't know. How could he possibly know? The screwdriver!!! He found it on the floor of the closet where she had thrown it with her jacket.

She knew he saw, but for the moment ignored, the screwdriver. "Why is your coat on the floor? You know I hate to come home to a mess in this cabin." His face was frozen in the earlier smile, but she could see the slight beginning of a twist to his mouth. And his eyes began to light with what she knew was excitement, anticipation of what was to come.

He walked towards the sofa where she sat, also frozen, waiting, knowing. When he was close enough for her to feel his body heat, he bent forward, grabbed her by the ankles and pulled her off the sofa. She started to cry as he dragged her across the floor. She could feel her back burning from the fibers of the rug digging into her skin.

When they reached the other side of the room, he grabbed her by her hair, opened the closet door, and said, "What the fuck do you call this?" as he pointed to the screwdriver on the closet floor.

Without waiting for her response, he shoved her into the closet. Her head hit the wall and she crumpled down below the clothes. She looked at him, crying, shaking, and said, "I don't know."

He screamed at her, "Pick it up and hand it to me!"

She did. He grabbed it and raised it with the metal end pointing towards her. "I should use this on you right now! I guess you haven't learned your lesson yet."

Todd closed the closet door with her in it and said, "Now stay in there. You do know what you're going to have to do to make up for this, right?" Shelly didn't answer. Coiled up in a fetal position she just lay there and cried on top of her shoes and coat.

Shelly knew she had to find a way to escape or she would die. But she couldn't answer the question she had asked herself for the past 13 months. How?

Chapter 2

Lynne's Story January 1997

THE 10TH DAY

Lynne looked in the mirror and ran her hand through her short blond hair. Her eyes were dark from lack of sleep and worry. She hadn't thought to put on makeup for weeks. She didn't recognize herself like this. Her body had no energy and she literally felt she could die from the total exhaustion she had been experiencing. There were times in her life when she had been tired from her job and being a working mom, but never anything like this. And this should have been a joyous time for her and her family!

Her baby, Kelly, had been home for nine days and Lynne's fear and concern continued to grow each day. Her tiny child seemed to have more and more difficulty finishing her bottles and her cry had become different over the last couple of days, strange somehow. It was more like short chirps rather than the typical sustained wail of a healthy child. Lynne would hold her, rock her, and try to sooth her into a few more swallows from her bottle, but it didn't seem to work.

She believed it would be another sleepless night and she was right. She lay in bed for a while, half asleep, but she listened for each sound, each movement from the small bassinette. She tried to banish the fear and focus only on the love she felt for her child. The fear finally triumphed, and she got out of bed and sat on the bedroom chair. She watched each breath, each tiny twitch as her baby dreamed of who could even imagine what, perhaps of the warm, wet days when she could hear the heartbeat of her mother, and had no struggle to breath, to eat, to survive on this planet.

At some point, Lynne fell asleep and woke with a stiff neck and pounding heart. Kelly was awake also making the strange crying sounds that triggered some biological warning system within Lynne's body. Surely this cry was NOT normal!

A little later that morning, after Lynne prepared a bottle, she snuggled with Kelly on the sofa in the family room. She looked at the tiny face and hands and prayed that this time she would take more of her bottle to make her body stronger and give her what she needed to grow and develop. Her prayers weren't answered. Kelly would barely drink even an ounce of the formula and Lynne thought she looked puffy. She understood her fear could be the result of imagination and worry, but she still picked up the phone and called her husband who had already left for work.

"I'm really worried about the baby today. She didn't drink her bottle, almost nothing, no matter what I tried." Her husband was a quiet, conservative man, who didn't always show his feelings, but she knew he was just as worried.

"I think you should call the doctor. We need some answers." Lynne could hear Luke's fear building below the frustration, the almost anger, in his voice. He and Lynne were convinced that Kelly had been sent home too soon, before she was ready to be released from hospital care.

A few minutes later Lynne had an appointment to take the baby in for a check-up early that afternoon. Her husband had come home from work to be part of the meeting with the doctor. She felt better as they walked through the door of the doctor's office. Doctor Mark had been her son's pediatrician and she liked and trusted him. He smiled as he walked into the examining room and took Kelly from her arms. He placed the baby on the scale and said there had been a modest weight gain. He listened to her heart and gently probed her tiny body.

"I think she's doing well," he said with a smile. "I think everything is going well."

"What about the puffiness?" Lynne asked. "She's changed over the past few days. I think she looks puffy."

"A lot of premature babies get puffy as they gain weight. There is recent documentation, which supports this theory. I believe that she's okay. And even though she doesn't seem to be drinking a lot, she has gained weight, so I'm not concerned. She's getting more than you realize or she wouldn't be gaining weight," Doctor Mark concluded.

Luke and Lynne felt relieved as they took their baby home. However, the doctor's words didn't provide comfort for long. Kelly's difficulty drinking her bottle continued and her little cries continued to trigger Lynne's biological alarm system. Soon the afternoon turned to evening and Lynne's heart began to pound. Her instincts told her that something was terribly wrong. But they had come so far with this baby! Lynne needed to believe that the doctor was right, that Kelly was ok. She struggled to ignore her instincts and tried to focus on what the doctor had said earlier in the day and not to panic.

As the night progressed, Lynne became increasingly convinced that the doctor had to be mistaken. Everything was not ok! The doctor's reassurances were well intended but obviously mistaken. She needed to talk to a doctor now! It was approaching 3:00 a.m. but Lynne couldn't wait. Her heart pounded and she could barely breath as she picked up the phone. She dialed the doctor's office, knowing that she would connect with the emergency service.

"This is Lynne Murray. My daughter, Kelly, is a patient of Dr. Mark and is a preemie. She's been home for 10 days and is experiencing increasing difficulty. She won't drink any of her bottle and now she's also stopped the crying that's been going on all night, but she isn't resting peacefully. As her mom, I know something is terribly wrong!" Lynne tried to control the panic in her voice so the nurse would focus on her words.

The nurse said she would reach Dr. Mark who was on call. Lynne was relieved to hear it was him. He had just seen Kelly that day. Thirty long minutes passed as Lynne's panic grew. The phone still didn't ring so she called the doctor's office again. This time she couldn't control the fear and panic in her voice.

"Why is the doctor not calling me? There's something wrong with my baby! I need to talk to him!" Tears poured down her face and Lynne knew she sounded hysterical but that's how she felt.

The nurse apologized and said she would have the doctor call as soon as possible. This time Lynne waited for fifteen minutes and called again. As before, the nurse could only offer an apology and promise to have the doctor call. Lynne's heart continued to pound as she paced back and forth from the phone to the bassinette, trying to breath, willing the phone to ring, needing comfort, or action. She was in agony as her hopes battled with her fears. She touched Kelly each time and prayed that she was wrong. Her husband and her son were sleeping in the bedrooms upstairs, unaware of the drama around them.

On one of the trips from the phone to the bassinette, Lynne noticed that the baby had stopped crying and had a fixed stare.

"Oh, my God! We need to go to the hospital!" she screamed.

Luke heard the scream. He jumped out of bed, pulled their son, Greg, out of his bed and ran down the steps. There was no 911 service in their community so they were all quickly in the car. Lynne held the baby close and watched her tiny face There was no car seat tonight.

Luke drove quickly but carefully. Their son's life was in the car also. It was about a 30-minute drive to the women's hospital, but it felt like an eternity to Lynne. She wished there was a way to teleport their car to the hospital to get help for Kelly. Every few minutes she would check to be sure her baby continued to breath by blowing into her face and watching for her to react to the breath. Each time she blew, Kelly would wince, and Lynne felt a brief, momentary sense of relief as she confirmed that Kelly was still there.

Lynne's feeling of panic continued to grow as they drove. She prayed that they would get to the hospital in time. They were driving across a bridge, still 15 minutes from the hospital, when there was no reaction to the breath and Lynne knew that Kelly had stopped breathing. She had been trained in CPR for infants and attempted to administer rescue breathing, but she was frantic. They were approaching another hospital, so she screamed to Luke to turn into the Emergency Room driveway.

They ran into the hospital and screamed to everyone who was there, "Who can help my baby?"

Chapter 3

Lora's Story January 1993
FIRST KNOWLEDGE

Lora had no memory at all of how that day began and, as is the way with the human mind, only a detached knowledge, rather than an actual memory, of the dark hours, weeks, and months immediately following the phone call. But she would never forget the call.

She knew she would have awakened early, for a Saturday, and showered in preparation for meeting the other members of the adoption group. She didn't remember where the group met or what they did that day. They probably walked through a business district and asked to place posters in windows. They were searching for women who were pregnant and considering abortion or adoption. They had committed as a group of 4 couples to work until each couple had adopted a baby.

Or rather, 7 of the 8 men and women had committed. Her husband wasn't truly committed, didn't feel the need for a child to complete their lives. She knew he felt relieved when the artificial insemination failed. Rick was afraid he would lose the lifestyle he loved. How could they travel, go to the theater, go out to dinner, go sailing every weekend, with a baby in their lives? How much money would be diverted from his pleasure? And so, though he reluctantly went to the initial adoption meeting with the other couples, he didn't go, never went, to the continuing Saturday meetings. He didn't walk the business districts and ask to place posters in windows. He went with Lora to meet the young woman who later said she would place her baby with them for adoption. But he didn't understand Lora's need, didn't want to understand, and he didn't smile as often now.

Lora did remember that she and Rick had planned to meet at home about noon, after the poster placement, and have lunch together. She wanted to talk with him because the previous night had been strange, and she still had an awful unsettled feeling. She had been angry with him and they hadn't spoken to each other on their ride home. She had gone immediately to their bedroom to sleep while he had remained in the family room and watched TV till the early hours of the morning. She wanted to talk to him. She wanted to repair the unsettled feeling. They lived a peaceful life and these feelings were alien to her.

Earlier the prior evening, she had waited for him in the lobby of the office building where she worked as a Human Resources Manager. She waited for over an hour, while she stood and looked out the lobby doors. Lora should have returned to her office to wait but she kept expecting to see his car come around the corner at any moment. He had dropped her off in the morning, with plans for dinner, and she had no way to get home unless she called a cab or a friend.

He finally arrived and she ran out of the building and slid into the front seat next to him.

"What's up? I've been waiting here for an hour! With nowhere to even sit! And why didn't you answer your phone?"

"Just involved in something at the office and I couldn't get away."

"But why couldn't you take a minute to call me?!! Did you even think about how many times I'd check the time and wonder where you were?! You knew I'd have no way to go anywhere!" She felt annoyed, even angry, alien feelings in her relationship with him, and she wanted him to know it. "It's Friday night, time to celebrate our weekend! Couldn't it wait till Monday?"

"No, not really. Not this." He didn't look at her as he spoke. Both hands gripped the steering wheel and he looked straight ahead. There had been no additional conversation, not even a discussion of where to go for dinner.

He had driven to one of his favorite restaurants where they took seats at the bar in the lounge. They ordered drinks and food and then he excused himself to go to the restroom. Lora sat sipping her wine and watched the evening news on the TV until she realized that he had been gone for a long time. She started to glance around the lounge and finally got up to walk around and look for him.

She found him on the phone in the entryway to the restaurant. When she walked up, he looked uncomfortable and motioned for her to leave.

"I'll be back to the seats in a minute."

She didn't move. She just stood there and listened.

"Well, ok. We can continue this at another time." He ended the call without his usual chatty conclusion, and he looked stressed.

"Who were you talking to?" she asked.

"Oh, just Jay. We have an issue with one of our business deals." But his answer didn't ring true to her. He seemed distant and didn't look at her while they finished their wine and ate the appetizers they had ordered. They left shortly after and hadn't spoken since. She remembered being unsure about what she expected as she headed back home that Saturday morning, but she knew she had felt uncomfortable and wanted to talk with him.

Rick wasn't there when she arrived home later that same afternoon so she would have done some small things to pass the time: play with their cat, Elrond, clean up the kitchen, watch TV. The phone didn't ring immediately. It could have been one o'clock or even two o'clock. Looking back, she had a feeling that she had been wondering where he could be and why he didn't at least call to let her know when he'd be home.

When she picked up the phone, she heard his voice on the other end. "It's me," he said.

"Where are you?" she remembered asking.

"You won't understand this, but I have to help a friend." He sounded like he was in a public place with a lot of activity in the background. "I won't be home till early tonight."

"Who is this friend?"

"It's no one you know."

"What do you have to help with? Where are you?" she asked.

He hesitated and a frightening feeling began to grow in the pit of her stomach. She sensed that there was a fracture in her life though she didn't know why yet.

"I'll tell you about it when I come home."

"No. Tell me about it now. Who is this friend?" After another hesitation, "Is it another woman?"

"Yes."

She didn't speak. She hung up the phone and the nightmare began.

Her brain tried to reject the possibility that this was reality. But she knew it was. On some level, she had known for a while now. She had reacted to a series of recent events without even realizing it. She had sensed his lack of interest in her and the decrease in the amount of time they spent together. She had begun to dress more provocatively at home. She had styled her hair differently. She had arranged special evenings at their favorite restaurants. He hadn't responded.

Lora began to cry and think about what to do. Who could she call? Where could she turn? Most importantly, how could she stop this nightmare? No one would believe that he was involved with another woman.

She picked up the phone and dialed frantically. She had to reach someone who could tell her this wasn't true, though she didn't really know what "this" was yet. She called Dr. Levy, the therapist they had met with before they began the insemination and then the adoption processes and left a message with his emergency service. She needed an appointment. She needed to talk.

Within minutes Dr. Levy returned her call and she struggled to remain calm enough to tell him the story. He didn't make it not true. He didn't give her a magic way to make the panic stop. He told her to take a shower; go for a walk; get out of the house and be with a friend or family member. He told her what to say and not say when she heard from him again, whenever that might be. He asked her to call the following Monday and schedule an appointment for Rick and her to meet with him. With the giving of all this advice, the fracture in her life became more real, and that wasn't what she so desperately wanted and needed.

Her sister, Jennie, was next. She was on the verge of hysteria as she told the story and Jennie said she would leave to come to her home. Then Lora called a locksmith with 24-hour service. She needed someone to come and change the locks on their home immediately.

Two hours later as she left the house with her sister, she scribbled a note to her husband and hung it on the door

---

Rick,
You won't be able to get in the house. I've had all the locks changed. I can't believe this is happening!
Lora

Praying that she was wrong, surely she was wrong about where her thoughts took her, she wanted him to understand why his key wouldn't work in the lock.

Lora felt overwhelmed with nausea. As her sister drove, she cried and screamed with sometimes unintelligible words coming from her mouth. She felt terrified. She didn't know how to live without him. She couldn't begin to imagine what her life could be like without him in it. She was 41 years old and her life with him had defined so much of her since she was 24. Her experiences with him were beyond anything she had lived in a childhood family with a happy, but very modest, lifestyle. Those experiences had taught her to be the person she was. If her fears were really true, it would be the loss of herself, not just the loss of him!

At about 6:00 p.m. that evening her cell phone rang while she sat in a movie theater with her sister and her nephews. She hadn't seen a thing. She sat there and clutched her phone, praying for it to ring, willing it to ring. He picked her up a few minutes later outside the movie theater. She took a deep breath as she climbed into the car and looked at him.

"Who is she?"

Chapter 4

Shelly's Story, Looking Back to October 1982

TRANSFORMATION

When the phone rang, Shelly answered it immediately. She had walked in the door just a few minutes earlier, and since then her parents had been complaining about Todd's repeated calls.

He started to drill her as soon as he heard her voice. "Where were you?!"

"At the mall with my friends." She partially reclined on the steps that led to the second floor of her parents' home, and nervously poked at the woodwork. She wasn't comfortable but the spot offered the most privacy she could find.

Shelly could hear the anger in his voice. "You know I don't want you going there without me!"

"Oh, come on. What am I going to do at the mall?" She tried to keep her voice light and teasing. She knew her parents watched and listened to everything she said.

He continued, even more angrily, "I just don't want you there without me! Period! Do you understand?!"

"Of course," she said. "I understand."

"You know I just care about you and all I want to do is protect you."

"It's ok. I understand."

But Shelly didn't understand. She was 18 years old and she didn't understand how this man had gained such control over her. In the evenings, lying up in her bedroom where she felt safe, she would try to think of ways to make him like her friends and family and for them to like him. She spent a lot of time defending him, explaining that they didn't know him the way she did. When she was with him every word that came out of her mouth had to be meticulously chosen so as not to upset him.

Sometimes she would try to get into discussions with him about her family and friends and explain what kind of people they were. In his car, he would listen as he drove and the more she said, the faster he would drive. His hand would rest upon her leg and, with every word she spoke, he would squeeze harder and harder. She would feel the beads of sweat forming on her forehead, her heart racing, her legs shaking. This was similar to the excitement she used to feel when she looked forward to their dates but, over time, it had changed to a feeling sparked by anxiety.

She remembered that excitement. One day, a few months ago, his car pulled down the road in front of her house. Just seeing his car made her heart start to pound. She knew the roar of the engine as he approached. His head emerged and she watched him extract his long legs from the car. He was tall, with shaggy blond hair, and a strong face. She remembered how much fun it was to talk with him. He was only 21 years old but seemed to know a lot about everything, especially history, geography, science.

He came to the door and said, "I've really missed you," and smiled.

She thought to herself, "Me? Didn't you tell me just a few months ago that I wasn't right for you?"

"I am so sorry for walking away from you. I didn't realize what my life would be like without you. I miss you! I miss our connection and the things we did together! I'd like to start over, if that's alright."

Shelly held her breath for a minute but inside she screamed to herself, "Say ok!. Say ok! What are you waiting for? Hurry up before he changes his mind!"

She couldn't understand why he would want to come back to her, but she didn't want to ask questions. Her feelings about her personal morals, her refusal to have sex with him, had been an issue for them. When they were dating, she had made it very clear to him that those morals would not change. She'd have to be sure he understood what it would mean if he resumed a relationship with her. She was a virgin and wanted to remain that way until she was ready to make the decision to have a sexual relationship. She wanted to be totally in love, with no doubts that she was ready, and he was the right person. Making love had to be about love! At least that's what she believed.

But she would deal with all that later. All she thought about at this moment was that, maybe he could be the guy she would fall in love with some day. So she replied in a voice that sounded shaky but, she hoped, convincing, "Why not? Let's give it a try. After all, what could it hurt?" And so it began.

She never told her parents about the frightening things that started to happen when she was with him. She hid from everyone the small bruises from the slaps, punches, and kicks he delivered when she said or did something that didn't please him. Questions from him followed each of her days at the Art Institute. "Who'd you talk to? Who'd you sit by? Guy or girl? Why'd you miss your bus? Were you talking to another guy?"

Instead of getting angry with him, the hold he had on her always took over. She found herself stumbling over her words to explain what she had done that day. But he always apologized when he heard her becoming upset.

Time passed and Shelly continued on with school while dreading going home after classes. She could see the disappointment and the anger in her parents' faces every time the phone rang as she walked through the door. If she wasn't there on time for his call, he became irate. He apologized only after he finished screaming at her.

Shelly could see it all happening. Her life, her relationship with this man, had become so strange. She felt like she owed Todd something. She didn't know why she didn't end it with him. It was unexplainable. She watched herself become unable to think for herself and make decisions without his approval. How had this become her?

Chapter 5
Lynne's Story January 1997
NIGHTMARE

A nurse walked towards them quickly with a frown on her face. "They are working on your baby but I'm afraid it doesn't look good for her." Lynne reached for Luke as the reality of the words spoken by the nurse began to wash over her.

"How can this be happening?" she screamed. Kelly had been in the hospital for 95 days before the decision was made to send her home. Didn't that mean that she was supposed to "make it?" The doctors said she was ready to go home! They would not have sent her home if they thought she would die! Kelly's own doctor had seen her that very morning and he sent her home saying that she was fine!

The nightmare continued to unfold. Every time a door opened, Luke and Lynne caught their breath, and looked up expectedly. They paced back and forth in agony, trying to remain calm enough not to wake up Greg. Lynne desperately wanted to be with Kelly, to see her little face, to help her to survive this crisis! She knew her baby needed her mother!

As they watched the minutes tick by, Lynne also flashed back to her 4 previous pregnancies that had ended before the babies were even born. She still grieved for those lives that were not meant to be. But this fear was so much worse! Surely it couldn't be that Kelly had come this far and would not survive! As each month of this pregnancy had passed, Lynne's hope grew that this time, this baby, would survive and be born. And now, tonight, Lynne's worst fears could become a reality.

Finally, the nurse came out again. This time she walked slowly, hesitantly, over to them. Lynne held her breath as she grasped Luke's hand, not wanting to hear the words she knew would come. Then the nurse whispered, "I'm so sorry. The doctors worked for 45 minutes to try to bring her back, but she is gone. She is so beautiful we didn't want to let her go! You have the right to see your daughter if you want to, but I need to warn you that she is badly bruised from the procedures the doctors used to try to save her. I would not recommend it!" There were tears in her eyes. And with the speaking of those words, the years that should have been theirs, together, as a family, melted away.

Lynne collapsed into her husband's arms. "No, no, no! Please don't let this be real!"

Then she wept. She wept for her precious baby who, after all of the ups and downs, had finally had enough. How could this be? This time their baby was supposed to survive and to grow! Why would God bring them this far and then allow Kelly to die?

After a few minutes, Lynne took a deep breath and looked up at the nurse, "I think you're right. We'll want to remember Kelly breathing and pulsing with life. Do you agree Luke?"

Luke paused and looked at Greg, now awake and with a bewildered face, then said, "Yes. I agree."

Greg was only seven years old, so Lynne immediately took him in her arms and struggled to find the words to explain to a young child. How does a child of his age understand death? How terrible that his first experience of death was with his sister. His experience of being the big brother had been so brief and not the picture that Lynne and Luke had shared with him when they told him about the baby that would join their family.

Thankfully a Social Worker came immediately and took them to a quiet room. He talked with Lynne for a few minutes then Lynne sat down with Greg and began to say the most awful words that had ever come from her mouth.

"Greg, you know how sick Kelly has been since she was born. We love her so much and she loves us so much. But she was tired of fighting to be ok. And God called her to come home. So she's gone home to be with God. God didn't want her to fight any longer."

Greg sat quietly while Lynne spoke, watching her face but not speaking. Lynne couldn't stop the tears rolling down her face but had to continue talking. She had to be sure Greg understood what had just happened.

"Greg, do you understand? Kelly won't be coming home with us tonight. She'll always be with us in our hearts, but we won't be able to see her. She's happy now so we need to find a way to be glad that she's not sick anymore and she's with God." Greg nodded his head yes, but Lynne saw more fear than understanding in his young face.

Lynne ached for her baby and for the life her child would never know. Her heart was shattered. She felt as though she were truly living in a nightmare. Maybe she would wake up and find out that this had just been a bad dream. But then family members began to arrive. Each minute that passed, each face that appeared, made this nightmare more real.

Dr. Mark also came and expressed his condolences, appearing to share in their grief. With tears in his eyes, he said, "I'm so very sorry for your loss. I truly believed she was going to be ok. I've heard all that happened through the night. I'm so, so sorry!"

"Doctor, why didn't you call us back earlier when we were trying to reach you! We knew something was wrong, but we couldn't reach you! I called and called, and you didn't call back! I didn't know what to do!" Lynne was angry and nearly shouting. The anger was so strong that, for the moment, it almost overwhelmed the grief.

The doctor quietly answered, "The batteries in my beeper were dead. I'm sorry!"

Lynne was shocked and outraged! How could the doctor on call not know that the batteries in his beeper were not working? Maybe if they had reached him Kelly would still be alive! She wanted to scream! She wanted to hit him!

Dr. Mark kept repeating, "I'm so sorry! You need to know I really believed the baby would be fine when I saw her in my office." There was a genuine look of despair on his face.

The doctor's continued apologies and explanations brought no comfort to Lynne, instead made her angrier, as she started asking herself who was to blame for their baby's death. Lynne replayed all the conversations she'd had with the baby's doctors and the nurses asking herself, "Why did this happen?" And then she started to remember….

Her thoughts took her back to last October. She stood at the bus stop as she watched Greg get on the school bus. To him it was an ordinary day. To Lynne it was a day of continued worries. She knew that she had not been feeling well and she he had an appointment with her doctor later that morning to talk about her concerns.

After Greg got on the bus, she walked back into the house and looked into the mirror. Her face was so swollen she barely recognized herself. She knew her legs and ankles were equally swollen. She felt very nervous, very frightened, about what the doctor would say, because she knew that something was terribly wrong.

"I'm going to the hospital for a checkup, but I am so afraid the doctor will tell me I need to stay," she thought. Her apprehension continued to grow and shortly after she drove to the hospital.

When Doctor Roberts walked into the examining room, Lynne could see the concern on his face. "Let's check that blood pressure." He took her pressure, not once, but three times.

"Your pressure is very high."

"How high?" she asked.

"High enough that I'm going to personally walk you down to Dr. Schmitt's office. He specializes in high risk pregnancies and I'd like to get his opinion, because you are also retaining so much fluid."

As the doctor quickly walked with her down the hall, he tried to make small talk, "How's your son? What grade is he in? What's your husband up to these days?" She knew he

36

wanted to distract her, to ease her fears, and she answered mechanically, not sure if her words even made sense.

Dr. Schmitt left after he examined her, and Dr. Roberts came back into the room and said, "You know, Dr. Schmitt and I are concerned about your pressure and the fact that you're retaining fluid. We agree it's best that we admit you to keep an eye on you."

Lynne began to shake, and she fumbled for her phone to call Luke. "I'm so scared!" she told him when he picked up and she explained what the doctor had said.

She was rushed into a room and immediately hooked up to many monitors. She was only 28 weeks pregnant, and very, very frightened. The doctors tried to comfort her, but she knew that in her case, "time was not on her side." The date was October 3 and her baby wasn't due until December 22nd.

The blood tests showed that her liver was still functional, but her kidneys were not working as well as they should. The doctors told her that they "wanted to keep a close watch" because when a woman becomes ill with pre-eclampsia, as she was, her condition could deteriorate very quickly. She began to receive injections to help develop the baby's lungs. The doctors hoped that this would improve the baby's chance of surviving.

Lynne felt only slightly reassured by what the doctors said. "You're in the best hospital possible in this area. If a woman were to go to another hospital with your symptoms, she would be transferred to this women's hospital."

When Luke reached the hospital and came into the room, he couldn't hide his alarm at the sight of her. Her face, arms, and legs were so swollen that she was distorted and almost unrecognizable. Luke didn't want to alarm her and tried to keep his voice light.

"So, what are the doctors saying?"

Lynne didn't know how to respond and just reached out for his hand. As they sat and held hands, she prayed silently and begged God for the life of her baby. "Dear Lord, you won't let this happen, will you?"

Chapter 6

Lora's Story January 1993

DARKNESS

As they drove away from the movie theater, Rick began to talk. He had a lot to say that sounded right to her. At least Lora needed it to sound right.

"Cutie, it's just a friend I made who needed some help. I've loved you for sixteen years. I still love you. Please don't blow this out of proportion."

Then more, "She's sick and alone. She thought she might have to go to the hospital." Then more, "So I went to Buffalo to help her." With each statement the picture continued to evolve, and Lora struggled to comprehend what he was saying.

"You drove to Buffalo and back today?"

"No, I flew."

Lora knew there were implications in this statement that she couldn't bear to think about. Over the next week, the story continued to develop. Rick gave her small doses of the reality, careful not to push it too far at any one time. She felt he looked at her and talked to her only to measure her pain and attempt to judge how much she could handle. He had flown to Buffalo to be with this woman because she was sick and may have needed to go to the hospital. The significance of his spending money, their money, to fly to be with her was more than Lora could consider.

Lora desperately tried to hang onto the tone of his voice when he said he still loved her. However, by the time she woke up the following weekend, Lora knew he was unsure if he wanted to continue their marriage. This woman, this friend, had become so important to him that he didn't know if he could give her up. Lora heard words coming from his mouth and they were the worst nightmare she ever could have conceived.

"I was on a business trip to Buffalo with Scott and we were out for drinks one night. I saw a group of women at the next table. They continued to glance at us, and we all started to talk. I'm sorry. I never wanted to hurt you."

And with tears in his voice, "I can't get her out of my mind. I dream about her all the time. I want to put our marriage back together but I'm not sure how or if there even is a way."

Then, "She's alone and afraid. She's had a tough life and an awful brutal relationship with a man. She's afraid of men. I started just wanting to help but...."

There was a look, a distance in his eyes that Lora had never seen before. It felt as though he had on a pair of dark sunglasses that prevented her from seeing into the man she thought she knew. He wouldn't let her in. He came home later and later each evening and sat staring at the TV.

Lora slept in the spare bedroom. Late at night she could hear Rick breathing in the next room and she wanted to be there next to him, snuggling close, cupped around each other. At times she would hear him, tossing, turning, crying out. She wondered what and who his dreams were about. She was afraid to know.

Each moment she was awake, and she slept little, waves of nausea moved through her stomach. On Monday and Tuesday she had somehow driven to her office but could barely function. She sat, stared out the window, and shook, partially from the cold of the day, but primarily because she felt emotionally destroyed. There were some moments when she felt numb to everything that had happened, probably an attempt of her brain to protect her. But the reality of her life would come screaming back and, at times, she could barely breath. Rick came home both nights, no travel scheduled. They sat, usually in separate rooms, with no conversation. As

Doctor Levy had recommended, Lora did not initiate any conversations about the events of the weekend, "the other", or what would happen going forward.

Lora had scheduled an appointment for them to see Dr. Levy on Wednesday. They had previously seen him several times as they tried to resolve their differences about whether to pursue insemination and later, after the procedures failed, adoption. Lora was terrified as they walked in to talk with him about "the other" and the state of their marriage. Dr. Levy asked the questions she had been afraid to ask.

"Have you had sex with this woman?" Rick answered, "No."

"Do you want to end your marriage?" He answered, "No."

"Are you willing to end your relationship with the woman?" He answered, "I don't know."

"Are you willing to stop seeing her until you and Lora decide the future of your marriage?" He answered, "Yes."

Lora breathed again. Dr. Levy suggested that they both continue to meet with a therapist but to do so separately. And so they stopped their lives while they each considered what to do, how to live going forward. They moved through the formalities of the life they had lived together. She could see concern in his face when he glanced at her. She didn't see happiness, or passion, or interest.

She wanted to push him away, thinking certainly he'd realize what he could lose and push to come back. She knew better though. He'd leave quietly, undoubtedly relieved at the ease with which he could get away and get on with living his present. He wouldn't look back. He had always lived in the here and now and she sensed that his here and now was with the other woman.

When Lora woke up that second Saturday she didn't know how to begin to live the day. She had already called the other couples they were working with and told them she couldn't do adoption posters that morning. At that point, she and Rick had made an agreement with a young lady who was pregnant to adopt her baby when the time came. The commitment among the couples working to adopt had been to work together until everyone had a baby. All thoughts of the agreements with the young pregnant lady and the other couples slipped away

Dark, dark days followed for her. In the future she would have a lot of trouble remembering what happened during many of those dark days. He would be gone, traveling on business he said. He would continue traveling to Buffalo where he said most of his business prospects were, but he promised that he had no contact with "the other" while they worked through their counseling process. The phone calls from him were erratic but there would be many notes as he came and went to destinations never clearly disclosed, with returns unspecified.

"Cutie, take it really easy, please. I'll call. Love you and Elrond."

"Cutie, I'll be at the Residence Inn, Buffalo tonight – unsure about tomorrow. Miss you guys. I'll call you later. Love…"

"Cutie, open the window for Elrond. I'll call you. Love you."

Lora continued to drive to her office each day where, thankfully, her direct reports worked to cover her continued inability to function. The overwhelming nausea also continued. Though she ate very little, she forced herself to drink water so her body wouldn't totally shut down. When Rick was home, she was determined not to show panic or despair in front of the man she had loved so fully. But she didn't have the answers to her life now and didn't know how to find them. How could she face a life without him?

Chapter 7

Shelly's Story, Looking Back to July 1983

PICNIC SUPRISE

One day Todd invited Shelly to go on a picnic. By this time, her mom and dad tried to limit her time with him, so they said, "No." Though she was 19 and out of high school, Shelly lived at home, and her parents controlled much of her life as they had always done since she was a child. Shelly knew they weren't going to change their minds about the picnic invitation, but she decided to go anyway without telling them. She was hopeful that some time together in a beautiful outdoor setting would enable her to talk calmly with Todd about the tensions between him and her family. She still believed they could all have a great relationship.

Shelly left a note for her parents as she slipped out the door and left with Todd for the picnic. Her mission was to finally stop the crazy life she'd been experiencing. They drove along the highway, and then onto country roads. She gazed at the amazing summer landscape of beautiful trees, blue skies, and fields shimmering in the sunlight. She felt the warmth of the sun coming through the window of the car. Todd smiled, laughed, and appeared to share her pleasure in the beauty of the day. She slid closer to him to enjoy the ride, feeling so happy about the day and so hopeful for the future.

As the drive continued, Shelly's thoughts drifted, and she started to think more about her mission. "This is the perfect time to bring up my family. He's happy. I'm happy. It should be easy."

Unbelievably, it was easy. Todd actually said he agreed with what she had to say about building a relationship between him and her family.

"You know, sweetie, you're right. We should all try to get along."

Inside she started screaming, "Woo Hoo! He finally gets it!"

He continued, "You are so beautiful, and I love you so much! I'd do anything for you!"

Shelly was in shock as she thought, "It's working! He does love me! And mom and dad are going to be so surprised!"

They had their picnic, laughed, kissed, splashed in the lake, as they enjoyed the day and each other. Too soon the sun started to set, and it was time to leave the park. Shelly couldn't wait to get home to talk with her mom and dad. She knew they would be upset with her for leaving without their permission or knowledge, but she believed it was the first step towards bringing them all together.

She thought, "I'll let them have their say and I'll take my punishment which will probably be a good grounding, probably till I'm 30." But she knew it would be worth it because everything would be great soon.

They gathered their blanket and picnic basket and walked back to the car holding hands. Todd said, "You know, I have a surprise for you."

"What do you mean, a surprise? You mean like ice cream, my favorite?"

Todd said, "No. This surprise is going to knock your socks off!"

Shelly's heart started pounding and all she could think of was the perfect ending to a perfect day. Maybe he would give her a ring and ask for a commitment!

She said, "Oh, yeah? If not ice cream, what kind of surprise do you have in mind?"

He said, "Oh, you'll see."

The warmth of the sun was no longer there, and the leather seats felt cold and damp from the windows being down. They pulled out of the park, singing to the radio, with Shelly feeling so excited and so in love. In her mind, all the bad stuff, the ongoing issues between Todd and her family, was behind her.

As they started driving, Shelly said to him, "This is the wrong way, isn't it?"

Todd responded, "No. You know I know all these back roads. And you do want your surprise, don't you?"

"Of course! You're the boss!"

They drove further and further. It started to get darker and darker and Shelly was concerned. "You do know where we are, don't you?"

"Of course. I told you. Don't worry. Just trust me!"

His words didn't reassure her. "Don't forget. I want to get home early enough to talk to my parents, so they don't worry."

Todd said nothing. He turned down a dark, narrow road, with only trees and a few cottages visible. Shelly had no idea where they were, and she began to feel frightened. Finally, as they turned a 90 degree bend, an interesting looking cottage appeared in a clearing. It looked like a small ski lodge or a summer home.

Todd pulled into the driveway, turned and looked at her, and said, "Surprise!"

"Oh, my gosh! You bought this place? It's beautiful! Is it really yours?"

"Kinda," he said as he led her to the door.

"What do you mean, kinda?

"You'll see. Come on. Let's hurry inside. I can't wait to show you the rest of the place."

They walked through the door and Shelly thought it looked perfect, including the fireplace in the sunken family room. "I can't believe it! It's absolutely gorgeous!'

"So you like it, huh?" He watched her face closely

"Of course, who wouldn't?"

He stepped away from her, went to the door, slammed it shut, and slid the dead bolt in place. He turned to look at her and his whole demeanor had changed. The light smiling look in his eyes was gone, replaced by the dark angry look that came over him when she talked about her family. The smile was still there but had transformed into a frozen caricature with no warmth behind it.

"Good. I'm glad you like it."

He walked towards her, grabbed her hand, and led her to the bedroom. The room was beautiful like the rest of the cabin and it had a small bath attached. There was a closet with bi-fold doors along the side of the bed. He opened the closet doors and repeated what he had just said, "I'm glad you like it ...because this is your new home, at least for a while."

She looked into the closet and saw that it was full of clothes. Her voice cracked as she asked, "What do you mean, my home for a while?"

He took a step towards her, so they were standing toe to toe, his head towering over hers. He pushed her onto the bed and stood with his arms folded. "Just what I said! Get used to it. You're not leaving, and neither am I!"

Shelly was afraid to move and lay there trying to understand everything that had just happened as he walked out of the room. She tried to slow her breathing and got off the bed to follow him into the family room where he had already lit the wood in the fireplace.

His back was to her as she asked, "You mean we're here for the weekend, right?"

He turned to look at her, the anger replaced now by a soft, calm voice. "Of course we're staying for the weekend. Don't worry your pretty little head. Let's have something to drink."

She followed him into the kitchen. When he pulled open the refrigerator door, it was stocked full of food, as if a family of 5 lived there. He pulled out two sodas and handed one to her.

"Come, sit by me. Let's enjoy the fire. I started it to take the evening chill off the place."

Shelly sat down and he pulled her close to him, placing his arm around her shoulder. She tried to measure his mood, contemplating the question she wanted to ask. It had been such a positive day! Surely the question would be ok.

"Do you think, maybe, I could call my parents, just to let them know where I am and that I'm ok?"

He started laughing and said, "But you don't really know where you are, do you?"

Chapter 8

Lynne's Story, Looking Back to October 1996

DECISIONS

Lynne was only 28 weeks pregnant, and she was very, very frightened. Within a few minutes of Luke's arrival, Dr. Roberts came in to talk with them about their options.

"We're facing a hard decision. We can wait to see how things go today or we can go ahead and deliver the baby now."

Lynne and Luke looked at each other for a long moment. They were both terrified to make the decision but knew that two lives were now at risk. Finally, Luke looked at Dr. Roberts and said, "This is the most terrible decision I've ever been asked to make. The lives of my wife and my child are both at risk. I'm terrified to act and terrified not to act. But, I believe we need to move ahead and deliver the baby now."

"Do you think we can wait a few more days?" Lynne asked. "Would it make a difference in the development of the baby's lungs?" She felt an overwhelming desperation to find any way to increase the odds for her baby. This baby had to survive! This baby couldn't join the others who didn't survive!

"Well," the doctor explained. "Studies do show that the more injections the baby receives, the greater benefit to the development of the lungs. I think we can wait overnight and see how things look in the morning."

Early the next morning Doctor Roberts came into Lynne's room. Luke had just arrived, after he first put Greg onto the school bus.

"Lynne, I've looked at your blood work and I think we need to move ahead now and deliver the baby. However, you need to know that, as much as I do want to be there with you, I was up all night with another woman who was in labor. So, if you decide to deliver today, I'd suggest my colleague, Dr. Sharon Miller, take over for me and do the delivery. She's an excellent doctor and will see that you get the best care possible."

"As much as I want you to be there, I want you to have your beauty sleep," Lynne smiled.

Dr. Roberts looked at Luke and said, "I just love your wife. As sick as she is, she still has her sense of humor."

He looked at Lynne, "Do you have a sister?" Somehow she smiled.

Things started to happen as soon as he spoke. Dr. Miller appeared in the room in less than 5 minutes to consult with Dr. Roberts. Initially, the doctors wanted Lynne to try to deliver the baby naturally. But when they reviewed the sonogram, it showed that the baby was lying sideways. That's when the doctors decided that a caesarean was necessary. They also thought the baby weighed about 2 pounds which was a good weight for 28 weeks. Lynne felt relieved with the decision, because she was so ill that the thought of going through labor was beyond her imagination.

"Are you ready, Lynne?" an anesthesiologist asked as she walked into the room.

A flood of emotions ran through Lynne as she realized that they were now moving towards an outcome of great joy or unimaginable heartbreak. Within a matter of a few hours, she could be holding a new life and putting a little face to the name they had chosen. But, what if it didn't go well? What if that life didn't survive? What if she didn't get to hold that new life? The fear battled with the excitement. Thankfully, she believed in her heart that they didn't have a choice about waiting to see what would happen. Her life and the baby's life were truly at risk.

As soon as Dr. Roberts left, Dr. Miller started to talk. "I want you to know that a resident is going to perform the surgery, but I will be right there, watching what is happening. You will still get the best care possible."

"Woah! I'm not sure we're comfortable with that. Dr. Roberts told us you would be delivering the baby. Why the change? This is a very delicate delivery. I don't think a resident should be handling it!" Luke stood face to face with Dr. Miller and was very upset about the change in plans. Lynne slowly drifted into a twilight sleep but still heard enough to know that she couldn't understand how they could let a resident perform the cesarean. They knew she was so sick, and the baby would be so small.

"Mr. Murray, I assure you, the resident is capable of handling the delivery. And, I will be right next to him. Now, please, let us proceed with the delivery! Step out of the room. We will come to let you know as soon as the baby is born."

A little later, a nurse called Luke into the recovery room and Dr. Miller began to talk to them. "You have a daughter! She was taken directly to NICU (Neonatal Intensive Care Unit) so you can't see her right now. Unfortunately, as the resident began the procedure, he accidentally cut the baby's ankle. I was right there with him, but the baby moved just as he began to operate. She required stitches which is unfortunate because it could be a source of infection."

Neither Lynne nor Luke said anything, each struggling to understand what the doctor said. Fear and anger again overwhelmed them, fear for the life they had yet to meet and anger at another mistake by another doctor!

"She weighs 1 pound 15 ounces," the doctor continued. "You know that's a real concern since she's only at 28 weeks gestation. And the medication you'd been started on to help develop the baby's lungs did not make a significant difference. She's also compromised with underdeveloped lungs." Though Luke and Lynne had known there were so many risks with the delivery of their child, it was still hard to comprehend all they heard.

And so, the tiny baby girl they named Kelly began her day after day struggle with her underdeveloped lungs and her fight for survival. Lynne didn't clearly remember a lot of the details, maybe because she chose to forget. It was the only way she could cope with the overwhelming and conflicting emotions of hope, fear and anger that defined her days. As the days began to pass, friends would tell her to keep a journal, but she didn't want to write it down because it made it more real. It seemed that if she didn't write it down, she could just float through each day and get to the next.

Lynne was taken to intensive care immediately following the delivery. As soon as she could leave her bed the next day, a nurse took Luke and her to see the baby. Luke walked and Lynne was pushed into a room filled with about fifteen incubators. She looked around, wondering which one held their baby. The nurse pushed her over to the incubator where Kelly lay sleeping. It was very difficult to see her because of all the wires and medical devices that were connected to her, keeping her alive. The wires and devices were, in turn, connected to so many monitors.

Kelly was so small, only slightly longer than a ruler. Still, Lynne could see her tiny features and she amazingly looked like her older brother, Greg. She had a very tiny hat on her head with just a little blond peach fuzz peeking out and a really tiny nose. She couldn't see her mouth because of the ventilator. She looked at Kelly's tiny body and felt amazed that she could even fight to survive.

Lynne worked with so many children who had been born prematurely. She knew about all the challenges they face in their day to day lives. Despite Lynne's hope that everything would turn out in Kelly's favor, she was also very aware of all the things that could go terribly wrong. She wanted to focus only on the joy of seeing her child but couldn't ignore the reality of all the possibilities.

"How can you tell when she's crying?" she asked the nurse. There was no way to hear any noise because of the ventilator.

"We can tell by looking at her," the nurse explained. She was very calm and reassuring. She dealt with this type of situation every day and it wasn't a shock for her like it was for them.

"How long will she be on a ventilator?" Lynne asked.

"It depends on how long it takes for her lungs to mature. It will be good for her to feel your touch. You can reach in. She'll know you are there."

Lynne stuck her finger through a small hole in the incubator and touched Kelly's little arm for the first time. Her skin felt thin and had the texture of very fine paper. She was asleep and Lynne wasn't really sure if the baby would feel that she was there. But it was so comforting to be able to touch her. And, hopefully the nurse was right. They had been connected for so many months. Maybe Kelly would sense her mom's touch, even while she slept. Maybe the touch would help bring strength and healing to their tiny daughter. Then Luke reached in to touch her. His hands were so large compared to Kelly's tiny body and it made it even more apparent how small she was.

Lynne sat there for a while and looked at her. She tried to just float and prayed that her daughter would survive. How would she get through the next days, weeks, months?

Chapter 9

Lora's Story, Looking Back to May 1985

VISIONS

She was 33 and he was 35. They agreed the time was now right for them to have a baby. Lora and Rick had been married for 6 years and their life together had been incredible! She felt that every day with him was a wonderful adventure! They loved to sail, to go to the theater, to eat in interesting restaurants, and to grow their own vegetables. They loved their cat, Elrond, and their small home. Most of all they loved to travel! Some of the trips were his rewards, earned for outstanding results in his sales position. Others were funded by their choice to travel instead of upgrading their home, or to save a little less. The choice was always clear to them, always "to do" rather than "to have."

Visions of that life swirled through her brain as she tried to imagine the next phase of her life with him and sharing that life with a child. With him she had climbed the Great Wall of China and walked the medieval walls of Dubrovnik. With him she rode a camel before the pyramids, the Glacier Express through Switzerland, and a sampan in Hong Kong Harbor. They strolled through the Parthenon, the ruins of Pompeii, and followed the way of the cross in Jerusalem. They dined in an outdoor café next to a Venice canal, at a farmhouse in southern France, and ate native food at a "tamaara" on an island in the South Pacific. They gambled in the casinos in Monte Carlo and spent hours admiring the art in the Louvre. They toured the Forbidden City, the Palace at Versailles, and the churches of Florence. Standing on Victoria's Peak, high above Hong Kong Harbor at night, they were mesmerized by the glittering lights of buildings and boats that illuminated the night sky. And there was, of course, their annual pilgrimage to the magical spot in Florida, with castles and princesses, with talking mice, ducks, and dogs, where you could do what you could dream.

The people they encountered were equally memorable. On the island of Patmos, she remembered the figure of a monk with a flowing white beard and a group of fishermen slumped in chairs at a sidewalk café. From the cold and blustery day when they visited the Great Wall, she could still see the image of an elderly woman who swept snow into a bucket and dumped it over the side of the Wall. On the island of Tahiti, she remembered the ageless, sunbaked woman who had arrived as a tourist countless years before and, like so many famous and unknown people before her, became permanently ensnared in the spell of the South Pacific. On a cruise ship in the Mediterranean, they laughed about the ship's officer who was obviously enamored with Lora, searched them out every evening, and attempted to monopolize her attention.

There were also the faces of those who shared their travels and, for a brief period of time, became their friends. Carl, an attorney from England, seemed to have jinxed every trip he had ever taken. When they met him, they were all stranded on a Caribbean island because their cruise ship had been commandeered by the British government to respond to the Falklands crisis. Bud, a retiree from a major oil company, was single and traveled with the widows of two of his friends. He shared his magic word, "Novshauskapop" which he used when someone spoke to him in a language he didn't understand. He said it made people leave him alone. Peter and June were a long-distance couple: she an aspiring actress from California, he a stockbroker from New York. Babette, multiple times divorced and presently unattached, was a former New Yorker who had moved to Miami. She was alone as she traveled through Europe with no reservations and no real plan. The visions of people and places went on and on, thrilling and amazing her.

And now, all that they loved would be shared with the child they were about to create. And so the planning began.

"Let's look for a special trip with lots of time to focus on what we want to accomplish!" Rick suggested as they sipped glasses of wine at the bar in their favorite restaurant.

"Ooh, that sounds great!" Lora agreed. "I think another cruise would be perfect! I can imagine lots of time for "togetherness" on lazy days at sea. Where would we want to go? The warmth of the Caribbean or maybe someplace we've never been before?"

"I like the cruise idea!" Rick smiled as he touched her hand and leaned forward to kiss her lightly. "Let's find somewhere new to experience as we have fun creating a new life!" He flashed the smile that always captivated and mesmerized her.

They researched cruise destinations, dates, and prices, and finally settled on a week at an interesting looking Bed and Breakfast in Vancouver followed by a 2 week Alaska cruise. They selected an outside cabin and a date in early June. When they reached Anchorage, the sun would rise a little after 4:00 a.m. and not set until close to midnight with twilight hours before and after. There would be very little darkness, something they had never experienced before.

One evening as the date for the cruise approached, Lora sat outside on their deck and waited for Rick to come home. She remembered a conversation a little over 7 years ago when Rick looked at her and asked, "Will you have a baby with me?"

Lora had been surprised. They weren't married, though they lived together, and had never talked about anything that could bring the commitment that having a child would. She had only dreamed about the possibility of a long-term, permanent relationship with this man. But a baby?! She wasn't even sure she wanted to have a child. A relationship with him, yes, definitely, but a child was something else.

Lora wasn't sure how to respond but finally said, "But we're not even married!"

He laughed and said, "Silly, of course that would be part of the plan!" He smiled and she found herself being drawn into his vision of their life together. Marriage would be part of the plan and they made the wedding happen. Now they would have fun making the baby part happen.

The cruise exceeded their expectations, with lots of time to work on their plan and lots of visions to add to their experiences of this planet. From the deck of the ship, they watched whales breaching. They sat beside a stream where bald eagles were fishing.

In Skagway they met a group of local citizens who dressed up like the days of Soapy Smith and the Gold Rush and came to greet each incoming cruise ship. They flew over glaciers and landed on a lake before one of them. In a small cabin they dined on Alaskan salmon, grilled over a wood fire. And most importantly, the nights, the mornings, the afternoons in their cabin were exciting, incredible, and possibly life creating!

After settling into their seats on the plane for the trip home, Rick looked at Lora and said, "If we didn't make a baby on that trip, we never will! How long will it be till we know?"

Chapter 10

Shelly's Story, Looking Back to July 1983

SETTLING IN

It was then Shelly knew she was in serious trouble and the nightmare began.

"Anyway, you can look around. Do you see a phone anywhere?"

"No, but surely...."

Todd interrupted her. "Surely nothing. You're with me. That's all they need to know. That's all anybody needs to know."

They continued to sit in front of the fireplace with their sodas. He behaved as though everything was normal. He turned on the TV and said, "Let's see if we can find a good movie or something."

Shelly tried to process everything that had happened that day. Despite all the issues between Todd and her family, despite the physical harm he had inflicted over the past months, she had still somehow believed he was everything she could ever ask for in a relationship. In a moment he had turned into someone she didn't know, didn't want to know. Then she had an idea.

"I need to use the bathroom."

"You saw where it is, just through the bedroom and to the right."

As she walked across the room, he said with a smile on his face, "If you look in the top dresser drawers, you'll find some pjs, socks, underwear, and sweats, all in your size. In the next drawers, you'll find the same for me. Why don't you just get ready for bed now? Maybe it will help you relax." She could hear what he said but it didn't really register.

He turned his head and continued watching the TV, as if nothing out of the ordinary had happened. Shelly felt close to panic when she got to the bedroom. She rushed to the dresser and very quietly opened the top two drawers. He was right. It was all there, all in her size. She hurried to the closet and opened the bi-fold doors. As she looked at the clothes, she saw everything from tank tops to sweaters, sandals to boots, all in her size. She dropped to the floor and trembled uncontrollably as she started to cry.

Shelly thought, "With his warped mind, he must have actually planned all of this as though we are a happy couple!" She knew they weren't a couple, but she was trapped. She didn't know where she was and neither did anyone else. She walked towards the windows to look at the bars on them. She had seen them earlier but believed they were there to keep people out during the off season. She now realized they were there to keep her in! And they were nailed shut as well. She was being held against her will! She was kidnapped! The only way out was through him!

Shelly tried to remain calm as she walked to the bathroom with clothes in hand. She slipped into sweats and a sweatshirt. When she opened the medicine cabinet, it was filled with new makeup, all her brands. She wanted to scream, to cry, to run for the front door. But she knew she had to control her impulse to run. She had to think and to plan. She had to be very careful and not cross his line.

The next few days felt as though they were children playing house, making dinner, hanging out, talking. She started to feel confident that he had calmed down. Then three days later he took her for a walk in the woods. She hadn't left the cabin since the day they arrived. She tried to look at and remember everything, where the cabin was located, what the surroundings were, but the woods were thick with summer leaves and undergrowth so she couldn't see far. She hadn't known the roads he had driven when they left the picnic, and nothing looked familiar now. He was happy and hummed his favorite song, as they walked through the woods without ever seeing another person or another building. She started to believe he wanted to show her that there was no one around, no way to escape.

On their way back to the cabin she looked up and saw that his car had a camouflage tarp over it along with branches and leaves. Her hopes that someone looking for them would see his car evaporated. No one could possibly know that anyone lived in the cabin. Fear overwhelmed and consumed her entire body. She felt her legs start to buckle. Sweat rolled down her back and she thought she could throw up.

The days passed slowly and turned into weeks. Everything was fine until she mentioned her family. If she even brought them up, she could see the anger grow in his eyes, his neck tensing up, and growing bright red.

It was now time for Shelly to start her next semester at art school. The dream of continuing school seemed almost impossible at this point. Still, she convinced Todd to drive her to a pay phone to make a call to at least ask to postpone her return to school. He agreed saying, "I'm glad you see it my way. Who needs stupid college anyway? All you do is meet people there."

Then in the same, mean, harsh tone he told her to turn around, pulled her hands behind her back, duct taped them together, and put a blindfold over her eyes, so there would be no chance for her to figure out where she was. They got into the car and he shoved her onto the passenger floor. He grabbed the paper from her hands with the info for her school and threw it on the passenger seat. Then he drove to a pay phone. She remained restrained in the car while he made the phone call and passed himself off as her dad. He told them they were going through a difficult time with a family illness.

She thought to herself, "Surely they will question him, and this will be my chance." But with no questions asked, they agreed to a leave from school.

He got back into the car and said sarcastically, "DONE! See, there's nothing I can't do."

Before they drove away, Todd removed the blindfold. His eyes glared at her, as she squinted to see his face. It was a look that she had grown to recognize and despise. Her hair raised on the back of her neck every time she saw it.

Then Todd smiled as he continued to gloat, "I told you there isn't a thing in this world that I can't do or undo."

All Shelly could do was cry as she shivered uncontrollably. She felt her bladder release and the warmth of urine as it ran down her curled up legs, through the seams of her jeans, and onto the floor of the car, until she sat in her own urine.

He remarked, "You better not have pissed in my car, or you're licking it up…. EVERY bit of it

She was numb all over. What he said didn't even register.

They drove back to the cabin and, once again, his whole demeanor totally changed.

Though he dragged her out of the car by her hair, the words coming out of his mouth started to become gentle and kind. He carefully removed the duct tape and took the gag out of her mouth.

When they walked into the cabin, Todd led her toward the bathroom where he began to fill the tub. She thought to herself, "What the heck is he doing?"

Then he started to undress her. "Now, Babe, you know I didn't mean any of that back there? Right?"

She couldn't bring herself to answer him. Again he asked the same question, and again she didn't answer.

Suddenly, after appearing so concerned and saddened by what he had said and done, he quickly pulled his hand back and slapped her so hard across her face that her entire body lifted off the floor. She landed on her back in the tub and her legs hung out over the edge. He grabbed them and squeezed her ankles so tightly she thought they were going to break.

"There, bitch, you want to treat ME with disrespect by not answering me? Wash yourself and be sure to scrub every inch of that disgusting body of yours. Your stench sickens me!"

The warm water covered her, and she slowly rubbed the washcloth over her body. She wanted the water to make her disappear. Later as she watched the water starting to drain from the tub, she wished she could just go along with it, silently and quickly, what a peaceful way to go!

Suddenly she could hear him approaching. The inner peace she had found in something as simple as watching the water swirl down the drain was gone. There was no longer a place for her to disappear from the hell she was forced to live. Again that overwhelming fear and feeling of nausea filled her body.

"What's he going to say? What's his next move?" His shadow came through the door before she saw his face and, in an instant, he was there with a sarcastic smile on his face.

Then like the psychotic person she now knew he was, he said, "All done sweetie?" He handed her a robe and panties. "Here slip into this and come out and sit by the only man who will ever love you. After all, who would really want you anyway? I mean, that's why I came after you, because I felt sorry for you. I guess I could call you my pet project. Right?"

She didn't answer right away. So he screamed into her face, so close she could feel his spit all over her. "RIGHT?" He repeated.

She struggled to get the words out but managed to say "Right, I mean…… you're right about everything."

He answered, "I'm finally getting through to that thick head of yours. See, who needs college when you have me to show you life, and the way it's supposed to be?"

She thought, "If that's the way life is supposed to be, my God, it's truly like hell here on earth."

He left the room, and she put on the robe as he instructed her to. When she walked into the living room, he was seated on the sofa.

She asked his permission, "May I sit on the floor in front of the fire place to get warm?"

Surprisingly, he said, "Of course. You don't need to ask my permission for that."

Shelly slowly curled up into a position on the floor as close to the fireplace as she could get, and as far away from him as possible. As she gazed into the fire, she couldn't stop wondering what her parents must be going through.

By 7:00 p.m. on the day of the picnic, Sue and George, Shelly's parents, had become worried. It had been about noon when they found the note and it was now a long day for a picnic. By 9:00 p.m. they were really concerned. By 10:00 p.m., they were panicked and drove to the police station to file a missing person's report. Their fear and panic turned to anger and frustration when they weren't taken seriously. The police wanted them to believe that Shelly was just out late with her boyfriend or had left on her own.

Her father insisted, "She wouldn't do such a thing. She's never given us any reason to worry."

The officer replied, "Believe me, this happens a lot. Youngsters who think they're in love and run away together. When they realize how hard it is to make it on their own, they come running back home. However, we definitely don't want you to leave here under the impression that we take this lightly. We'll keep our eyes open. We want you to contact us the moment you hear anything. Other than that, Sir, there's nothing we can really do at this time."

Shelly's parents knew they had to continue to try on their own. Their next move was to contact Todd's parents. After they tried to reach them by phone several times the next day, they decided to go to their home. When George knocked at their door, a woman slowly opened it and they could see a man standing in the background.

"Hello" the woman said. "Is there something I can do for you?"

"We would like to talk to you about our daughter, Shelly, and your son. May we come in?" Sue tried to sound calm and friendly. She wanted their cooperation.

Todd's mother turned to look at his dad, as if she needed his permission. They both hesitated. Shelly's parents continued to stand there, waiting. Finally, Todd's father came to the door. "You can come in, but I don't know how much we can tell you. What exactly do you want to know?"

Shelly's father replied, "All we're asking for is the truth. What happened to our daughter and your son?"

"What do you mean what happened?" Todd's father asked. "Our son does as he pleases, and we have no problem with that. We haven't heard a thing. Did something happen? Maybe you need to keep better tabs on your daughter. Now if you don't mind it's getting close to our suppertime, and we like to keep a strict schedule around here. If not, the work just doesn't get done."

Shelly's dad started toward Todd's father, but her mom stopped him. She pulled him out the door and towards their car.

"Oh my!" Sue said when they were seated in the car. "Now we understand where Todd gets his disposition! I wonder what they know."

Their faith in God was a significant part of their lives, and Sue turned to her faith for strength to get them through this terrible time. Multiple visits to their priest and his contact with Todd's parents brought no information either and only added to their desperation.

But Shelly knew none of this as it happened. All she knew was that she should have listened to her parents. How could she have been so naive to think that someone like Todd could ever change for anyone or any reason?

Chapter 11

Lynne's Story, Looking Back to November 1996

KANGAROO CUDDLING

After that initial visit, Lynne spent time with Kelly at least twice a day. She needed someone to take her in a wheelchair because of the caesarian and because her blood pressure was still elevated. A nurse would take her to see Kelly during the day and then, when Luke would come to visit, they would go to see her together. They continued to reach into the incubator to touch Kelly and hopefully impart strength and healing. They each continued to battle in their own ways with their fear and anger.

When Kelly was 5 days old, Lynne was released from the hospital. Going home after delivering a baby was a wonderful day for most mothers. For Lynne it was incredibly difficult to go home without Kelly. She felt as though she left part of her soul behind. She saw other couples leaving with their full term, healthy babies. She felt like other people stared at her thinking, "Look at that poor lady leaving without her baby." She knew that there was no possible way they could know what she had gone through, and was still going through, but she felt that her pain was so strong it had to be visible on her face. She was the type of person who couldn't hide what she felt, and she was in agony for both herself and their tiny child.

Since Lynne was on leave from her job as a Mobility Instructor at the School for Blind Children, she was able to be home in the mornings to put Greg on the bus and to be there when he got home. She was concerned about him. Lynne knew it had been a difficult time for him in many ways since Kelly was born. She and Luke had spent a significant amount of time at the hospital with Kelly though they tried to keep life as normal as possible for Greg. Still, there had been fewer family dinners, fewer movies, fewer bedtime stories, and significantly fewer smiles. The hugs continued but Lynne believed that Greg could see the fear and anxiety in their faces. They would take him to see Kelly for short periods of time each week. Lynne was sure he didn't fully understand everything that was happening. He had occasional questions about Kelly and when she would come home. But Lynne knew he mainly just wanted his life and his parents to return to normal as any child would have wanted.

As soon as the bus pulled away each day, Lynne would make a phone call to the nurse on duty to check on Kelly's status. Then she would get her electric breast pump and start the process that took at least twenty minutes, ten minutes on each breast. Lynne was really pleased because she got a lot of milk that she could take to the hospital for Kelly. At this point Kelly couldn't have it because she was on IV fluid but the nurses reassured Lynne that, once she was ready, she would be given it through a feeding tube inserted into her tiny nose. They had to wait until her stomach and intestines were ready to accept the nutrition. Until then, they kept it frozen.

Unfortunately, when Kelly's doctors began to introduce Lynne's breast milk, she developed NEC. This condition is common among premature babies whose intestines are not fully developed. It's similar to an adult colitis but it can be fatal to such a small baby. So, even though Kelly's body needed the breast milk, her intestines couldn't handle it and they had to stop giving it to her for about 10 days. She was back on IV fluids and Lynne felt like they had taken a giant step backwards in the survival of their baby. The doctors continued with all the medication they could administer through IV but it felt so disheartening that Kelly couldn't get the nutrition they knew she needed.

Despite the disappointments, the nurses and the doctors encouraged Lynne and Luke to hold Kelly against their skin.

It was called "kangaroo cuddling." The first time Lynne got to kangaroo cuddle Kelly was incredible.

She walked into the room and the nurse said, "Would you like to hold her?" It was already a couple of weeks since Kelly had been born and Lynne had only been able to touch her so far. She began to cry.

The nurse told her what to do to prepare. She had to remove her shirt and her bra.

"Do you mean I have to sit there naked?"

The nurse laughed, "No, you'll put a hospital gown on and leave it open in the front so Kelly can feel your skin. We'll cover you with a blanket."

Then the nurse brought a rocking chair over so Lynne could rock Kelly while she held her.

"What about all the wires and monitors?" Lynne asked.

"Don't worry. When I hand her to you, we'll be sure everything is arranged so her monitors will stay in place."

As Lynne removed her clothes, she shook with anticipation. She wished Luke was with her for this incredible experience. She sat down in a rocking chair and the nurse gently lifted Kelly out of the incubator. The nurse handed her to Lynne and Lynne said, "Here I go again," as the tears started streaming down her face. The nurses were accustomed to her tears by now.

Lynne couldn't see Kelly's face because she held her against her body. The only thing she had on was the tiny hat and tiny diaper. It was amazing to Lynne that someone so little could be alive. It felt like holding a baby doll that had soft skin and a beating heart. But Kelly was alive! She and Luke had created this tiny pulsing life and she prayed that the pulsing would continue, and that Kelly would soon be strong enough to come home.

After what seemed like a very short time, the nurse said, "Lynne, it's time to put Kelly back in her cocoon." She had only been able to hold Kelly for about ten minutes. She couldn't maintain her own body temperature yet and it was vital to keep her warm.

Lynne reluctantly handed Kelly back to the nurse and watched as she laid her down. It was at that moment that Lynne started to think that Kelly might make it. The nurses thought she was well enough for Lynne to hold her! She had to be getting stronger. Hope and optimism started to overcome the fears.

The day that Lynne first saw Luke holding little Kelly became etched in her mind. He was a big 6'3" man getting ready to hold his tiny baby for the first time. The nurse asked him to remove his shirt so that he could hold her against the skin on his chest. He was also directed to wear a gown, so he didn't have to sit there half-naked.

Lynne could see her husband shaking as the nurse handed Kelly to him for the first time and saw tears in his eyes as he reached for her. As he placed her on his chest Kelly seemed to disappear because she was so tiny. The only evidence of her presence were the wires coming out from beneath his hospital gown. He sat, rocked her, and talked softly to her for about 10 minutes before the nurse said it was time to place Kelly back in the incubator. He looked at Lynne and said, "That wasn't long enough. When will I be able to hold her longer?"

The next Saturday, Greg was invited to a birthday party that started early in the afternoon. Since Lynne was able to spend more time with Kelly during the week, she stayed home to drop Greg off at his party while Luke headed to the hospital early. Having time to spend with Greg was also precious to Lynne because she needed to have a good sense that he was ok. She made his favorite pancake breakfast and they watched Saturday morning cartoons together. It comforted Lynne to hear Greg's giggles as they watched Scooby Doo, his favorite. It reassured her to get a glimpse into his life that somehow retained a sense of normalcy. Lynne didn't want to feel that Greg spent his days consumed with worry about his sister.

After dropping Greg off at the party, Lynne headed to the hospital. The song by Donna Lewis that always reminded her of Kelly was on the radio. It captured some of the emotion that Lynne felt for her tiny baby. It spoke to their special connection of love that Lynne knew would be eternal. It had become "their song."

When Lynne got to the hospital and walked into the NICU she was surprised to see Luke standing over Kelly and washing her with a tiny sponge.

"Luke, what are you doing?!!"

"I'm giving Kelly her first bath today! How special is this?"

Lynne thought to herself, "Wow! This is a good sign! Kelly must be improving." But at some level she was still afraid, and a voice inside wondered, "Was she really?"

Chapter 12

Lora's Story, Looking Back to June 1989

SOLO ACTION

"I've had it with the tears! It's not meant to be!" Rick walked through the door one night to find her crying again. She knew he didn't want to see tears, couldn't comfort her tears. He was frustrated that he couldn't convince her how wonderful their life was without a child.

"We have a great life! We travel, go to the theater, go sailing, have dinner in great restaurants, and have total flexibility. What more do we need?!" He looked at her and flashed the smile that had always drawn her into his visions.

Lora's voice quivered as she tried to reply, to make him understand. "But our lives will be incomplete without a child! How can we feel good about lives that have been devoted to just having fun? I want to take care of a child! I want to love a child and feel that special love in return! How will we feel when we draw our last breaths, if our lives have only been about ourselves and having fun?" Lora walked towards him and tried to put her arms around him, but he pushed her away.

"I won't continue to watch your drama! It's time to accept that a baby is not going to be part of our lives! We tried to make it happen, but it didn't! Let it go!" His face was hard now and his tone was cold. Rick left the room and Lora didn't follow. It was one of many recent nights that Rick chose to sleep in the spare bedroom. He left on a business trip the next morning without saying a word to her. Lora went to her office as always and tried to focus on other people's problems, tried to bring resolution to the workplace she supported, tried to draw comfort and hope from those resolutions. There was no call from him that night. She sat with their cat and tried to see a way to bring happiness to them both.

A few weeks after their wonderful, potentially life creating Alaskan cruise, Lora had walked out of their bathroom knowing there was no baby growing inside of her. She felt disappointed but not upset. There was lots of time for them to create a baby and lots of fun to be had while they tried to create a new life. In the meantime, she knew her wonderful life with Rick would continue. And so it did, with continuing hope for a pregnancy and continuing disappointment.

In June 1987 they decided to consult a doctor. It was then 2 years since the Alaskan cruise. There was still no urgency but they both were surprised that there was no baby considering their continued intense efforts. The test results weren't good. There were no apparent issues with Lora's fertility, but Rick's sperm count was very low, probably too low to conceive a child. The doctor was still hopeful they would be successful over time but didn't feel artificial insemination was an option for them, unless they used a donor. Initially, there was absolutely no sense of urgency. In fact, Rick and Lora laughed when they responded to the doctor's question.

"How do you think your marriage will be impacted if you are unable to conceive a child together?"

"No impact!" they both agreed.

"We'd love to have a baby," Lora continued. "But we have a wonderful relationship and an incredible marriage. That won't change!"

It had now been about 2 years since they first consulted the fertility specialist and Lora was approaching her 38th birthday. Until this year, Lora truthfully thought she would be happy with her life whether or not she had a child. When Rick had first asked if she would have a baby with him, Lora wasn't even sure that being a mom was something she wanted in her future. Somehow that had changed recently, and Lora had become overwhelmed with the desire to have a child. At some level she recognized that her intense desire was undoubtedly linked to her mother. Her mother had died when she was 38 years old. As Lora approached her 38th birthday she began thinking more about all the things she wanted from her life and trying to recapture her connection to her mother. She believed she could only find that special connection with a child of her own.

Unfortunately, at about the same time the desire to have a child grew stronger in her, Rick decided that maybe he didn't really want to have a child after all. And so, they looked at each other, and the rest of their lives, with no idea of how to resolve their dilemma. The home they shared became filled with arguments and tears. They discussed, and eventually battled.

At this point, the fertility specialist could offer no options other than artificial insemination by an anonymous donor. Lora was willing but Rick wouldn't even consider that option. He said he would consider adoption but definitely not the insemination process with a donor. And so, after talking and talking with each other about their different visions for how to live the rest of their lives, after consulting multiple times with a therapist who could offer no real resolution, after Lora's feeling of being isolated from Rick continued to grow, after continued lonely nights with no contact from Rick, Lora decided to make her own decision. She decided to move ahead with artificial insemination by a donor, with or without Rick's agreement.

Lora was also open to the idea of adoption but, first she wanted the full experience of feeling a life growing in her. Then they could adopt another child as well to create their family. So she scheduled the procedure and waited for what she hoped would be the right time to tell Rick. She hoped that he would somehow agree now, and they would be able to return to a life of love, fun, adventure as she attempted to conceive a child in another way. There wasn't a right time.

It was a Friday night and Rick was home for dinner. They had finished eating, sipped some wine and avoided the topic of a baby. Lora took a deep breath and said, "I need to tell you something. I've scheduled an insemination procedure for Tuesday next week. I hope you'll come with me."

Rick slammed his glass down so hard that Lora saw wine splash onto the table. "I don't want you to do this! Do you understand? How could you think it's ok for you to do this without my agreement?! I told you I would agree to look into the possibility of adoption as a compromise. But I don't, do not, want you to have an insemination! What's wrong with adoption?"

"Nothing, nothing, of course! I've always wanted to adopt a child, several children, since I was in high school. But we can do both. We can watch a child grow in me and we can adopt also! Let's experience both ways to build a family!" She reached out to touch his hand, but he pulled it away.

Rick looked at her and said very slowly, "No! I don't want you to do this! I don't agree. Don't do it!" He got up and left the room. A few minutes later, Lora heard the garage door go up and he drove away. He came home late that night and there was very little conversation the next two days.

Lora was determined to go forward with the insemination. She believed it would be ok once a child started to grow inside her. She believed he would become excited once a new life became a reality. They had talked about having a baby before they even talked about marriage. She had to make it happen. It would be a whole new adventure for them to share. He would thank her one day for making him a father!

The following Tuesday Lora left her office in the middle of the morning to head to the hospital for the procedure, alone, without Rick. He was at home, in their bedroom packing a bag, when she got there later in the afternoon.

"I hope you're going to tell me that you decided to respect my wishes and didn't do it." He continued putting clothes in the bag and didn't look at her.

"No, I had the procedure. Maybe we'll be parents in 9 months!" Lora smiled and hoped his reaction would not be what she expected and feared. "Please, please, please be excited about the possibility of finally becoming parents together. Incredible things could be happening inside my body now! I love you and desperately want this adventure for us!"

There were no words from him as he turned, grabbed his bag, and walked from the room. Contact from him was erratic over the next few weeks, including over weekends. Lora kept telling herself that the anxiety about their relationship would be worth it when they celebrated a baby on the way. He had so much love to give a child. Together they would experience a connection so basic to human life on earth.

Despite her attempted optimism, Lora's anxiety grew as the days passed. She would soon know if the procedure had been successful. She needed someone to talk with about her feelings and one morning went into the office of her colleague, Helen. Helen listened to Lora's story, only some of which she already knew.

"Lora, I can hear how much you want to have a child! I understand that. But, do you understand how much you are risking by taking these steps without your husband's agreement?"

Chapter 13

Shelly's Story, Looking Back to August 1983

RAPE

It was another evening and Shelly again sat and gazed into the fire, still wondering about her parents, as Todd walked up behind her without making a sound. "Penny for your thoughts?" he said.

He frightened her so badly that she was afraid to turn around and look at him. He sat down next to her and slowly pulled her hair back off her face. She felt frozen, unable to speak. She didn't want to say anything for fear he would lash out again.

He repeated, "I said, penny for your thoughts."

She thought, "Say something. Say something." Finally she said, "I'm really not thinking anything other than how warm this fire feels."

He responded, "It is nice, isn't it?" Then he said with the same soft tone in his voice, "Are you sure you're happy? I mean, you wouldn't be thinking about your parents and being at home now, would you?"

His voice sounded so sincere she thought, "Maybe he's finally reaching out and understanding how badly I want to go home to my family. He's never sounded so concerned."

So she tried to answer him as delicately as she could, "Well, you know how much I love my family and I would love to see them…."

Before she could finish her sentence, she saw the back of his hand coming towards her face. With no time to react, she felt the blow hit the side of her head. She flew onto her left side. Her hair was in her face but through it she could see him pull his leg back and she felt a blow to the small of her back.

Then he got down into her face and said with a whisper, "Wrong answer. Will you ever learn?"

Answering himself, he said, "I don't think so. You stupid bitch! How dumb do you think I am?!"

He walked away into the kitchen and she heard him open a beer. She lay there, afraid to move, knowing she should be feeling the physical pain, but unable to because of the fear.

He returned to the living room, beer in hand and said, "Get the hell out of the way. I'm trying to watch TV. I don't need your fat ass in the way."

Shelly crawled across the floor and laid in a fetal position for a while. It seemed like hours passed but it was probably just a few minutes. Then she very slowly crawled into the bedroom, climbed up onto the bed, curled up in a ball, and fell asleep crying.

She woke up suddenly to find him on top of her, his hot breath in her face. All she could smell was the stench of the beer and the heat coming from his unclothed body. He started saying, "You love me, right? You love me, right?"

She wouldn't answer. She couldn't answer. She couldn't stop him. She could feel his hands all over her body, as he ripped her clothes off, touched, and probed There was no gentleness in the hands that roughly groped a body never yet explored with love and tenderness. His breath was steamy on her body and she could hear guttural groans that she understood signaled pleasure for him.

She thought, "This can't be happening! This can't be happening!" She was still a virgin and didn't want her first time to be this way. With his left hand he grabbed both her wrists and pulled them over her head. He then straddled her naked body and with his face close to hers said again, "You love me, right?"

She didn't answer. Tears just rolled down the side of her face. She tried to mentally slip away, saying to herself, "He may be able to take my body but he will never have my heart and my mind." Then she was back when he smacked her across the face and thrust himself inside her with no concern, with perhaps even pleasure, for the pain she felt. As he continued penetrating her, slamming into her, he kept screaming, "Say it! Say it!" She could feel his spit hitting her in the face.

She finally said it and he pulled himself out of her, ejaculated all over her face, and smeared it through her hair with a smirk on his face. Shelly would never forget the smell and the stickiness.

Todd then said, "There, bitch, now say that you don't love me."

He rolled off of her and walked boldly and proudly into the bathroom. She became physically ill. She quickly grabbed her clothes off the floor and vomited into them so it wouldn't be on the floor and she wouldn't get into trouble.

When Todd came out of the bathroom, he had showered. He looked at her and said in a calm and loving voice, "I'll take those and you can go get a shower now, Babe. I warmed it up for you."

She found the strength to pull herself off the bed and ran into the shower. The first thing she did was to get under the water and wash her hair. No matter how hard she tried, she felt she couldn't get clean enough. At this point, a part of her mind told her that this would be his chosen weapon of power. She was afraid this treatment would continue until she could find a way out of there. She had to focus on escape and find that way out.

The rapes continued over the next few weeks with no restraint now. He acted as though her body was his to take for his own pleasure whenever he felt the desire. She was afraid to resist but couldn't hide the reality that she felt only fear and no pleasure. She tried not to do or say anything that would excite his desire to physically dominate her.

He believed he had instilled such intense fear into her that she wouldn't even try to escape. One day, he needed to leave for a while. He felt comfortable that he had enough control over her that she wouldn't dare to try anything. He walked to the door saying, "Now, Babe, you know I've got to go for a while, but I'll be right back. Are you ok?"

She said yes. Her voice shook because she thought this might be her chance. She walked him to the door. He said, "Remember, the door locks behind you if you walk out." It was a warning not to leave the cabin.

She said, "Yes, I know."

He winked and gestured with his hand in the position of a gun. He got in the car and pulled away. She knelt on the sofa and watched his tail-lights go down the road. It would get dark soon and he knew she was afraid to be in the woods at night. Would she ever find the courage to try?

Chapter 14

Lynne's Story, Looking Back to November 1996

HOMECOMING

Being able to kangaroo cuddle and bathe Kelly was at least a start and it gave Lynne and Luke hope. It had now been 2 weeks since she was born, and Kelly began to show slight improvements. She was moved into a bigger neo-natal unit where she soon developed a blood infection. Several of the other babies in the unit also developed the same infection. There were rumors that the illness may have been caused by poor hand washing from one of the caregivers! Lynne and Luke were again outraged when they heard this latest news of another occurrence that threatened and potentially could have ended the life of their daughter.

Still, Kelly slowly rose above the illnesses that so many preemies succumb to during their fragile beginnings. She was finally moved to one of the "Con" nurseries where babies would go when they began to show steady improvement.

"I can't believe that Kelly is well enough to move upstairs," Lynne excitedly told her new friend Cindy. Andrew was Cindy's tiny baby who seemed to follow little Kelly as she was moved from one area to the next. Lynne and Cindy had become very close friends as together they experienced the fears and worries of having a child in the neo-natal unit.

"I'm so happy for you and your family! Cindy told her. "You've waited a long time for this."

Not everyone provided encouragement and support about Kelly's progress. One of the nurses who had taken care of

Kelly for quite a while stopped Lynne in the hallway the same day and said, "You'd better tell your husband to chill!" Lynne looked at her to make certain that she was teasing. She was not!

"What do you mean?" Lynne asked.

The nurse looked her in the eye and said, "He asks too many questions!"

"He's trying to learn and understand everything that's happening with Kelly, the machines, the medications, her ups and downs," Lynne cried. "If that was your baby fighting for her life, you'd have a lot of questions, too." Lynne quickly walked away from her, shaking with disgust.

"How dare she?!" she wanted to shout aloud, to anyone who would listen. She was so proud of husband and how he faithfully went in to see Kelly every day after work.

The days slowly became weeks, then months. Before they realized it, Halloween turned into Thanksgiving, then Christmas and then New Year. There were so many times they thought they would lose her during the 95 days Kelly was hospitalized. Despite the moments of hope and optimism, the fear and anxiety took a physical and emotional toll on Lynne. She had difficulty sleeping and eating. She lost weight and, at times, couldn't focus on the most basic functions of her daily life. Every waking moment was filled with worry about her tiny child. Her attempts to float through the days didn't protect her from the overwhelming emotions. In the past, time had slipped by quickly for Lynne. Now each hour, each day, crawled slowly into the future.

But Kelly continued her fight to breathe and to grow and she began to respond to Luke and Lynne when they held her. One morning when Lynne walked into the room, she heard the tiny cries that she knew came from Kelly. She didn't need to see her to know. The biological connection between Lynne and her baby was so strong that her reaction to that tiny cry was immediate.

As she walked towards Kelly she said, "Who's making all that noise?!"

Astonishingly the crying stopped, and Kelly turned her head towards Lynne's voice. Her daughter recognized her mother's voice! The connection between them was confirmed! It was amazing to see that such a tiny human being could respond to the love from her mother.

And then the doctors began to talk about when Kelly would be ready to go home. Lynne and Luke still had so many concerns. They were worried that she was not "ready" to come home. They knew she was still so fragile and required so many different medications.

Soon the news came that the doctor had set a date for Kelly to go home. It should have been a reason to celebrate but Lynne's and Luke's fears continued to grow. Kelly had started to "spit-up" immediately after her feedings. She had never done this before. Because the feedings followed her medication, this was very concerning.

When Lynne mentioned this to one of the nurses and then to a doctor, the response was the same. They just brushed her off saying, "All babies spit-up." Even when Lynne gently reminded them that this was a new occurrence for Kelly, they did not seem concerned and the date to take Kelly home remained unchanged.

Lynne was definitely worried! Beyond worried, she was frightened and panicked. She and Luke would be responsible for administering seven different medications to Kelly using tiny droppers! They were worried that with her spitting up she would not keep down the medications.

One of the nurses, Debbie, approached Lynne in the nursery one day. "I really don't believe Kelly is ready to go home yet. I know you are concerned, and I agree with your concern. Your daughter has made a lot of progress, but she is still too fragile to leave hospital care. It's a huge undertaking for the two of you to provide the care she needs."

"Oh, thank you for speaking up!" Lynne said. "I'm so happy that she'll be able to have more time here before she goes home. We were so worried about being able to care for her."

"No, no, I'm sorry! I've spoken with Kelly's doctors and told them about my reservations," she said as they stood talking. "But the doctor I just spoke with was adamant. He said that Kelly Murray is going home."

Lynne looked at her and felt the fear rising again.

"Mrs. Murray, she's slowly gaining weight and maintaining her body temperature outside of the incubator. That's good. The doctors have the final say. I don't mean to increase your worries. I just wanted you to know what I thought in case you want to talk to the doctor again before she's released." Debbie gave her a hug and walked away.

The conversation added to Luke's and Lynne's mounting fears. The nurses knew Kelly so well, day in, day out, with more constant contact than the doctors, and Debbie was concerned. Luke and Lynne tried talking to the doctor again, but he would not reverse his decision. They ended up feeling it was out of their hands and they had no other option but to take Kelly home on the scheduled release date.

The night before they brought Kelly home they both were asked to stay with her in a room near the neo-natal unit. It was designed to simulate them being at home with her by themselves though the nurses were there if they needed them.

One of the hospital staff took them into the room to settle in before they brought Kelly to them. Lynne looked around the room. There was a huge stain on the floor in the bathroom. There were dirty dishes under one of the twin beds. Her husband looked at her and said, "They expect us to bring our baby into this dirty room? Whose home is this supposed to simulate?!" They told a staff member and they at least removed the dirty dishes, but Luke and Lynne were still very unhappy with the conditions.

A little later a nurse brought Kelly to them. They had notes about her medications and feedings. There was a phone in the room they could use to call for help if they had difficulty. They were assured that someone would come immediately if they called. It was an uneventful night, and everything went smoothly with no spitting up that night. Lynne felt that it helped to have this time with Kelly in the hospital, but she knew it didn't really prepare them for what they were going to have to do when they got home.

The next morning they had all of their written instructions and medications. The nurse told Luke to go get the car and pull up to where the new moms would leave with their babies. It was bitterly cold and snowy and very windy. He pulled up and parked, thinking to himself, "This has to be one of the coldest days of the winter and we have to take our tiny baby home." Kelly was only 3 lbs. 11 oz. that day.

A few minutes later, Luke, Lynne and Kelly were walking out to the car. Lynne got in the back seat with Kelly and they adjusted the car seat before taking off for home. Lynne was both excited and nervous, but the nervousness outweighed the excitement. They were responsible for the care of this tiny baby they believed wasn't ready to come home. But they also felt they were at the mercy of the doctors who insisted she was ready to come home. Lynne prayed they were right.

Still, there was also a sense of relief to know that Kelly would finally be home, and they wouldn't have to travel back and forth from the hospital every day. They were also happy that grandma and grandpa would be waiting at home with Greg.

Lynne thought, "It's finally the real beginning of a new life for our family! But how many days will go by before the worry will fade and I can truly enjoy my baby?"

Chapter 15
Lora's Story February to March 1993
Continuation from Chapter 2
SWEDISH FISH

Thoughts of Rick holding "the other", kissing her, moving in her, ran constantly through Lora's brain. He said, "No, it wasn't happening." But Lora didn't fully believe him. She imagined the poor, frightened, abused woman – afraid of men. And he…strong, gentle, kind, loving… making slow, tender, passionate love to her, asking her to tell him if he hurt her. Lora remembered his approach, his words during her first connections with him and felt certain it would have been the same with "the other."

She became increasingly obsessed with this intruder in her life. Rick told Lora her name but to Lora she would always be "the other." She was a few years older than him. He could barely disguise the pride in his conquest as he talked about her. She loved Disney World like he and Lora always had. She sold Mary Kaye cosmetics and he had started to help her with her finances. She was divorced with two children.

Lora looked back at her notes in her day planner and realized all the time he had spent in Buffalo over the last several months. She studied his old cell phone and charge card records to search for clues about "the other" and about his activities. She looked for any phone numbers that were in the Buffalo area and began to call them. Most of them were business numbers.

When she found what seemed to be a home phone number, she solicited the help of one of her co-workers and friends, Guy, who was very charismatic, with an outgoing personality. He devised a pitch as a vacuum cleaner salesperson and made the call.

"Hello, is this ….?" Guy said her name.

"Hi, my name is Guy." Two thumbs up! It was her!

"I was given your name by a friend of yours who thought you might be interested in purchasing a new vacuum cleaner and I sell the best on the market."

The call went on for several minutes. When he hung up, Guy looked at Lora with a sad grin, "She's not going to buy a vacuum cleaner, but she sounds cute."

Through her studies of Rick's charge card, Lora learned the names of the restaurants where he had dined in the Buffalo area. She found checks made payable to "SB" in his checkbook and screamed with rage at him for having given their money to "the other". She studied a hotel bill from a convention he had gone to in Atlantic City a couple of months ago and found a notation that two keys had been given. She knew "the other" was with him, though he denied it.

Lora continued to drive to her office most days, though she was rarely functional. She attended class one night a week for her Human Resources Master's Degree but often left part way through the class. She saw Dr. Levy twice a week. He worked to coach her through this terrible, humiliating time while her husband saw his own therapist to help him choose between his girlfriend and his wife.

"Don't question him. Don't pressure him for a decision. Don't show your own emotions to him. The fact that he hasn't left at this point, most likely gives you the edge."

The only time she felt hunger was when she drove back to her office from the doctor's office. She would drive through a local fast food burger restaurant and order a huge burger with large fries. Those two huge meals weren't enough to keep her from rapidly dropping weight. On the nights Rick was home with her Lora would try, sometimes successfully, to interest him in sexual encounters. She hoped to make him feel passion if not love. The successful encounters still brought physical pleasure for her but no emotional joy or satisfaction.

Lora was never sure when to expect Rick at their home. His schedule remained erratic and she didn't believe she really knew where he was despite his notes and her calls to multiple hotels looking for reservations in his name. When he was there, the home phone would ring frequently and they both often chose to ignore the ringing, undoubtedly for different reasons. When Lora did decide to answer it, she would often just hear the click of someone hanging up.

One Friday evening in mid-March, Rick pulled into the driveway just as it began to snow. Weather forecasts said it was a huge storm that had formed over the Gulf of Mexico and would have a significant impact on Pennsylvania over the next few days with 2 feet or more of snow accumulation. This Friday night was typical of some recent weekends for them, cooking together, a little strained conversation, then sleep in separate bedrooms

By early Saturday morning, the snow came down hard and the significant accumulation started. There was no discussion about Rick going anywhere. There was a very different feel to the day, as though they were disconnected from everyone else and all the drama of the past months. Lora felt light and peaceful, but she was still surprised when Rick threw her coat at her.

"Let's go play in the snow!" he laughed.

Within a few minutes they were outside, dressed in coats, boots, gloves and hats. They threw snowballs and made snow angels while they sprawled on the ground. Lora giggled and laughed as she threw snow into his face and ran to try to escape the snow flying towards her. When she sprawled on the ground again, Rick joined her and suddenly rolled on top of her. Lora didn't resist his embrace or kiss.

"Let's finish this in the house," Rick suggested, and they were in their bedroom within a few moments. Their joining was intense and passionate with new and unexpected sensations and feelings. It felt this way the few times they had connected recently, but this time Lora felt happiness also. It almost felt as if the past months had not happened. Lora felt no intruder on this weekend, no "other."

By Sunday the snow had stopped, and they worked together in the afternoon to clear the driveway. Monday began to loom, and Lora could feel her mood changing. After coming back into the house, she sat alone in the family room until she heard him call her name. She walked up the stairs and found him in their bathroom. Candles were lit, champagne was poured, the tub was full of water and bubbles. Rick began to remove her clothes and soon they were in the tub together with the magical feeling of the day restored. The love making was amazing again, in ways Lora had never experienced with him. She couldn't totally stop her thoughts from contemplating how and why it had changed. Who else had he kissed and caressed, nibbled and sucked in this way? Who had taught him the new techniques? "The other" was back!

After the make-believe weekend of the blizzard, Rick's absences and Lora's panic resumed. She couldn't believe she had allowed herself to connect with him as she had over that weekend. She felt stupid and embarrassed. She also felt a desperate need to know where he really was and with whom, so she contacted a private investigator. The investigator said he could follow Rick from their home on one of his business trips and report back to her on where he went and who he was with. It would be pricey but at least, her business friend Wise Helen said, she would know for sure what happened on his trips to Buffalo. Lora decided against the investigator, not because of the price.

Wise Helen didn't buy his story about no contact with "the other" but was, true to her nickname, wise enough not to push too hard for the reality she believed she saw. One morning Lora walked into her office and saw a small bag of Swedish Fish lying on her desk. There was an unsigned note stapled to the bag. "If it smells like a fish, it probably is a fish!"

Lora read the note and slid the bag into the back of her desk drawer. She wasn't yet ready to accept the reality of

Wise Helen. She was, in the midst of emotional turmoil, waiting for him to make up his mind. She didn't know if it was really even possible to go back even if he decided he wanted to, but still she waited. She was so afraid of the future, but she had become calmer now. She started to find ways to survive and prepare for the final, overwhelming hurt when he would choose "the other".

In some of the quiet moments she wondered, if she had known 16 years ago, that her relationship with him would lead to this point, if she would have walked away at that time. Or, would she still have opted for the 16 years? She knew the price of love could be great. She had grown and changed because of her love for Rick and the life they had lived together. Would she give that away to spare herself the pain of these days? She didn't know.

At home alone many nights, Lora would sit and remember the life she believed she had been living and imagine the life she now knew Rick had been living. She hadn't known what all the trips to Buffalo meant. Now she could only imagine what he had been doing, how he had connected with "the other", how he longed to stay there with "the other". Lora knew that feelings were strange, funny, living entities. Once gone, once changed, could those feelings ever find their way back again? Her heart was afraid not. She believed he could easily replace her face and his feelings for her with another similar face. He would continue to be his charismatic, charming, engaging self. He would continue to live the life he had been afraid of losing if a child became part of their life.

Rick was a man who would walk into a room and others would be drawn to him, to his smile, his arrogance, his gift of words. He was a master showman, but he revealed little of the essence of his person. At some level, she had always believed that she was a prop in his life. He had chosen her to help build his image. She had the right look, a very nice income, a willingness to live his vision of life. He selected her in the same way he had selected an expensive sporty car, his drink of choice, his designer clothing. She was a prop and props could be easily replaced, couldn't they?

Chapter 16

Shelly's Story, August 1984 to October 1984

Continuation from Chapter 1
MOTHERLY LOVE

Shelly remained coiled up in that fetal position. She lay there and cried on top of her shoes and coat, with the questions she had asked herself over the last 13 months still rolling through her brain. It had taken a year before the fear of continuing to live with Todd overcame her fear of running through the woods alone. Although this attempt to escape had been unsuccessful, she knew she had to find a way out or she would die.

She struggled to gain her composure as she lay on the floor of that closet. Then she could hear Todd's footsteps approach. She shook so badly she felt her teeth chatter. The steps got louder and louder until she could sense him standing there right outside the closet door. She froze as the hairs on the back of her neck rose. She could feel the beads of sweat roll down her spine. Who would open that door Jekyll or Hyde????

Then she heard him speak in a calm soft voice, "Babe, are you going to come out and sit with me? I really miss the warmth of your body next to mine."

Shelly cringed. She didn't even want to be in the same room as him, let alone sit next to him. But she managed to simply answer, "Sure. I would love to come in and sit with you."

Shelly spent most of her time putting on a smile for the monster she lived with while, in her mind, she tried to devise a plan to get away from him. It would be very difficult since he rarely left her alone. He watched her every move. Sometimes she thought he could actually read her mind. It was then that she started to think to herself, "I'm going to have to be smarter about playing this game. He can't read my mind, but my face shows everything I feel inside. That's how he knows what my next move is going to be, and that's what sets him off." Shelly knew she had never learned how to conceal her thoughts and feelings, but she would now. She would win at this game!

One day Todd went out for a few minutes, just long enough for her to take a deep breath without him judging her or accusing her of something ridiculous. When he returned, he acted as though he was in a hurry. He carried boxes into the house and quickly started throwing his clothes into them. He tossed her a box and in a rushed voice said, "Well, Babe, we're going to relocate. Gather your things together. Bring only what you need, and we'll come back for the rest of our things later. And, DON'T ask me any questions. GOT IT?" "

Yes", Shelly replied softly, "I got it".

They didn't speak as they hurriedly got their things together and threw them into bags. This was totally unexpected, and Todd gave no indication of where they would go or why, but this was a glimmer of hope for Shelly. "Maybe now I'll be able to find a way out of this nightmare." she thought.

It wasn't long before they were on the road. This time there was no duct tape over her eyes. She could see and feel his agitation. He was fidgeting in his seat and continually looking at the rear view and side mirrors. He drove very fast as always and didn't seem to care if she saw where they were. She wondered why he didn't care.

"Don't think for one minute that this is over! You're not going home to your precious family! We're going to my house and my parents aren't very happy with you!"

Without thinking Shelly answered, "Not happy with me?" Todd answered, "Ya you! They know how conniving you can be. After all, I would have never done anything like this unless you pushed me into it."

Shelly quickly responded, "That's crazy!" Before she could finish speaking he slammed his fist into her jaw. Shelly flew against the passenger window. When her head hit the glass, she lost her vision and she couldn't think clearly. Her eyes were open but for a few seconds she couldn't see anything. Once again it felt as though she floated above herself and watched everything happen.

The chill of the window glass against her face brought her back to the moment to hear Todd say, "Awe Babe, now you know I didn't mean to do that. You just made me react in a way that I couldn't control. It was all you. You made me do that. If you would just be a good girl that wouldn't happen. Now try not to upset me and I won't have to react that way."

Shelly sat there with tears rolling down her cheeks as they continued on their way to his parents. He had his hand on her leg and slid it back and forth squeezing softly as he drove. She tried to stay as still as possible and not make a sound so she wouldn't upset him in any way.

It wasn't long before they turned off the main road onto a very narrow dark dirt road. The car rattled as they drove over the bumps and divots and moved along slowly until they approached what looked like a pull off along the roadside. However, it wasn't a pull off. It was the driveway to his parent's home. The house appeared to be a spacious white farmhouse with black shutters. It was surrounded by a large open lot and Shelly could see a barn behind the house. The home looked welcoming with its beautiful flower beds flanking the wraparound porch and a stone walkway leading up to it.

As he opened his car door, Todd said, "Well, Babe, here we are."

Shelly looked up and smiled. "This is so quaint," she said, trying to please him, as she climbed out of the car. She followed behind Todd and hung her head, as though she was his servant, as though he owned her. A short round lady stepped out of the door and walked down the steps toward them. Her hair was silver grey, pulled up in a bun on top of her head. She wore an ankle length floral dress with a white apron. Shelly had never met either of Todd's parents previously.

"Hi Todd, it's so good to see you! Hello Shelly." Her tone cooled and her voice dropped off as she said Shelly's name. "Let me help you with your bags." She reached for Todd's bags but ignored Shelly who struggled to carry her bag up the walkway.

By the time they reached the door, Todd and his mother had talked about the weather and their farm. Shelly kept quiet as she continued to drag her bags into the house.

"Todd, I have a room all ready for you, as always," his mother said smiling at him. She looked at Shelly with a glare and in a stern voice said, "And yours is over there, girl! You won't be sleeping with my son."

Shelly approached the room hesitantly as his mother stood there, watched, and said, "Well, go on! There's nothing hiding in there that's going to get you! Get your things settled in and come out to the kitchen."

All Shelly could say was, "Yes, ma'am."

Todd looked at her with a slight smile then walked into his own room. Shelly walked through the door of her room. It was dark and dreary. It had a musty smell with a hint of moth balls. The curtains were drawn and admitted very little sunlight. They were heavy and old-fashioned looking, hanging from hooks at the top. Despite how dark and dreary the room was, she was still relieved to have her own room, away from him.

Shelly walked over and pulled the cord to open the curtains. As she did, she saw thin bars that were made of wood. She then ran to the other side of the room and pulled the cord for the other window, only to see the same wooden bars. She just stood there, feeling like a prisoner. She was a prisoner, his prisoner.

Shelly was startled as she heard his voice say, "Looks like you're stuck with me." He stood in the doorway and smirked at her.

She replied, hesitating for just a moment, "Yes, it looks that way."

Todd walked away as Shelly dropped to a sitting position on the bed. She pulled her knees up to her chest, her face in her hands, and she started to cry. In her mind all she could think was, "Will this never end? I want to be home in my room, on my bed!"

She wiped the tears from her eyes and started to put her things in the drawers as she had been told until Todd showed up at her door again.

"Ready, Babe? Let's go see what's cooking!" He sounded excited, as if they were there for a special dinner.

Shelly responded quietly, "Sure. I'll be right there." She'd been hearing her stomach growl, but she didn't feel like eating anything. She put on a fake smile and joined Todd in the kitchen.

His mother stood at the sink, washing lettuce for a salad, with her back to them as she barked out orders. "Set the table! Come on, you two! And get yourselves something to drink."

Since they had a farm, there was always a huge jar of milk in the refrigerator. It wasn't pasteurized so it had a film of fat that lay on the top. Todd shook it up, excited to swallow the first sip as if he were a child drinking a delicious milkshake. He looked at Shelly and said, "Do you want some?" He shoved it under her nose as he smirked.

Shelly said in a quiet voice, "No thank you." She hated the taste of milk, any kind of milk, and he knew it. He sat and laughed as he gulped down his first glass.

Shelly filled a glass with water for herself and wished dinner was over so she could just go to her room. She wanted to get away from the smell of any food. She wanted to get away from them.

A few minutes later Shelly heard the sound of a tractor crawling up the hill and into the yard. It was his dad. He came through the door and stomped his feet to get the mud and cow dung off his boots.

"What's for dinner, woman? I'm starved." He didn't even acknowledge that Shelly was there. He was a heavyset man who looked older than what she would have thought he was. His skin was worn and wrinkled from the sun. His mouth scowled. He wore a flannel shirt and green work pants that were dirty and had an awful smell to them.

"Oh, just sit down. It's coming right up."

Todd's mother put the food on the table, a roast with potatoes and carrots, a salad, and bread. As they ate, it was silent. No one said a word. The only sound was that of the silverware clinking against the plates. Todd and his father ate with their faces down close to their plates, as if they were animals shoveling food into their mouths. It made Shelly cringe. She had taken a little of each item and forced herself to eat it all so that she wouldn't appear rude and ungrateful. There would have been severe consequences for that.

After the dinner, Todd and his father moved to the living room to watch the news. Shelly and Todd's mother did the dishes in silence, just as they had eaten dinner.

As they finished and Shelly sat down, Todd looked at her and said, "Go in and get a bath."

Shelly asked, "Now?"

Todd's face got red and his forehead tightened as he said in a raised voice, "No! Tomorrow! Yes, now! I knew I was right. You really are dumb, deaf, and stupid! Now go, before I drag you in there myself!"

Shelly got up and caught the sight of Todd's mother's face. She laughed and his father said, "That a boy! Don't give them an inch! They'll always want a mile!" Shelly lowered her head and walked into the bathroom. She was grateful she had barely eaten at dinner. Her stomach was in knots. She didn't want to get sick for fear of him hearing her.

After her bath, Shelly walked back into the living room. It was dark and dingy. Everything was in gold and green colors. There was a fireplace at the far end of the room and a TV in the corner. His parents each sat in their own chair. His father sat by the window, next to a small table that held the telephone and the TV remote. His mother's chair was positioned to face the TV but behind his father's chair. Shelly and Todd sat next to each other on the sofa along the wall until he told her to go to bed. This became the norm, day after unending day.

Shelly was expected to do chores with Todd, clean the chicken coops, collect eggs, and shovel cow manure. It was the price they had to pay for room and board. Time passed slowly, days turning into weeks.

One afternoon Todd and his father sat on the side porch while Shelly washed her hands to prepare for dinner. She suddenly heard them talking loudly and yelling so she went out to see what was happening. As she opened the screen door, she couldn't believe her eyes. There, in front of the house, stood her bother and brother-in-law.

Todd screamed, "Leave! She's not coming with you!" as he pushed Shelly in front of him and said, "You tell them to go! Now!"

"My God, it can't be! Could this be my chance? Can I go home?" Shelly thought as a cold sweat washed over her body. She wanted to run down the steps and into the car that was parked behind the two men. She wanted to finally escape the nightmare! She had dreamed so often about the day someone would find her and she could go home.

"Shelly!" Todd screamed again.

"Ummmmmm," Shelly muttered.

It was then that she felt a sharp pain in her back, and she could hear the hammer of a pistol being pulled back. Todd's dad said, "Do it!"

Shelly didn't dare refuse and yelled, "You need to leave!"

Her brother yelled back, "Shelly, this is your only chance! We're not coming back for you!"

"Just go!" Shelly yelled.

After a brief pause while Shelly's brother stared at her, the two men turned and walked towards the car. As they got into the car, she could hear her brother say, "Unbelievable! She wants to be here! That little whore didn't even have the decency to let our parents know where she was!"

After they closed their doors, Todd looked at her and said, "Good job!"

Shelly was overcome with waves of despair and hopelessness. Without a word she walked back into the house and hung her head as tears rolled down her face. Todd and his dad stayed on the porch to be certain the men left. After they drove away Todd, Shelly and his parents all continued their daily schedule as though nothing had happened. Inside her world was crumbling more than she could ever imagine. The despair she felt made her want to scream but she had to hide her feelings to survive. An escape had been so close, but she was forced to let it go. Would she ever have a chance again?

Later that evening, the phone rang, and Todd's father answered it. Shelly was in her room, but she could hear him speak though she couldn't understand what he said. When he hung up the phone, she heard him call Todd into the room. He spoke quietly and she moved closer to her door so she could hear what he said.

"That was your brother, Ed. He needs you to do a run for him tomorrow. He wants you to meet him at the airport at 7:00 a.m. You'll pick the merchandise up there and deliver it to Jack down at the docks." Shelly knew what this meant. Todd was being asked to run drugs for his brother. Along with everything else, this was one more thing for her to fear. To his family, this was a regular occurrence. To her, it was something she only knew about from the movie thrillers she had seen on the big screen.

Shelly heard him agree and start walking towards her room. She quickly got back into bed and picked up her book as though she was reading. Todd walked into her room, "I have to take off early tomorrow. You'll be staying here. Mom will have chores for you to do."

Shelly looked up and quickly said, "Ok." She dreaded the thought of being home all day by herself with his mother. But then, the thought occurred to her, "This may be my chance!"

94

As the sun came up, Shelly could hear Todd pull out of the driveway. Within a few minutes, his mother showed up at her door, carrying a bucket. "Well, here we are. Looks like we have the day together. I planned to have you help harvest pumpkins today, but I don't believe I can trust you as far as I can throw you. So, it looks like you're spending the day in here. You'll need this because you're not going to be able to go anywhere." She tossed a bucket towards Shelly. walked out and locked the door behind her.

Stunned, Shelly sat on the bed, and looked at the door, as she thought to herself, "I can't do this anymore! I've got to get out of here!"

She started to rummage through the drawers, hoping to find anything she could use to pick the lock. In the very back of a small drawer in the vanity, she found a metal nail file and thought it might do the trick. She walked to the door and started to fiddle with the keyhole to see if there was any way to pop the lock. Despite her best efforts, she had no luck. She sat on the floor, dismayed, but still thought, "There's got to be a way."

Then she looked up at a shaft of sunlight and thought, "The window." She knew she would have to get past the wooden bars but decided to try anyway.

Pulling back the curtains, she was able to slide the window partially to the side, but the wooden bars were still there. She took the nail file and started to pry around the nails. When they were loose enough, she kicked them the rest of the way out. She quickly pulled herself up on the windowsill. As her heart raced, she lowered herself to the ground.

In a split second, she felt a poke in her back. It was his mother holding a shotgun. "Going somewhere?"

The old lady forced Shelly back to her room. She poked at her with the shotgun and laughed. "This is going to be an interesting night here. I know my son, and he is going to have some fun. You must be wanting it! You couldn't be stupid enough to think you could get away! You must be missing it! He won't disappoint you!"

Shelly shook as she moved back into the house and towards the bedroom. Through the fear she thought, "What kind of a mother does this? What kind of a woman does this to another woman? What kind of a mother enables her son to live the life he lives? Now I know why he is the way he is. His whole family has issues. They're all disturbed! They're all crazy!"

As Todd's mother shoved her back into her room, she saw his dad secure the window she had tried to escape from. He chuckled to himself as he worked. When he finished, he turned to look at Shelly and his wife. He raised his eyebrows and grinned as he walked past them and out the door. Shelly couldn't comprehend how his parents could both know what their son would do when he got home, and both enjoy the anticipation.

"Now you can sit here until Todd gets home, then he can deal with you! Think about that, why don't you. I hope you have fun!" His mother looked at her with a cold stare and twisted smile on her lips. She slammed the door behind her as she walked out of the room.

Shelly curled up on the bed, in a seated position, hugging her knees, rocking back and forth. She was thinking about it, and she was scared. She knew exactly what would happen to her. "I know he's going to beat me! What do I do? Can I fight back? But why? I can't escape. He has all the control. Why did I try to get away? He's going to be furious!"

She knew why she had tried to escape. Somehow there was still a little fight left in her. She thought back to the fire at the cabin the first night he had raped her. That night, she had sat and watched the flames fade, but the coals remained hot. In the middle of all of it, a single flame flickered.

She thought to herself, "I will never let him take all of me. My fire inside will always have a flicker of hope left." And so, it had been that very flicker that had moved her to attempt to escape today. It would be that same flicker that she believed would pull her through the beating and rape that was to come.

A little later she heard Todd returning home. She still sat curled on the bed when she heard his car pull up the driveway and the car door slam shut. She could imagine the look on his face and how it would change when he learned what she had done. She could envision the gleam that would come into his eyes and show his excitement. She sometimes wondered if he had ever connected with a woman without force, without violence. Had there been other women subjected to rape and abuse by him? Did he know how to express love without instilling pain and fear? Could he love with gentleness and tenderness? Did he even know what love meant? Were beatings and rapes the only way he felt excitement and sexual satisfaction?

But at this moment Shelly was focused only on what would to happen to her. Her heart pounded. Her body was covered in beads of sweat. She struggled to breathe as she heard his mother's voice explain to Todd what had happened that day. His mother's voice was shrill as she described detail after detail, choosing words to encourage his anger. "That little bitch, sneaky, ungrateful, needs to learn a lesson…" Shelly sat, frozen, stared at the doorknob, waited for it to turn, and thought about what she knew was about to happen.

Suddenly the door burst open without him even turning the knob. He had pushed or kicked with so much force that he broke the latch. He moved across the room in an instant. He pulled Shelly off the bed and threw her onto the floor. He dragged her across the floor by her hair. She felt him lift her by the throat and slam her against the cupboard door.

Shelly could hear his voice scream at her and his spit hit her face but somehow she removed herself from it all. Her body was being beaten and slammed but it was as if she had lifted herself from that body and watched from above. Her body experienced the pain, but she would not allow her mind to go there. It was an act of self-preservation. It was the only way she had mentally survived the ordeal over the last months.

When the beating finally subsided, he threw her back onto the bed, tore at her clothing and threw them on the floor. He began to rape her. "I'm sorry I hurt you! You know I had to do that! I can't allow you to leave me. I can't imagine a life without you! Why would you push me to do that?"

Shelly remained silent, removing herself from what was happening to her body. There had never been a time when he approached her sexually without pain and violence. This was the sum of her sexual experience.

"You are my life, you know! Please try to understand that." Finally it was over, and he collapsed on top of her. As he pulled himself off of her, he continued, "I need you to obey me and, if you don't, well, then you know the consequences. I do all of this because I love you and you should be grateful! If I didn't love you, who would? I mean, look at you! You're nothing but a disgusting whore! Now get yourself cleaned up."

He walked out of the room as she lay there, and tears rolled down her face, but she remained silent. Pulling herself up off the bed, she walked into the bathroom. She had become numb to the beatings, the insults, the rapes. This was her norm now. It had become expected more than feared.

As she bathed, she could hear his father saying, "It's about time you got control over her. Gotta keep them in line." Todd and his mother laughed.

"Do you think this is the last time that bitch will try to leave you?"

Chapter 17

Lynne's Story, Looking Back to Early January 1997

PUFFINESS

The ride home felt like an eternity because of all the things going through Lynne's mind. Thoughts swirled, happy thoughts and unwanted thoughts, as she flipped from excitement to panic.

"The doctors feel Kelly is well enough to come home. That's wonderful! She'll get to sleep in her own home. We'll be able to hold her and cuddle her whenever we want to. Greg will be able to connect with his sister."

"But, I'm so scared about taking care of her. How can I do this? What if I make a mistake? Even the nurse was concerned about sending Kelly home!"

"Ok, you have your master's Degree. You can do this!"

"But intelligence has nothing to do with taking care of her. What if the nurse is right? What if Kelly shouldn't be home yet? What if it doesn't go well for her?"

They finally got home, and Lynne saw Greg's little face looking through the window as they pulled up the driveway. Her parents were there, waiting with Greg, as they carried Kelly into her home for the first time. Lynne's mom was anxious to hold her, but she was also very nervous because Kelly was so tiny. Still, Lynne placed the baby into her mom's arms and began to unpack all the supplies they had brought to care of Kelly.

Lynne's parents stayed for a while, until they got settled in, but too soon they drove away, and Lynne started to feel very overwhelmed and frightened. She knew that it was up to her and Luke to do what was needed to help Kelly grow and thrive. They had a small bassinette in their bedroom where Kelly would sleep. Lynne wondered how much sleep she herself would get. She was afraid to take her eyes off Kelly.

As soon as Lynne's parents left, Kelly began to cry. Lynne looked at the clock and knew it was time for her feeding. While Kelly was in the hospital, the nurses tried to have her on a feeding schedule. She took breast milk, but from a bottle. Lynne warmed the bottle in the microwave and tested it carefully to be sure it wasn't too hot. She kept Kelly swaddled in blankets so there was more of her to pick up.

Lynne sat down on their couch and tried to get comfortable to feed Kelly. She was hopeful that the spitting up after eating would stop now that she was home. She was so little. She could only take about 2 ounces at a time. She drank slowly but finished the bottle and went to sleep. Lynne felt relieved that she hadn't spit up. The next few days were good. Two visiting nurses came to weigh Kelly and to check her vital signs. The nurses said that everything was going well.

On the fourth morning Lynne woke to hear Kelly crying. Amazingly, Lynne was so exhausted that she had found brief times to sleep. The sound was a tiny little cry, almost like the squeak of a baby kitten. Lynne had become such a light sleeper that she heard Kelly's every move. She knew that it was time for Kelly to eat so she took her downstairs to give her the medication, prepare her bottle and settle on the couch to feed her. The house felt very cold and Lynne turned up the thermostat to make it a little cozier.

Lynne had continued the pattern of giving Kelly medication first, then following with the bottle. Kelly had seven different medications each of which had to be administered with a syringe. Lynne gave her the medication in their kitchen where she could work under the overhead lights. She brushed the tip of the syringe against Kelly's lips to get her to open her little mouth and slowly depressed the syringe so that she wouldn't choke. Kelly took the medication easily. They were lucky that it wasn't difficult.

After giving the medication, Lynne carried Kelly into the living room and got comfortable in the corner of the couch. Kelly took the 2 ounces with no trouble. She had finished the bottle and was still snuggled in Lynne's arms when Lynne saw the milk coming back out of her mouth. It was a significant amount and looked enough that it could be the whole 2 ounces. This meant that the medication had probably not been absorbed.

Lynne felt panicky and reached for the phone to call the hospital. She had the number to call directly into the neonatal nurses.

"Hi, this is Lynne Murray. My daughter, Kelly, came home a few days ago after being in the hospital for 95 days. She's on 7 different medications and I'm concerned because she just spit up after taking the medication."

"Well, all babies spit up," the voice replied.

"But I'm concerned that she didn't get the medication. She needs the diuretic for her lungs. Her lungs aren't healthy."

"I'm not concerned about this," the voice said. Lynne felt like she was brushed off, but she knew the visiting nurses would be coming soon and she could talk to them.

Later that morning, around 10:00 a.m., one of the visiting nurses came. She introduced herself as Kathy. She seemed very friendly and interested in how they were doing and how Kelly was doing. She weighed Kelly and said she was pleased that she had gained some weight. She took her vital signs and said she thought she was doing well.

At her first opportunity, Lynne said, "I'm concerned that Kelly spit up right after I gave her the medication and her bottle this morning."

"I think it's ok as long as she doesn't do it all the time, but you should track it."

Lynne felt a little reassured but still worried. She knew she wouldn't feel better till Kelly could take the medication and always keep it down. Still, she was comforted by the words of the nurse until the next time Kelly spit up later that day.

Again Lynne called the hospital and asked to speak to one of the nurses who was familiar with Kelly, and again was told, "All babies spit-up!"

"But I don't think you understand! She can't be keeping her medication down. She needs that medication to survive! I'm worried and I'm frightened!" Lynne didn't know what else to say to convince the nurse how serious this could be for Kelly.

"Mrs. Murray, you need to stop calling with the same questions. We have babies here who need our attention. Absolutely call if something different happens. If not, you can talk with the visiting nurse when she comes." The voice was cold and sounded annoyed.

The visiting nurses continued to come. Each would evaluate Kelly by weighing her, listening to her lungs and asking general questions. They all seemed pleased with Kelly's progress, which gave Lynne and Luke increasing confidence. Kelly had slowly continued to gain weight and the nurses didn't seem to be concerned about her spitting–up.

And then, there was the appointment with Dr. Mark on day 9 and his terribly flawed assessment of Kelly's condition. Lynne left that appointment feeling reassured that Kelly was making slow and steady progress. But at some level she still questioned, "Was she really?"

Chapter 18

Lora's Story March 1993

TRUTH

Rick rarely picked up the phone in his hotel rooms when Lora called, no matter what the time. He always had an explanation for where he was and what he was doing. He called her at home on off hours when she normally wouldn't have been there, apparently hoping to just be able to leave a message. She was often home now as she waited and hoped that he would call.

One Thursday morning, when Rick was again in Buffalo, she called his hotel room at about 6:15 am, before she left to drive to her office. There was no answer. After the third try, she called the front desk and asked to leave a message for him.

"Please tell him that, if he's interested in saving anything, he'd better get his ass back to Pittsburgh tonight."

Lora was always on the edge of hysteria and had begun to act and speak in ways that were foreign to her. She hoped that her message would embarrass him. He had always been a private person, so professional, so concerned about his appearance and the impression he made on others.

When she got to work, she tried again and still there was no answer. She walked into the office next to hers to find Wise Helen. "Helen, I need your help!"

Wise Helen looked up, "What's happened now?"

"I've been calling him since 6:15 this morning and there's no answer in his room! What if something has happened to him? What if he's had a heart attack from all this stress and conflict? I'm so scared! I need to find out if he's ok Will you help me? I can't do it myself."

Wise Helen hesitated, then said, "What do you want me to do?"

"Would you call the hotel and tell them that you're his mother and he hasn't been answering the phone and you're worried about him? Ask if someone can go and check his room to be sure he's ok."

"Oh, Lora, do you really need me to do this for you? Can't you guess where he might be?"

"No, no! I can't guess! I need to know for sure what's happening. I can't continue to live like this! Please call for me! I'm so upset. I can't pull it off myself. Please, Helen, please!"

Wise Helen made the call for her and handled it beautifully. "Hello, my daughter-in-law has been trying to contact her husband, my son, who is a guest at your hotel. He's not answering, and we're concerned about him because he's had some health problems recently. Could someone go to his room and check to be sure he's not in need of help, but unable to pick up the phone? Thank you. I'll wait."

A few minutes later, Helen hung up the phone. "They said there was no one there and the bed had not been slept in."

"Where is he? Where is he?" Lora cried. But, of course she knew where he was, or at least who he was with.

Rick called at about 12:30 when Wise Helen was in Lora's office. His voice sounded tight and controlled.

"Lora?"

"Yes."

"I got your message and I don't appreciate you leaving that kind of message with the hotel clerk". He sounded angry. "I must have been out getting coffee when you called. I haven't done anything wrong."

"Helen called the hotel for me this morning and pretended that she was your mother. They had your room checked and the bed was never slept in."

Silence. Then, "I don't want to talk about this on the phone. I'll see you when I get back to Pittsburgh."

"No, no! I want to talk now! Where were you? You just lied to me! Where were you?"

"Alright, you're right. I didn't sleep at the hotel last night. It was "the other's" birthday yesterday. I took her out to dinner and slept on her couch last night. Nothing happened."

"How fucking stupid do you think I am?!!" She had never before in her life used the word "fuck." The door to her office was closed but she was sure others outside could hear her voice. She didn't care.

How far had they come that he could think it might be ok for him just to take his girlfriend out to dinner for her birthday, as long as he slept on the couch? How much had their lives changed? How could she have allowed this to become "normal?" Wise Helen had repeatedly warned her not to accept this reality.

Wise Helen would say, "As human beings, we can become accustomed to almost anything. Don't let this situation become normal for you or it will take you much longer to get out of it."

Lora tried to lower her voice and speak calmly. "You have driven me to the point that I now use the word fuck in my office at my job. I have allowed myself to live in this insanity to the point that I am out of control. People outside my door can probably hear me screaming. You lie to me repeatedly. You tell me about your girlfriend's birthday. Cancel the rest of your appointments and get back to Pittsburgh if you are interested in saving anything." She hung up and began to cry.

When Lora got home from work there was a message on the answering machine from him.

"Cutie, I need to install a system at Wicker Lumber. I can't get home till Friday. Please, please don't do anything rash. We need to talk. I love you."

She didn't hear from him again on that Thursday. There were a few messages from him on Friday asking her to please pick up the phone if she was home. Then, there was nothing. By 9:00 p.m. that night she realized that he wasn't coming home.

On Saturday morning she was desperate to know where he was. She called the phone number for "the other" and left a message for him to call her. When she called again, "the other" answered.

"Let me talk to him."

"He's in the shower. You know how mornings can be!"

"Then I'll wait. I think it's time you and I talk anyway. I need to know what he's telling you."

"No. I can't talk while he's here. He'll be leaving soon. I'll call you back then so we can both understand the truth."

Lora's phone rang in less than an hour. "The other" began telling the truth as she knew it.

"I'm sorry that this is happening to you. I don't know you and I'm sorry if you're hurting, but he and I love each other. He's coming home to tell you that your marriage is over. He's going to get his things and find a place for us to live. He's been to see a lawyer and he's going to file for divorce on Monday."

Lora said little. She couldn't totally comprehend the words she heard and what they meant about the life her husband continued to live. How many times could she struggle to comprehend what was happening in her own life?!

"Lora, he's crazy about me. All my friends can see how he feels about me. I ask him why he loves me, and he says he loves me because I'm fiery and crazy."

"How did you meet?" Lora asked.

"We met right before Thanksgiving. I was at a bar with some friends and he was with his friend, Scott. Scott started talking to me first. Then he said I should talk to his single friend. When I was ready to leave, Rick walked me to my car, tried to kiss me and asked if he could come home with me. He didn't have a wedding band, so I believed he was single. A month later I learned that he was married but by then you were separated"

"We were never separated," Lora said. Apparently there were lies to "the other" also.

"How can that be? He used to call me every Saturday morning to tell me how much he wanted to be with me, and we'd talk for hours. Where were you if you weren't separated?"

With that question, Lora realized they had been separated, not physically, not legally, but they were living different lives. Every Saturday morning she had worked with the other families to make the adoptions happen. At the same time he had built a relationship with another woman.

"He called me for weeks afterwards before I'd agree to see him again. I constantly picked up messages from him even when you were in Cancun together. He told me he couldn't get this strange person off his mind while you were there."

The more she talked, the more Lora realized that she didn't know this person "the other" described. She believed her husband had loved her. Their marriage was the center of both of their worlds. He wasn't interested in other women. They had the best marriage any two people could have. Their friends were envious of their life and their marriage.

"The other" continued, "He's always been very gentle with me. Even something small, like the touch of a hand, he allowed me to give to him when I was ready."

"Lora, I don't want to hurt you any more than you're already hurting, but he wants to make a life with me. He told me he wants to marry me as soon as he can get a divorce. This is not a casual relationship. He's in it for the long term. I have waited my whole life for someone like him." "The other" sounded bubbly and excited.

"You know, he treats me like a queen. He's always fussing over me, hanging up my coat, opening the door for me. I'm always telling him to just relax. He took me to this beautiful bed and breakfast last week for my forty-fourth birthday. The place was named Tara."

It was another punch in the stomach. It became increasingly difficult for Lora to breathe. She had picked up a brochure about Tara, hoping that she and he could spend a weekend there and try to reconnect. One day she couldn't find the brochure. He denied any knowledge of it and she had dropped the idea.

"I know you left him a message at his hotel in Buffalo while we were at Tara. You told him to get his ass back to Pittsburgh if he wanted to save his marriage. I offered to take a bus back to Buffalo if he wanted to go home and try to work things out with you, but he wouldn't let me do that. He told me he was where he wanted to be."

It was another punch! The night he lied about taking "the other" to dinner for her birthday and then sleeping on her couch! Lora realized he must have checked into the hotel in Buffalo, so he would be registered if she called, and then left to take "the other" to Tara for her birthday! Dr. Levy was right! There was no end to the deceptions. He was a pathological liar.

"He was ready to tell you weeks ago, but he felt bad for you and couldn't do it. The week he was in Cleveland for that meeting, I was with him. I've done a lot of traveling with him. He planned to come home last Friday night and tell you. We checked into the Marriott Courtyard and, when he left, he promised to be back in an hour. He didn't come back till the next morning and he hadn't told you. He told me he's worried about you and what you'll do. He cares about you and is worried about you. He loves me!."

The Mexican dinner on Friday! Lora had made one of their favorite recipes and had waited anxiously for him to come home. When he did, he was distant and distracted. She now understood! "The other" was sitting at the Marriott Courtyard waiting for him. On Saturday morning, they had talked for a while and he told Lora he would go to Buffalo and end it with "the other". He actually drove her back to Buffalo.

"The other" continued, "He told me he always called you "angel." He calls me "cutie." He says, "I love you tons."

Lora's words! "I love you tons," using her phrase, her words to tell "the other" how much he loved her. Lora didn't tell "the other" but, yes, he had always called her "cutie" not "angel." How easy for him to never slip with names!

And then what was probably "the other's" final maneuver to be sure there was no way for Lora to save her marriage, "You know, he's done this before. I'm not the first person he's been involved with. I'm just the first one he fell in love with." And she proceeded to tell Lora about his lifestyle with girlfriends in multiple cities, with gambling and prostitutes, with a naive wife at home waiting.

"He almost didn't marry you because of the woman in Ohio. But he didn't have to choose. He was able to have you both for as long as he wanted. I can't believe you never knew, never even suspected." She talked on and on, so sure of herself, and what she knew of Lora and her life with her husband.

"You are so professional. You wear suits. You are Ms. Corporate America. You're quiet and reserved." She delivered each statement like a slap in the face. "I saw your photo. You're beautiful but that's not enough for him. I'm artistic, outgoing, and impulsive. He and I have a special connection. We laugh and have fun together. We're both Italian and love talking about family traditions and our grandmothers. I told him if he ever does to me what he's done to you, I'll cut his penis off."

"It took a while for me to trust him enough to sleep with him," she continued. "But, he was so patient, so gentle, it became easy for me. He told me to let him know if he ever hurt me." And then one more measured dose of pain, designed to be sure Lora understood that it was impossible to save her marriage, "Remember, if you make love with him, he has done the same things to me."

"He's coming back to Buffalo to get me later this week and take me to Pittsburgh for the weekend. We're going to a retirement party together on Friday."

Lora started laughing at that point. "Interesting! Looks like we will finally get to meet. He and I are going to a retirement party on Friday also. A man I've known for a long time is leaving the company. He called me personally to be sure I planned to be there."

Lora began to tell "the other" just a little of the story she had been getting from Rick and what had been happening at their home. She told "the other" just enough to let her know that he had lied to her also.

"He tells me he wants to end his affair with you but needs to do so carefully because you are very ill, and he's concerned about the impact it will have on you. He wants to be with me for the rest of his life, but he needs to be sure you will have support when he ends his affair with you. Has he told you we're planning to take a European river cruise together? Just to reconnect, heal, and find our way back to the life we love?"

"Oh, and remember, if you make love with him, he's done the same things to me, many, many times. We are still married, and you know what married people do!"

Before Lora was even finished, "the other" began to cry and scream, "No, no, no! You have to believe me! He has promised me a life!"

"He promised me a life too, a long time ago. So why would I not believe you?"

Chapter 19

Shelly's Story, November 1984
APARTMENT LIFE

Shelly had spent most of her days locked in her room. This day was the same. She had been awoken by the roosters at sun-up. On some mornings she would lay there and pretend that it was her farm. She envisioned herself riding the horses through fields of daisies and purple flocks. The sun would be warm on her face and the wind would softly blow through her hair. Then reality came flying into the room.

"Let's go!" Todd said.

"Go where?" Shelly asked.

"That's not for you to worry about. I need you dressed, and your things packed and you out in the kitchen in 20 minutes. Let's go! Hustle!"

Todd left the room but returned in a second saying, "And you know what will happen if you're not!"

Shelly quickly pulled her bag off the shelf in her closet and packed the few things Todd allowed her to keep in her room. She ran into the kitchen with time to spare.

Todd said with his smirk, "Hey, there she is. See what happens when you follow the rules?" He kissed her lightly on the cheek. He took her hand and her bag and led her down the porch steps and to the car. As he threw the bag into the back seat, he said, "Turn around." It was his evil, cold voice again.

Shelly did as she was told, anxious not to do or say anything that would make him angry. He duct-taped and blindfolded her saying, "You know where you belong." He shoved her onto the floor by the front seat. "I don't even want to hear a peep out of you! Do you understand?"

Shelly nodded her head. The car started with that familiar roar that seemed to burn through her ears. It had become a sound she hated.

He drove quickly. The car rumbled down the road and picked up speed. The tires screeched at every bend. Shelly could feel each turn and bump in the road. At first she was fearful of the speed they were going. Then she thought, "Maybe he'll manage to wrap this thing around a tree. Maybe he'll be killed. Maybe I'll be killed and then it will all be over today!" She knew it was sad to think that death would be a better place than where she was. But, to her, it would mean peace. Peace was something totally unreachable for her.

After it felt like they had driven for miles and miles, the car came to a stop. Todd got down close to her face and said in a strong voice, "Stay here, and I mean it. Don't move a muscle."

Shelly doubted she could move at all at this point. Her neck was kinked to one side. Her arms and feet had fallen asleep. She felt as though needles were pricking her legs and she could not reach the blindfold. Trying to move was not an option.

Todd returned to the car, a little winded. "We're here. I'm going to undo your blindfold and tape. If anyone asks, we're happily married, got it?"

"Yes. I got it."

When Todd removed the blindfold, it was hard for Shelly to see. The light burned her eyes at first. Then things began to come into focus. In front of her she saw a long set of concrete steps that led down to a cream-colored apartment building. There were at least 4 other buildings close to them. But, the one in front of her was positioned the furthest from the road and along the wood line. It was Autumn now. The leaves had changed and started to fall. It was incredible that she had been with him for over a year since that dreadful picnic day.

"It's beautiful," she thought. The sun shimmered on the leaves in shades of crimson, gold, and orange as the wind blew gently. Even in all her turmoil, Shelly could see the beauty God had created.

People passed them as they walked down the steps to the apartment building. Shelly saw each and every one but would not have been able to say what they looked like. She stared straight ahead to avoid making eye contact with them, while she smiled and held Todd's hand. For a few minutes it almost seemed right, the two of them walking hand in hand. Everything had started to feel as though it was normal, their normal.

"Maybe it's not too bad," she thought. "Maybe if I do exactly what he wants me to do, he'll change. He did say that it was because of me that he acts the way he does."

As he opened the door to enter the building, Shelly could smell someone cooking spaghetti sauce and it reminded her of home. That was a feeling that she quickly dismissed because of where that feeling would lead her.

After walking down a few flights of steps, to the very bottom of the building, there was a door that led out to what appeared to be a small yard before a wooded area. They turned left into a hallway and stopped by the first door on the left, #301.

Todd opened the door and yelled, "Home sweet home!"

After Shelly stepped through the door, it slammed shut behind her. She walked around and saw a small apartment furnished with a sofa, coffee table and small tv in the living area. A small dining table to the right was positioned outside of a tiny kitchen. There was a door that led to the bedroom and the bathroom.

"Well, what do you think?" Todd asked.

Shelly swallowed hard and quietly responded, "It's nice."

"It's not just nice! It's what you'll be calling home from now on. Our home!" He had a strange smile on his face as he dangled a key from his hand.

"See this?" he continued. "This is the key to your happiness. It all depends on how you act, if this is really a home sweet home. Come on, take it! I said take it!" His voice had become harsh.

Shelly reached for the key and he quickly yanked it away.

"You will never have a key to this place. Do you see that door? It locks as soon as it closes behind you. When I leave and come back, you had better be here, inside this apartment."

He placed his hand softly on her cheek and smiled at her. His hand moved back to the small of her neck and he pulled her close as if he was about to kiss her gently. Then his hand yanked the back of her hair and pulled her head back. His face turned angry as he said, "So, don't get any ideas. You can't leave here without me knowing! Got it?"

"Yes." Shelly said softly.

Todd yanked her hair even harder still and screamed, "What?!!"

"Yes! I said yes!" Shelly replied.

She was locked up like an animal again. It was a basement studio apartment with 2 small windows so very little light came in. It smelled musty and it was cold. She walked into the bedroom and opened the closet door. There were her clothes and shoes, just like before.

"How does he do that?" she wondered. It was a déjà vu moment again, only this time there were people living around her and that gave Shelly hope.

In the kitchen, as she opened the cabinets, all the cans were perfectly stacked with the labels facing forward. His mother had hers the same way. She had taught her son well. Everything had to be exactly the way he wanted it, the tablecloth, the towels in the bathroom, the quilt hanging on the bed. Anything out of place would result in a beating.

A few minutes later Todd told Shelly that he had to go out for a while. She sat on the sofa and tried to collect her thoughts. She could hear people walking in the apartment above her and could still smell the spaghetti sauce.

"This time, I'm really not alone. How can I get out of here? I have to get away from this narcissistic animal, but how?"

Chapter 20

Lynne's Story January 17, 1997

GRIEF

Three of them were back in the car, driving home again, without their baby. Greg fell asleep immediately. There were no words to share between Lynne and Luke. She held the blanket to her face, the blanket they had wrapped around their baby on their frantic drive to the hospital. Lynne inhaled deeply to remember the smell of their baby, to memorize what she would never experience again. Tears rolled down her cheeks, but they were silent tears. The man next to her, the man driving the car, her husband, stared ahead as he drove but she could feel the emotion he tried to contain.

Lynne could barely walk as family members helped her into the house and carried their sleeping son to his bedroom. She settled onto the sofa in the family room.

"Can I get you something to drink?" Lynne's dad was very scared for her and very worried about how she would cope with such a tremendous loss. But she couldn't see the worry on his face or hear the tone of his voice. She couldn't think of anything or anyone except for the tremendous emptiness in her arms and in her soul.

"Lynne, can I get you something to drink?" her dad repeated.

"Um, no, no. I don't want anything."

She tried to remain sitting but couldn't. Their home was full of memories, memories of excitement, joy, worry, fear. She got up and started to walk around the first floor, looking around, touching pieces of furniture as she walked, and thinking, "The last time I touched this table, Kelly was here with us. The last time I looked out this window, my daughter was in our home. The last time I walked down those stairs, I carried Kelly with me."

"Lynne, what are you doing?" Luke was there, at her side, in anguish himself over the loss of Kelly but still focused enough to be concerned about Lynne's behavior.

"Oh, Luke, she was here with us yesterday! She was here with us the last time I walked through these rooms! She will never be here with us again!" Lynne slumped onto the floor, shaking and crying. She knew there would never be an end to the ache, never be an end to the tears. The pain of her miscarriages paled compared to this agony! There was an overwhelming void deep in her soul that she knew could never be filled.

"I know! I know!" Luke started to cry also.

And then she heard "Lynne, Lynne, listen!" It was her mother down on the floor next to her. "Kelly is here with us. I can feel her. She'll always be here with us. I know it hurts in a way I can't even begin to comprehend! Just try to hold on. Just try to breathe. We're all here with you! God will help you through this!"

Lynne tried to focus on the words, tried to believe it could be ok again someday. On some level, she knew she was grateful for the love and support surrounding her. She knew she loved everyone gathered there for them. She believed Kelly was an angel and with God now. But the thoughts brought no comfort.

Lynne's dad stood in another room talking to Luke. "We'll stay here tonight. It's getting late and I know neither of you have eaten. Do you know if there's something here we can cook for you? Should we go out and get some food? What can we do to help?"

"Thank you. I think there's food in the fridge that we can heat. I don't know if I can eat anything now but please find something for yourself. I appreciate the offer, but you don't need to stay tonight. We'll need to be alone." Lynne heard the words and understood her husband's need for privacy for his grief.

Later, after everyone left, Lynne and Luke sat on the sofa in their family room. They snuggled close and held hands. The void in their hearts and minds was overwhelming. So much of their recent life had been centered on caring for Kelly. Neither knew what to do next. Neither could find the words to comfort the other. Time passed in some undetermined fashion with neither of them moving. But then Lynne could feel the tightening of Luke's muscles. He looked straight ahead but she could see his jaw harden.

Without a word to her, Luke got up from the sofa and walked up the stairs. When he came down, he held the bassinette in his arms. He walked past Lynne, still without a word, and carried the bassinette into the backyard. She could hear the sound of crashes and wood splintering but didn't rise to watch.

She continued to hold the blanket and cry while the flames from the bassinette lit the night-time sky. How would they ever find a way to face tomorrow without her?

Chapter 21

Lora's Story March 1993

ADMISSIONS

After the phone call with "the other", Lora left to go to a friend's house. While she was there, Rick called.

"Let me in." He apparently thought Lora was in their home, not answering the door.

"I'm not home. I'll call you when I get home, or maybe I'll call you tomorrow, or maybe I'll have my attorney call you." She had never given him a key to the new lock. He could only enter the house if she was there to let him in.

"Please listen to me. I need to talk with you now. I need to tell you some things. Please tell me where you are. Let me pick you up so we can talk."

Lora hung up without replying. A few minutes later, she saw his car pull up in front of her friend's house. Good guess! He sat outside the house and called her cell phone. She didn't answer and he continued to dial and redial her number. Finally she decided to remove the drama from her friend's home. She walked out to his car and slid into the passenger seat.

"How much do you hate me?" he asked as he put the car in gear and prepared to drive away.

"Stop. Don't drive anywhere. I'm not going with you. What do you want to tell me?"

He took a deep breath and said slowly, "I've lied about everything." He didn't look at her and didn't continue to speak.

"I've figured that out. What else do you have to say?"

"I'm sorry. I don't know what I want. I know you talked to "the other" and have her whole story. But I haven't been truthful with her either. She doesn't know how I still feel about you. Please come home so we can talk."

"Why would I ever want to do that," she laughed. "How stupid do you think I am? I have nothing to say to you and there's nothing I want to hear from you!"

"Please, we both have so many years invested in our relationship! Won't you give us one more time to talk through what has happened. I know you won't believe this, but I love you! I've loved you since those first days when you were 24. I need you to understand and then you can do what you need to do."

Lora finally agreed to drive home to continue the conversation. She got there before he did. He was undoubtedly on the phone, spinning a story for "the other". She left the door unlocked and sat down on the loveseat with Elrond. Rick walked in a few minutes later, opened a bottle of wine, and poured a glass for both of them. He pulled a stool from the kitchen and perched opposite the loveseat. She could see there were tears in his eyes which infuriated her. She was the one who had suffered for weeks, for years though she didn't know it till now! He was the one who had lived the secret life! He was the one who didn't know what he wanted! As their life had always been, it was all about him!

She screamed, jumped up, and dumped her glass of red wine over his head. "You are out of time! You need to make a decision this weekend!" She cried and sobbed. She couldn't believe she still spoke as though he had the choice to make! She didn't know how she could even consider continuing a marriage with him! How could she ever find trust and peace with him again? But she was desperate! She was exhausted! She went to the bedroom where she finally fell into a restless sleep.

She woke up about 7:00 a.m. the next morning. She found him already awake in the family room and asked for his answer.

"I don't know how to answer you" he was teary again. "I don't know how I can leave you, but I don't know how to tell her. She doesn't deserve this. She has a horrible week to go through. She's going for a leukemia test on Tuesday. I promised her I would be there with her. She's depending on me."

"What do you mean, she's depending on you?!! I'm your wife. Whatever you may have promised her, you promised me a lot more and a long time ago. You can't be with her this week and be married to me. You can't get through the next week without making a decision and delivering a message to one of us. Don't forget, I talked to her too. I know she's upset and won't allow it to continue either."

He kept repeating the same things, "I don't know how to tell her. I love her too, but I can't leave you. I could make a life with her if things don't work out for us."

Finally, about mid-afternoon, he made the call to her. "I'm not coming. I can't leave Lora"

Lora could hear "the other" screaming and crying from where she sat on the steps. It made her want to throw up to hear him call her, "cutie" and say, "I do love you." They talked for about two hours while Lora listened to every word he spoke. He told "the other" he didn't want to hurt her. He cried but was silent much of the time. "The other" did most of the talking.

Lora sat and tolerated his outpouring of emotion for this woman. She didn't know what to think, though, by then, she should have known. She should have begun to "see" but she didn't. She wouldn't allow herself. She felt shaky and humiliated, but she still couldn't consider that her life going forward would be without him.

She didn't know if she would be ever able to put the marriage back together, not just because of his relationship with "the other" but because of what she'd learned about him and the way he lived his life. She knew he was not the person she believed she had married. However, he had defined her life for so long she didn't know how to begin to define it for herself. She didn't want to give up. She was afraid to give up.

She couldn't walk away. She somehow felt that this fiasco of a day had been a victory for her. She still refused to acknowledge the true picture. A small part of her wondered if the road back to a good marriage could be any more difficult than finding a new road on her own. She couldn't understand why she allowed herself to be in this position, waiting for him to make a choice between her and his girlfriend. How could she possibly allow it to be his decision after all that had happened?! But nowhere in her was the anger, or the courage, or the self-esteem to admit that her marriage was over. Any of the emotions that could have helped her were overshadowed by an overwhelming fear.

The farce continued as the next week crawled slowly by. He told her he called "the other" on Monday to be sure she would keep the doctor's appointment but that he hadn't returned any of her other calls. He had a hard time sleeping. He whimpered and talked in his sleep. He said he had a huge knot in his stomach. When she asked him why, he refused to answer the question.

On Friday morning, Lora woke him early, before her normal 6:00 a.m. departure for her office.

"What now? Where are you going to be this weekend?"

"What? What time is it? What are you talking about?"

"I need to know where you are going to be this weekend. I can't go to work not knowing if you are going to be here tonight."

He sighed and looked past her as he said, "I've been thinking about going to Buffalo."

Lora walked out of the bedroom and called her office. She said she would not be in that day. After she hung up, he walked down the stairs and they started to talk again. How many times would they say the same things?

"Cutie, I love you both. I'm really messed up and I don't know what to do." He cried and looked an emotional mess.

"You have to make a choice. I am not going to live one more day like I have since the end of January."

"If I go to Buffalo, you might never let me see or talk to you again."

"You're wrong. There's no "might" about it. If you leave, we're history. I don't ever want to see you or talk to you again. I won't live like this." She was not as strong as she tried to sound.

"OK, I'll pack some things," he said. "Do you hate me?"

"Yes, I hate you."

"Please don't say that you hate me."

She started telling him the things that Dr. Levy had said about him. "You're really sick and you're a pathological liar." She screamed, "You let me live a joke for the past week! There's no way we could ever put this relationship back together! I'm having my phone number changed so there's no way you can get in touch with me. Now, get out!"

"When can I get my stuff?"

"Call one of my sisters and she'll make arrangements for you to get into the house under my terms."

"Will you take a call from me later?"

"No. I have nothing to talk with you about. What would you have to talk with me about?"

Finally, she walked out to go to an appointment with Dr. Levy.

"Good-bye, sweetie. I'll see you in court. I hope you have a good life," she said as she left.

When she got home after her appointment his car was in the garage. She walked in and looked at him.

"Why are you here? I didn't expect to find you here. I don't want to see you. I've already said my good-byes. I didn't think I would have to face it again. Please leave."

"I don't want to leave. You know I love you. I just need some more time to deal with this situation. Can I call "the other" in private?"

"No, you can't call your girlfriend in private from our home. You can call her in front of me and tell her you're not coming. Tell her you're never coming! Tell her you are staying with me and it's where you want to be! Tell her your affair is over!"

He dialed his phone. "Hey, it's me. I'm not coming today. No. I can't talk about it now. I'll call you in the morning. No. I can't."

There was little communication for the rest of the evening. He sat rigidly in front of the TV with a glass of Jack Daniels, and then another, and then another. She opened a bottle of wine and had a glass, and then another, and then another. Later in the night she heard him trying to sleep in the spare bedroom. She heard him tossing, moaning, then gasping for breath.

Lora woke early the next morning. She wanted and needed something to happen. Still, she let him sleep late because he had told "the other" he would call her in the morning. She slipped quietly into the spare bedroom and sat next to him on the bed. She looked at him for a long time, at his face, the face she had loved for so long. She realized that she didn't know him, not really. She was no longer sure who or what she loved, or if it was even love. She was humiliated to be waiting for him to make a choice. But she still believed she needed him in her life.

When he finally awoke, he touched her face.

They woke up again after noon. "What now?" he asked.

"It's time."

"Time for what?"

"It's time for you to pack your shit and get out!." Lora said as she jumped out of bed. "That's never happening again!"

"If there's any way you could possibly still want me, I don't want to leave."

Lora took a deep breath. "I love you. Through this nightmare I have always been willing to put 150% into making our marriage strong again. We have a lot of things to work through. But, if we both want the same thing, we can make it work. If we can survive this, we can survive anything."

"I just have one more thing I need to take care of. I need to drive to Buffalo to tell her face to face. Please understand. I need to do this."

"Are you kidding me?! If you walk out that door, we are right back where we were yesterday. If you want to stay, it's on my terms. Just call her and tell her what you should have yesterday."

"Ok. How about this. Let me drive up today to tell her. Then you fly up tomorrow and we'll drive back together."

"Doesn't work for me. If you need to see her, how about we drive up together and then the three of us meet to explain to her what is happening?"

They talked and talked, and the day got later and later. Lora turned to wine again to help her keep calm, one glass and then another.

Finally, he picked up the phone, called "the other" and told her he wasn't coming. Lora could hear the screams again. "The other" screamed that he didn't have the courage to tell her face to face and he let her think all week that he'd be there. He had talked with her all week though he didn't tell Lora so! Then he said he'd come and face her. He'd be there in five hours. Lora screamed "No!" She grabbed his phone and disconnected the call.

"Why did you do that?! She's upset! She's alone!" He started to shout, and his face contorted with anger.

Lora walked up to him and stood on her tiptoes till she was almost eye to eye with him. She said quietly and slowly, emphasizing each word, "YOU CAN'T GO to Buffalo if you want to be in this marriage. You need to MAKE YOUR CHOICE!"

"Ok. It's over with her! I'm done! I can't go on like this." His shoulders slumped and he let out a huge sigh.

And then, when Lora said nothing in reply, "It's just that I didn't end it with her in the right way! I should have told her face to face. She's a good person who needs help. I didn't get to help her in the way I wanted to! I'll never see her again!" His hands shook as he cried about his girlfriend to his wife.

Lora had never seen an emotional outburst of this intensity from him. This was not the self-assured, always in control person she had lived with for so many years. She picked up her glass of wine and dumped it over his head. A waste of a good wine! He wasn't the only one out of control! As she walked up the stairs, Lora was teary also but still with enough presence to wonder, "How long till he calls her again? How long till he sees her again?"

Chapter 22

Shelly's Story, November to December 1984

BUILDING TRUST

"How can I get away from this narcissistic animal?" Shelly wondered desperately as she walked into the kitchen to make a cup of tea. "Obviously, fighting and rejecting him isn't working. What if he thought I was really going along with this? What if I made him trust me? What if…????"

A few months passed uneventfully while Shelly continuously had a smile on her face to maintain the façade of loving to be there with Todd. One day Todd returned home from the side job he worked with his friend, Marty. Shelly had never met Marty but Todd was always going somewhere with him. Shelly had the feeling that Marty was a decent guy, just by the way Todd spoke of him and his wife. She also didn't believe that Todd had told them about their situation. To everyone on the outside, Todd was such a great guy, always willing to help and lend a hand. Little did they know!

Shelly greeted Todd with a smile, "I think I'm going to like it here!"

Todd looked at her with wide eyes and half a smile. "Oh, yeah, what makes you say that?" Shelly felt he chose his words to test her and she thought quickly about how to respond to continue the farce.

"I don't know," she said. "It's just starting to feel like home."

Todd smiled, grabbed her around the waist as he pulled her to him and kissed her hard. "It's so good to hear you say that! You have no idea what that means to me! Now, what's for dinner?'

Shelly responded with the best fake smile and upbeat answer she could while she hoped that he didn't suspect her plan. After dinner, Todd went to get a shower. This had continued to be her "M.O." and he bought it so far.

The laundry room was at the end of the hallway, and Todd had started to let her do the laundry when he wasn't home. She had to prop the apartment door open with a rock, so she didn't get locked out. Shelly thought many times about trying to run but Todd had convinced her that he had eyes everywhere and she believed him. He even told Shelly that the people who lived there wouldn't help her because he paid them to report her every move. She was convinced that she had to play the game so well that no one would know what she was up to.

One day, as she carried laundry back to the apartment, Todd came home and greeted her at the bottom of the steps. She flashed a huge smile and he responded with his own smile, saying, "Hi, honey, it's good to see you so happy!"

Shelly thought to herself, "It's working! He's starting to believe!"

It was close to Thanksgiving now and Shelly ached to be home. On the holiday she and Todd ate alone in their apartment. Shelly made a huge meal, as though 20 people were expected for dinner, because that's what Todd wanted. The turkey may have smelled like her mom's, but nothing tasted right to Shelly. In her eyes, nothing was right and yet she managed to work through the day, while she held onto the hope that she would be home for the next holidays to come.

The nights were the worst since he expected her to have sex each night. She pretended to enjoy it. Each and every time she would separate her mind from her body. As her body went through the experiences of him pawing at her and thrusting himself into her, she was mentally and emotionally somewhere else. He didn't seem to notice that she accepted but didn't enjoy their sexual connections. He collapsed and slept as soon as they were finished, while she showered and scrubbed her skin as though it had been exposed to a disease. Her skin was always red and raw afterwards, but she still felt as though she was never clean enough.

It was December now and it would soon be Christmas. One day Todd showed up with 3 old dusty boxes. He came through the door and laughed, saying, "Ho, ho, ho!"

"What have you got there?" Shelly asked.

"These, my dear, are our Christmas tree decorations."

The boxes smelled musty and when Shelly opened the flaps on a box, there were several ornaments that were broken. "Where did these come from?" she asked. She suspected the boxes were from his family's house.

Shelly's voice must not have been as upbeat as Todd thought it should be. He said, "What do you mean, where did these come from? Don't worry about it. Just be grateful," he said, and grabbed her cheeks, squeezing hard. Todd was always defensive about his family. "You are grateful, right?"

"Yes, of course," Shelly answered.

"Good, because I started to think the bitch was back!"

"No, of course not," Shelly said softly.

"So, let's go! Get your boots on. We're going to cut down the first Christmas tree for our new home." Shelly did as she was told.

It had been snowing and the ground was lightly covered with a blanket of white. They rode in silence as Shelly looked at the lights on the homes and businesses. She could see a family decorating their Christmas tree as they passed by. Oh, how her heart longed to be home! Her mom was probably baking while her dad sampled and got scolded for stealing cookies from the cooling rack.

Shelly could feel the tears running down her cheeks as she thought, "I'm sure my sisters are home wrapping gifts for our family and friends while our favorite Christmas carols play in the background and the aroma of ginger and cinnamon fills the air."

She wondered if all the work she had done to get Todd to trust her would pay off, telling him how wonderfully sweet he was, what a great provider and lover he was. She didn't know.

What she did know was that, if he saw her crying, the results wouldn't be good. So, she quickly dabbed her eyes to keep him from noticing the tears.

It wasn't long before they reached the Christmas tree farm. It was beautiful. White lights glistened in the snow that draped the fir trees like soft fluffy blankets.

"Well, we're here!" Todd said. "What do you think? Doesn't it look like a winter wonderland? This is going to be the perfect Christmas!"

Shelly stood there and absorbed the beauty of what she saw. The air was crisp that night. She could feel it in her lungs.

"It truly is beautiful! How do we choose just one? They're all so perfect!"

"Oh, it's easy," Todd said. "You just walk through until you see one that gives you that Christmas feeling in your heart. You know, just like when we were kids and saw the tree lit up on Christmas morning for the very first time."

"Oh, that feeling," Shelly thought. She wished so much that she could go back, turn the clock back, but she couldn't. She needed to stay focused. "Of course I remember that feeling. Who wouldn't?"

They walked hand in hand through the rows and rows of trees until Todd stopped and said out loud, "This is it!! This is the one for sure! I can feel it, can't you?" Sadly Shelly felt nothing but didn't dare let him see her lack of feeling.

"Yes! I can feel it! This is it!" she said with a smile.

Todd quickly climbed under the tree and sawed until they could hear it crack and fall to the ground. "Timber!" he said. He sounded so giddy, as if he was a child.

How wonderful it would be if they were a couple in love and happy. But the abuse and feeling of wanting to be away from him loomed over her like a dark, heavy cloud. She wished she could love him, especially at times like this. She loved seeing him so excited and lighthearted, almost like a glimpse of the person he could be. At some level she still hoped that maybe she could help him be that person.

Todd tied the tree to the roof of the car. Then they talked and laughed about being kids at Christmas while driving back to their apartment. When they arrived, Todd released the straps on the tree, and they carried it down the steps to their apartment. Before she knew it, Todd had the tree in the stand.

"Bring some water in for the tree, Babe," Todd said.

"Sure." She obeyed his command as usual.

Shelly turned on the radio and found Christmas carols as they began to decorate the tree. The lights went on first then the bulbs, but her favorite part had always been the icicles. She placed them strategically on the branches as if creating a painting.

"Voila," she said. "Finished!"

Todd stepped in from the kitchen. "Not quite," he said.

"What do you mean?"

"What's a tree without the star on top?" He pulled out a round thing that to Shelly didn't even look like a star.

"No, wait!" Shelly ran into the bedroom and, from under the bed, pulled out a box that contained a star that she had made using cardboard, aluminum foil, and glitter.

"I've got it right here," she said.

Todd took it from her and placed it on top of the tree. "Now it's perfect," he said. They were both proud of the masterpiece that stood before them.

"How about some hot chocolate?" Todd said.

"Of course. What could be better?" Shelly said as she headed to the kitchen to warm the milk.

"Perfect?!" she thought. "This isn't perfect. Perfect would be decorating the tree with my family and the room filled with love and laughter."

"Here we go," she said, carrying the hot chocolate in on a tray. "Steaming hot with marshmallows, just the way you like it."

Todd had a big smile on his face. "Thanks, Babe! Let's sit and enjoy the tree together." As they gazed at the tree, tears started rolling down Shelly's face.

"Are those happy tears I see?" asked Todd.

Shelly knew what her answer should be. She opened her mouth and before she realized what was coming out of it, she stood up in front of Todd saying, "No, these aren't happy tears!" She could hardly believe what she heard herself say.

Her mind screamed, "Stop! Stop! Stop! You're going to ruin everything!" But she couldn't stop. Her brain told her one thing, but her heart told her something else. "This Christmas is not perfect, but you could make it that way. The best gift you could give me is to take me back home to my family! That's what Christmas is, Todd! Family, love, and kindness not being isolated in a two-room apartment with you!"

As soon as her mouth stopped moving, Shelly knew she would pay a significant price and she did. Todd stood in front of her, enraged. His eyes lost the glistening, giddy look she had seen earlier. It was replaced with evil. Fire burned in his pupils as if he could shoot hot daggers from them.

In one sweep, Shelly's feet were lifted off the floor. She flew into the Christmas tree. Crash! The tree toppled over, and Shelly landed in the middle of it. Lights flickered, bulbs broke, and icicles flew through the air. When everything settled, Shelly felt her skin burning from the glass fragments that had cut into her back, neck and arms. But he wasn't done!

Todd screamed intelligibly in her face as he yanked her up from the smashed tree and dragged her by her wrists across the floor, through the bedroom and into the bathroom. He had a bad habit of not flushing the toilet after relieving himself. He lifted the lid and the seat, grabbed Shelly by the hair, while he screamed, "Did I just hear shit coming out of your mouth?! Do you know what we do with shit?"

He shoved her face into his feces while he flushed the toilet and continuously screamed at her. At this point Shelly could no longer hear what he said. Just as before, she had separated herself from her body. Physically, she gagged and cried, mentally she couldn't hear or feel any of it. Finally, Todd yanked her face from the toilet and dragged her back into the living room. He screamed out orders to clean up the mess that she had caused. Then Todd walked out the door and slammed it behind him.

Shelly lay there while Christmas carols still played in the background. She found the strength to pull herself up from the floor and made her way into the kitchen. "What have I done," she thought. "If I would have just kept my mouth shut, he wouldn't have done this."

She took Lysol wipes from under the kitchen sink and scrubbed her face over and over again. She cried as she pulled the glass from her arms. She didn't know how much time passed. Everything had become a blur to her as she cleaned up the mess. She had just about finished running the sweeper when she could feel a presence behind her.

It was Todd. He yanked the cord from the wall stopping, the sweeper. He grabbed Shelly by both arms and pulled her close to him. She trembled as she heard him say, "I'm so sorry, Baby. If you wouldn't have said what you did, none of this would have happened. You do understand that, right?"

Todd kissed the top of her head, with her hair still wet from the toilet. As he squeezed her tight, she could feel what was left of the glass shards cutting deeper into her skin. Her shirt was wet and bloody, but it didn't faze her. He released her and straightened the tree in the stand. Shelly stood there, afraid to move. Todd then took her gently by the hand and led her back to the bathroom. He undressed her while she stood still like a mannequin.

"You need to climb into the shower, Babe. Let's get you cleaned up."

Shelly, still silent, did as she was told. Todd washed her hair and her body, being careful he didn't push too hard on the glass that remained in her back. After showering her, he led her to the bedroom, laid her face down on the bed, and picked the glass shards out of her back. She drifted off while tears cascaded softly down her cheeks.

The next time Shelly opened her eyes it was morning. She awoke alone in the bed and could smell pancakes cooking and coffee brewing. She slowly pulled herself of out bed and wrapped herself in her robe. She walked into the kitchen and saw Todd standing there, smiling, as he flipped pancakes.

"Good morning, Gorgeous!" he said. "How'd you sleep? Like a baby I'll bet."

Shelly just smiled and sat down at the table. She looked over to the corner where the Christmas tree stood. Todd had put it back together the best he could though the star at the top hung off to one side. All she could do was stare.

The next evening Shelly was sitting at the table when Todd came home and tossed a newspaper in front of her. He grabbed Shelly by the hair and shoved her face towards the paper, screaming, "Read!" Shelly didn't know why at first until she saw the headline in the Gazette.

It read, "Window Shot Out of Back of Station Wagon While Man Drives to Work."

As she continued to read, her stomach churned.

"Mr. Ziegler was traveling to work in the early morning hours and a bullet narrowly missed him as it shattered the back side window of his station wagon. He managed to keep control of the car as he continued driving to a lit, safe place to pull over."

Suddenly Todd yanked Shelly's head back as he looked in her face and screamed "See what happens if you try to leave me? You were lucky this time! If I wanted to kill him, he would be dead! Don't push me, Shelly! You did this! And if he would have died, it would have been your fault! Get it? "

Shelly began to cry uncontrollably and said softly, "Yes, I get it."

As she tried to calm her breathing, she wondered, "What else is this mad man capable of?"

Chapter 23

Lynne's Story January 1997
WHO WOULD THEY BE?

Lynne thought there would be no sleep that night. The anguish of coming home without Kelly had been overwhelming. But, finally, sheer exhaustion took her to a restless twilight of nightmares, terrors and visions of a baby's face. When she woke up early the next morning, she didn't know how to begin living the day. But she knew she had to find a way to get out of bed, to walk into the room across the hall, to give comfort to the little boy who slept there. She had to find a way to laugh with him again, to share the joys of his life, to maintain the family that would help him grow into a strong adult. Lynne also had to support and love Luke and help him to heal.

Before she could move to do any of that, they had to bury Kelly.

Though it was still very early, Lynne called Rose, who was one of her closest friends and also a doctor on the staff at the hospital where Kelly died. As soon as Lynne said "Hello" she could hear Rose crying.

"Oh, Lynne, I am so sorry! I know what happened! I've been waiting to talk to you, to come and cry with you! I'll be there in a few minutes."

As Rose promised, she was there within a few minutes. They hugged and cried together as Lynne told the story of the previous day. "I don't understand how this happened. She was just at the doctor's office yesterday! He said she was doing well! How could he be so wrong! How can she be gone?!"

Rose listened for a while and then said, "There are some things I need to tell you. Honey, I'm the doctor who examined

Kelly's lung tissue last night. Her lungs were so badly diseased. I can't believe the doctors allowed her to go home with you. But you know, I believe she wanted to be home with you and her dad."

Lynne couldn't fully comprehend the words she heard. Her brain swung from the anguish she had been feeling to rage that Kelly's doctors had insisted on sending her home.

As Lynne listened to what Rose said, her thoughts also went back to the conversation she had with a Nutritionist at the hospital when Kelly was home and having difficulty keeping her formula down. The Nutritionist had found that the instructions Lynne had been given for mixing Kelly's formula were wrong. As a result, Kelly had been given too much sodium in her formula. It was another significant mistake on the party of the hospital's medical staff!

Later that day, it was time to go to the funeral home to make arrangements for Kelly. She was so tiny. Lynne couldn't imagine how she would be buried. Luke's brother, Josh, accompanied them. As they sat in the office and waited for the director of the funeral home, Josh said, "I can't imagine what you're going through, the pain of your loss. But, if I can be here and help in any way, this is where I need to be." Lynne heard the words and, at some level, appreciated the thoughts and the offer of help. But Josh was right. No one could imagine the feelings unless they had lived this nightmare. No one could understand how the world looked to her now, the unbearable hopelessness that gripped her soul. No one could share the ache in her arms where Kelly should have been cuddled.

The funeral director came in and sat down with them and Lynne tried to focus on what he said. Through the painful discussion of the details, they decided it would be a one day viewing the next day with the service at the funeral home the following morning. Lynne couldn't bear the thought of anything dramatic in a church. She couldn't bear the thought of the tiny casket being carried down the long church aisle. Instead, they opted to have the priest from their parish officiate the service at the funeral home. Lynne's mother had found a beautiful dress that was on a baby doll she had bought for Kelly. Incredibly, it was the right size for Kelly and would fit her perfectly. They decided to have her buried in it.

Somehow the rest of the day passed. Lynne couldn't always remember from one moment to the next what she was doing or why she had walked into a room. The only thought beyond her ache for Kelly was her love for Greg. It was the only thing that kept her moving. She knew she had to talk with him, to hug him, to be sure he had food. She had to find a way to smile at him and help him believe their life would be ok.

That night, she and Luke lay in their bed, not touching, not sleeping, not communicating. Even the physical presence of her husband brought no comfort to Lynne. They were each living their own nightmare, not yet knowing how to draw comfort from each other. At one point, he tried to pull her close to him, but she resisted, knowing she couldn't go where that embrace might lead.

The next morning, when Luke and Lynne walked into the viewing room with their immediate families, they slowly approached the tiny casket, needing to see but also afraid to see. They hadn't seen Kelly's face since the frantic drive to the hospital. Lynne couldn't believe how much their daughter looked like a beautiful baby doll. She even had pink lipstick on her tiny lips. Lynne reached out to touch her face, wanting to touch but afraid to touch. The touch made the nightmare even more real. Her baby was cold. Her baby would never smile again. Her baby wouldn't learn to wobble as she took her first steps. Her baby would never smash spaghetti across her face and through her hair. Her baby would never learn to say, "I love you mom!"

Thoughts swirled through Lynne's brain as their families began to slowly approach. "How does a person get through this day, much less the rest of a life? How can I prepare to say goodbye to my daughter?"

Their family members were all worried about Luke and Lynne. Everyone wanted to help but weren't sure what to do or what to say. Many of them were crying as they hugged Luke and Lynne and offered their condolences. By later that day, the line of friends and family wound through the funeral home and spilled out into the parking lot. There were so many people who were touched by Kelly's story.

Lynne knew she should be grateful for the words, the hugs, the sympathies. She listened to their carefully chosen, well intended, words, "unspeakable, unimaginable, overwhelming, inconceivable, unthinkable," and tried to find the gratitude. But she wanted to scream instead, "You don't understand! You can't fathom the pain and agony! We will never heal! Your words can't comfort us!" She didn't scream but she couldn't stop her tears and she couldn't begin to conceive of the path to healing that they so desperately needed.

The next day was the funeral. It was a day Lynne didn't want to wake up to. Beyond the terrible feelings of loss, there was also a looming fear of what life would bring without a baby struggling for her life, and now with the loss of a baby to mourn.

Too quickly the room was full of family and close friends and it was time to begin saying goodbye. The priest led the group through a condensed version of the service that would have taken place in a church. It was hard for Lynne to even follow what he said. She continued to look at Kelly, thinking, "This is the last time I'm going to see her."

Luke and Lynne held Greg's hand tightly. They were both so concerned about what was going through his mind. How much did he understand about what had happened on this day? Did he grasp the full concept of death? Did he realize he would never see his sister again? How would this impact him?

After everyone else had said their goodbyes, it was finally time for them to step up. Lynne knew this moment was inevitable but couldn't fully conceptualize what was about to take place.

Luke leaned over and whispered to Greg, "Walk up with mom and me. It's time to say goodbye to Kelly."

The three of them stepped forward to look at her little face one last time. Lynne and Luke each reached out to touch her tiny arm as tears streamed down their faces.

Greg said, "Goodbye little Kelly. We'll see you again in heaven."

Lynne didn't want to walk away. She wanted to freeze this moment and hold onto Kelly forever even though she couldn't hold her in her arms. The time ticked away, no one wanting to interrupt these final moments. Luke and Greg stood next to Lynne, neither moving.

Finally, Josh walked up to them and whispered, "It's time to go." They walked to their car, a different family, a family Lynne didn't know. Who would they be now?

Chapter 24

Lora's Story April 1993

REVELATIONS

Nearly 3 months had passed since the revelation about the life that Rick had been living. Three months that were filled with hope, lies, drama, crazy sex, despair, and Rick's mother, Eleanor. She and Lora had never been close. When Eleanor had learned that her son had been dating Lora, and they were living together in his home, she had done everything she could to stop their relationship.

Before they had even met, there were multiple phone calls from her with a variety of accusations and threats.

"I will destroy you if you don't leave my son alone!"

"Why is he even involved with you? Does he feel sorry for you?"

"I never want to know you and I never want you to know me!"

"Leave his home immediately or I will call the police on you!"

"He has a lovely girlfriend who we love very much! You may be a piece of ass on the side, but he will never break up with his girlfriend!"

At some point, Eleanor very, very reluctantly accepted the fact that her son would marry Lora. She was a smart woman and her relationship with Lora had suddenly become cordial, though cool. There were no feelings of love from either woman but after the marriage there were regular family visits, even family travel together. Two different types of love motivated them. Still, there were always comments about the way Lora "cared for" her son. His clothing wasn't as white as when she had done his laundry for him. Didn't Lora know that her son loved his lasagna layered with sliced hardboiled eggs in addition to the sauce and cheese, parmesan cheese only, not the ricotta cheese that Lora used? And she always brought toilet tissue when she came to their home because she had heard Lora laughing about her mother frequently forgetting to buy it when she went grocery shopping. Lora's family had occasionally used newspaper.

The phone calls from his mother resumed after the conversations with "the other". She cried, but was accusatory, and wouldn't accept that any fault lay with her son.

"What did you do that pushed my son to this other woman?"

"What did you NOT do that pushed my son to this other woman?'

"You know, sometimes a woman just needs to accept what has happened and put up with it."

"Give it time for him to get her out of his system and let him find you waiting."

Lora had ended those conversations as quickly as she could, sometimes with angry words. Sometimes she was very tempted to tell Eleanor about the ground deer meet. Lora's dad was a hunter and had often given them deer roasts, deer chops, ground deer meat. Eleanor always insisted that she would never eat deer meet, did not like the taste, would never like the taste no matter how it was prepared.

Lora was tempted to say, "And do you remember the pasta sauce I frequently made when you came to dinner? Remember how yummy you always said the pasta sauce was? Guess what type of meat was in it?"

But she didn't. Not because she was a kind person but because she was an exhausted person with no energy for any additional conflict in her life.

At this 3 month point, Rick's travel schedule was erratic, supposedly because of business commitments. He had stayed at their home again last night but left early in the morning, before she was even out of bed. He didn't look good when he walked back into the house that evening, but she was hopeful that the upcoming weekend would help begin the healing process. They had reservations at a lodge on Skyline Drive in the Blue Ridge Mountains of Virginia. She was anxious to pack and be ready to leave. Lora had suggested the weekend away to give them time together away from everyone and everything that had been going on in their lives. They needed time to talk, to explore their relationship, to find if there could be a way to reconnect. Rick didn't appear excited, but he did agree to go which Lora hoped was a positive sign.

"I have my bag upstairs and I've started packing so we can leave early tomorrow. I don't know what you have here and what you have "wherever", but let's be ready and try to take advantage of the full day."

"We need to talk," he said. "Grab a glass of wine and let's sit down." The look on his face was nothing she had ever seen before. There was no light in his eyes. She could see the darkness, though he looked at the floor, the door, the window, the cat, anywhere but at her. He picked up the bottle of Jack Daniels and poured himself a drink.

"No. I don't want a glass of wine." She was afraid of that look on his face and the tone in his voice. "Just tell me what we need to talk about." She perched on the edge of the stool in the kitchen and felt her heart beating rapidly.

"I don't know how to tell you this. I'm so sorry. But I need to go to Buffalo. She's pregnant with my baby and she's losing the baby. I can't let her lay there and bleed alone. I need to be with her. You and I need to reach a compromise about this weekend." His voice shook and there were tears in his eyes. Tears because he said he and "the other" were having a baby together and she was losing the baby!

At first, Lora couldn't understand what he said. Her brain wouldn't wrap around the words, perhaps in an attempt to protect her from the anguish that would come. But then, slowly, the words began to coalesce, and she couldn't stop the understanding. She began to work through the change in her view of the world.

"They hadn't been able to conceive because his sperm count was too low, right?"

"They had tried everything, but he couldn't provide enough sperm for artificial insemination, right?"

"They had an agreement with a young lady to adopt her baby when the baby was born. He wasn't excited about it, but it happened, right?"

"He didn't really want a baby, right? He had become angry so many times when she pushed for a child, right?"

"He couldn't be having a baby with "the other". It wasn't possible! Right?"

"There couldn't be tears for a baby with "the other", right?"

And then she understood and something in her ended. So much became clear now. "The other" was going to have a baby, his baby, the baby that should have been Lora's! Her connection to him was one Lora had never been able to achieve. "The other" was fiery, and crazy, and she had been carrying his baby. He thought he would be a father. They believed they would be a family.

There were no tears, no hysteria, no love, just the last piece of the picture. She looked at him with new eyes. She looked at her life, their life, with new eyes. She looked towards her future with horror.

"So now you understand it all and why it's been so hard for me to end it with her. I don't know if it's obligation, or guilt, or probably a little love as well. But I've loved you for so long and I still do. Please don't make any decisions until I get back. Let's push the weekend away back a week. Let's figure it out together. Let me help her through this crisis and I'll come back to you."

There was nothing to say. Nothing she could agree to. No way to stop him. Lora walked out of the kitchen and into the bathroom where she flushed her wedding band down the toilet. "How symbolic!" she said aloud.

Then she followed Rick into their bedroom and watched as he began to throw clothing into a bag, a bag that had been a gift from her. She started pulling shirts out of his hands, screaming, "I gave you that! You're not taking it to her!"

He grabbed another bag and quickly transferred the clothing to that bag. "I'll be back sometime tomorrow, and we can talk. I love you. Don't do anything crazy. Take it easy, please, really, really easy."

And he was gone. That quickly. She sat on the snuggly sofa with her cat next to her and had a glass of wine, and then another, and then another, and, at some point, she slept.

There were phone calls and messages the next day. He had a 3:15 flight scheduled that Saturday afternoon.

"Please be there to talk with me when I get back. I love you!"

The next message was a 6:00 p.m. flight that day, and then an 8:00 a.m. flight on Sunday. She slowly began to throw his remaining clothing into boxes.

Lora drove to the airport on Saturday afternoon, in her small, older car that was purchased second hand from a car rental agency. It wasn't even red, her favorite color. He had always been Mr. Flash, with the new, upscale, sporty cars.

She drove slowly up and down the rows in the parking lot. Back and forth, back and forth, looking, looking for the flash car. And, finally, there it was. She stopped her car in the aisle, pulled his from the parking spot, and replaced it with her car. She drove away in the flashy expensive car, with the roof open and the radio playing loudly.

The quickly scribbled note she left on the seat read, "Surprise! Would you ever have believed I'd have the spirit to find a new car for myself in the middle of all the drama? ☺"

Chapter 25

Shelly's Story, February to April 1985

CLICK

Christmas had come and gone. The routine of Todd going to work and Shelly dutifully staying at the apartment, washing clothes and constantly cleaning continued. Shelly's mind never stopped thinking about how to get out. Todd had threatened to kill her family if she ever asked to leave again and after his actions at Christmas she believed that he would. So she was careful to think before she spoke and to act the way he expected her to, while always wishing every kiss was their last.

Shelly still felt sorry for him at times. She couldn't stop the thought that his issues, and all the terrible things he had done, weren't his fault. But then the thoughts of all that happened would flood her mind and she would realize that she couldn't help him. He was beyond any help she could give him. However, she could help herself.

Shelly slowly started to regain his trust. He had started to believe she had finally accepted that she wasn't going back home, that HE was her family now.

Every day Todd came home with stories about Marty. "Hey, Babe, do you believe that Marty is getting a puppy? I told him he's crazy."

"Oh, really," Shelly said. "I don't know. I think a puppy would be sweet."

"Yeah, until he pisses on the floor."

"True," Shelly said. "But we're not the ones who are going to have to clean up after it. We should go play with it while it's still a pup. You know, just like grandkids. You go play with them and get them all wound up and then go home and leave them with their parents."

Todd laughed, "You got that right!" He paused and then said, "Well, I'll talk to Marty. Maybe we can swing by their place some night and see the pup. Anyway, I'd like you to meet Alissa, his wife. I think you two would hit it off."

That caught Shelly's attention. Careful not to sound too excited, she replied, "Well, that would be nice. I'd like to meet her."

Todd got up from the dinner table and went to take a shower. Shelly's heart flipped with joy and excitement. "Oh, God! I can finally get out of these four walls. But should I tell her what's going on? Will she tell Marty what I say? I don't know! I don't know!' Shelly paced the floor back and forth as her thoughts continued, "I think first I'll just talk with her and feel out the situation. If I behave myself according to Todd's standards, then maybe he'll want to take me back another time."

It was a Thursday night when Todd came home from work and said, "Well, guess what we're going to do this weekend?"

"I don't know. What?" Shelly answered, trying not to be too hopeful.

"We're going to see Marty's pup and, if his wife is home, I can introduce you."

"Oh, that sounds like fun! I can't wait to see that puppy!" Shelly said.

Inside her stomach was flip flopping. "Finally," she thought. "Finally, I get to talk to someone other than Todd."

The next day Shelly got up early, shortly after Todd had left for a job. She took a shower, washed and styled her hair, gave herself a pedicure and a manicure. She laid out an outfit on the bed so it would be ready when it was time to go. Time ticked by slowly, but Todd finally walked through the door at ten after five. This was the first time Shelly was happy to see him since before he ran with her.

"Hi babe, are you ready to see the pup now?'

"Yes, for sure," Shelly said.

"Let me get cleaned up and we'll head out. Marty asked us to join them for dinner at their house."

It wasn't long before Todd was ready to go. Shelly could feel the excitement in her chest. Her heart pounded rapidly. If he noticed she would say it was from the idea of playing with a pup but really it was because she would actually have another woman to talk with.

As they drove away from the apartment, thoughts of becoming friends with Alissa kept filling her mind. "How am I going to start this? What do I say first? Will she be receptive? Stop, Shelly", she told herself. "Just take it one day, one minute, one thought at a time."

"What's up with you? Why are you so quiet?"

Shelly jumped when his voice interrupted her thoughts. For a split second she feared that maybe he knew what she had been thinking. "Oh, geese. I'm just excited, I guess." She cringed, hoping he would believe her response. "I didn't realize Marty and Alissa lived out this far," she said, continuing to try to divert his attention.

They finally reached the small town of Greenville where a large sign read, "Welcome to Greenville, Home of the Mounties." The town was small and appeared very quaint. Mom and pop shops lined the streets in Victorian style and white lights adorned the fronts of the buildings and the trees. It gave Shelly a warm feeling. It felt like going home. For a second that sad, hollow feeling stirred in her heart. They made a right and then a left and pulled in front of a beautiful yellow Victorian.

"We're here," Todd said. "This is it! Hop out. They live on the second floor."

They walked up the front steps to a set of large white double doors. Todd pressed the buzzer and waited for Marty to answer.

"Hey there. I'll be right down," Marty's voice came through the speaker with a happy sounding tone.

Shelly could feel her palms sweating. As the door opened, Marty was standing there smiling. "Hey, guys! So glad you could make it. Hello, Shelly!" Marty said. "Alissa is really looking forward to meeting you."

"As I am to meeting her," Shelly replied. She thought she may have sounded too formal, but it had been a long time since she had the opportunity to meet someone new. She was nervous and wanted to make the connection that could be so important.

The house was split into two apartments but that wasn't apparent until you stepped inside They walked through the doors and up a flight of stairs. The comforting aroma of fresh baked bread filled the air. They could hear the pup excitedly whimpering as they approached, and Marty opened the door.

"Hello," said a sweet soft voice. It was Alissa. She was very petite with long blond hair and stylish cat glasses. Marty introduced them and the puppy jumped excitedly between their legs as they handed their coats to Alissa.

"So glad you could make it," Alissa said.

Shelly smiled and said, "You have no idea how glad I am to be here."

"What's that supposed to mean?" Todd snapped.

It had become an awkward moment for Shelly. Apparently, Alissa felt it also. Before Shelly could respond, she quickly ushered them into the living room, introducing them to the puppy. "This is Rusty."

Shelly sat down on the floor and started playing with him. "Hello, sweet baby," she said. "Oh, my goodness, you're so happy, aren't you? He's so sweet!" Shelly said in Todd's direction.

But it was Alissa who answered as she strolled back from the kitchen with snacks. "He is so playful and loves any attention he can get. Dinner will ready shortly so have some munchies with your drinks," Alissa said.

"Is that homemade bread that smells so delicious?" Shelly asked.

Alissa laughed, "It is! I'm hoping it's delicious. It's only the second time I've made it. The first one didn't come out too bad if I say so myself." The girls both giggled at her comment. Shelly started to feel comfortable and even hopeful.

"She's so sweet and down to earth," Shelly thought. "This could be the start of a great friendship and my ticket home if I play my cards right!"

"Can I help you with anything?" Shelly asked.

"Oh, no, I have everything under control," Alissa said while looking at Rusty. "At least when it comes to dinner! Those two can shoot the breeze about their cars and their work. You and I are going to play with this wild puppy! He wants some attention!" There was laughter all around the room and the evening continued with a pleasant feeling.

Todd and Marty spent the evening talking about cars and work. When dinner was finished Shelly said to Alissa, "The lasagna and the bread were delicious! Let me help you clear the dishes."

"I'm glad you liked it! Thanks for the compliment and the help" They chatted about so many things as they did the dishes: scrapbooking, cooking, what was new in fashion and so much more.

Then Alissa asked suddenly, "Are you and Todd ok?"

Shelly felt her body flush from head to toe. She was afraid this was a test. Did Todd put Alissa up to this? She answered with her voice shaking, "I'm not sure what you mean, are, we ok?"

"Sorry," Alissa said. "It's just the way he jumped down your throat when you got here. And he kept shooting you looks at the dinner table that appeared to have you hanging your head. What's up with that?"

Shelly stood there trying to figure out if it was a sincere question from Alissa or if she was baiting her for Todd. She responded with, "Well, you know Todd. He always needs to be in control of his surroundings." She hoped it was a vague enough answer. Shelly could feel her hand shaking as she continued drying the dishes.

Alissa walked over to her, put her hand on Shelly's shoulder and asked, "Are you alright?"

Shelly couldn't hold back the tears as she looked at Alissa. "Oh, please, please, don't tell Todd I'm crying!"

"For heaven's sake, I wouldn't dream of it! But you need to calm down before he walks in here. I noticed he doesn't like you out of his sight, at least not for more than a few minutes."

By her tone, Shelly could see that Alissa was annoyed with him. Alissa had Shelly sit down at the kitchen table and gave her a cool cloth for her eyes. "Is it something I can help you with?"

Shelly thought to herself, "You have no idea what a loaded question that is!" But she responded with a simple, "I'll be alright."

Before Alissa could say anything else, Rusty ran into the kitchen with Marty and Todd following close behind. "What's going on in here?" Marty asked.

"Oh, just dishes and girl talk," Alissa answered as she shifted her eyes towards Todd.

Todd responded, "Oh, yeah, what kind of girl talk?"

"Just the usual," Alissa said. "Clothes, make up, that kind of stuff." Alissa followed his eyes to where Shelly just sat there with her head down, gazing at the floor. Shelly was afraid to look at either Alissa or Todd. He could usually read her so well.

"Well that sounds interesting!" Marty said laughing as he nudged Todd in the arm. "How about it, Todd?"

"Oh, yeah! Really interesting," Todd said still not taking his eyes off of Shelly.

It had become very awkward for everyone and after a moment Alissa said, "Anyone for dessert?"

Suddenly they could hear a bell ring from the other room. Alissa had hung a bell on the front door for the dog to ring when he had to go outside.

Marty said, "Oops, that's my cue. Rusty has to go outside. Come on, Todd, you can be my entertainment while I wait for him to do his business."

Todd sounded reluctant but said, "Sure, why not?" Shelly felt sure he was afraid to leave her alone with Alissa any longer.

As they walked the dog outside, Shelly helped Alissa in silence, neither of them knowing what to say. Then they both started speaking at the same time. "You know,.." Alissa started. "I wanted to…" Shelly started to say at the same time. They giggled as they both said, "Go ahead."

After a moment of silence, Alissa spoke first, "You know, if there's anything you ever need, just give me a call."

Shelly studied Alissa's face. It appeared warm, comforting and genuinely concerned. She said, "Oh, it's ok. I'll be fine."

Alissa said in an annoyed, yet friendly tone, "You know, I don't mean to sound rude, and please don't take this the wrong way, but there's just something about Todd that doesn't set well with me. I can't put my finger on it."

Shelly just smiled a half smile and didn't answer. Alissa continued, "I mean, he's nice enough but he's a bit edgy."

It was at that point that Shelly reached across the table and grabbed Alissa's hands saying, "Alissa, can I tell you something?" There was a lump in her throat and her stomach was flip flopping, but she knew it was now or never. Would she ever have another chance?

Alissa's eyes widened and she said, "Sure, anything."

Shelly started with, "I need your help."

But before Shelly could say another word she heard Todd's voice yelling, "Shelly, where are you? We gotta go!"

Shelly immediately jumped out of the kitchen chair and darted towards the doorway. Alissa grabbed her by the wrist and said, "But wait! You wanted to say something!"

At the same time Todd walked through the doorway into the kitchen and Shelly ran into his chest. Todd looked down at her with a coldness in his eyes and said, "Yeah, Shelly, you were about to say something. So say it!"

Shelly stuttered a bit and managed to come up with, "Oh, yes, I wanted to thank you, Alissa, for such a nice evening. Dinner was great! Everything great! So, thanks again!"

Shelly tried to act as if nothing was going on, but Todd placed a hold on the back of her neck and tightened it as she spoke. Alissa watched their facial expressions while she struggled with what to do or say next. She seemed to sense the tension rising in Shelly the moment Todd's voice came through the door. After a moment, she got up from the chair and said, "Here, let me get your coats for you."

Shelly said thank you and moved into the living room with Todd continuing to tightly grasp the back of her neck. She broke away from his grasp as she dropped to the floor to pet Rusty.

"He's going to miss all this attention after you guys leave!" Marty joked.

"I'll bet," said Shelly as Alissa walked into the room with her coat and purse.

"Here you go! You're going to need this tonight," Alissa said. "Sorry it took so long for me to bring yours out. I was looking for Todd's coat. I forgot he already had his on! Well, anyway, thank you both for coming. It was so very nice having you here."

She hugged Shelly and Todd and they walked down the steps and out the door with Marty following behind, saying, "I hope you guys enjoyed yourselves this evening. Hey, Todd, don't forget to give me a call in the morning about the part we need for that job we're working on."

Todd answered, "Yeah, I won't forget. See you tomorrow."

Shelly was extremely nervous as they slid into the car. "He's mad," she thought. "But maybe I'm just being paranoid."

Todd shifted the car into gear with a hard yank, 1st, 2nd, 3rd gear. By the time it reached 4th gear, Shelly knew the night had just begun. She tried to be upbeat, hoping to soften what was to happen by saying, "Well, that was really nice!"

Todd just stared at the road without a word.

"I really like Alissa," Shelly started to say.

But before she could finish, Todd looked at her and yelled harshly, "Save it, Shelly! You'd better hope I didn't hear what

I thought I did. Marty will tell me everything you and Alissa talked about. You can bet on it. And when he does…."

Todd didn't finish. He just stared ahead and drove. Shelly knew she hadn't been able to say anything to Alisa about her situation before Todd walked in so Marty should have nothing to tell Todd. So why was she trembling inside?

They reached their apartment and walked silently to their door. Todd opened it and Shelly followed him in. She walked into the bedroom and reached for her pjs on the bed. When Todd walked in behind her, he commanded in a stern voice, "Turn around!"

Shelly did as she was told. Todd yanked the pjs out of her hand, threw her down on the bed, and climbed on top of her. "I think I'm going to fuck you tonight, just so you don't forget who you belong to. Got it?"

He grabbed her hands and held them tight with one hand while ripping her clothes off with the other. Shelly had known he would do something to her tonight. "Did it have to be this", she thought.

"Don't even think about speaking, looking at me, or enjoying any part of what I'm about to do to you! This is punishment for something I think you said to Alissa. And if I find out that's not the case, well then, it's just a bonus for me!" Todd said, smirking at her.

Before he penetrated her, Todd opened his nightstand, pulled out a 38 revolver and laid it next to her face. "You see that?" he whispered into her ear.

Shelly nodded her head yes.

"Look at it," he instructed. "Don't take your eyes off of it." Then he thrust himself inside her.

Shelly immediately shut herself down. She shifted herself out of her body again to somewhere else. Yes, she could feel him all over her, but he could not control her thoughts. That's the one thing that still belonged to her. Time passed without Shelly moving a muscle.

Suddenly her thoughts were yanked back to reality when she felt something between her legs that wasn't familiar. Todd said to her, "Do you feel that?'

Before Shelly could answer she heard, "Click." She realized it was the barrel of the gun he had shoved inside her.

"Click," she heard again. Her mind screamed, "What is he doing? Is this how he's going to kill me?"

Then Todd said, laughing, "Do you know how many rounds this gun holds?"

Shelly shook her head no.

"It's funny. I think it's six. Click." He pulled the trigger again. "You see there's only one bullet in here and for the life of me I can't remember how many times I've pulled this trigger." He then pulled the gun from between her legs and put it against her temple. Shelly closed her eyes tightly and cringed. Todd said, "Was that four or five times?"

"Click!"

?????

Chapter 26

Lynne's Story, January 1997
THE DAY AFTER

Lynne didn't want to begin living what would somehow become her family's normal. At some level she didn't want the hurt to stop, didn't want to find a way to heal. Lack of pain would mean that she had accepted life without Kelly. Healing would mean that Kelly had become part of the past. She didn't want friends and family to go on with their lives and stop thinking about her precious daughter. She didn't want them to forget that Kelly had smiled, had cried, had wiggled her toes, had grasped her mom's finger. She wanted Kelly's brief life to remain significant to those who loved her.

Last night, at home after the funeral, had felt surreal. It had been such a long, emotionally draining day for everyone. Lynne and Luke's parents asked if they wanted company that night but looking at their parents' faces they both knew that their parents needed rest also. After their parents left, Greg did some homework and watched TV. Luke carried wood in from the backyard and started a fire in the family room fireplace. Later, Lynne heard him in the garage, doing something for some unknown reason. She sat and stared at the TV for a while and then walked upstairs into what would have been Kelly's room. She touched the small dresser and the crib set up for when Kelly would have become big enough to sleep there. She looked at the tiny clothes in a dresser drawer but couldn't think about packing and donating them. She pulled a sleeper from the laundry bin and inhaled, trying to capture and memorize the scent of Kelly. The pain that enveloped her felt overwhelming, and her tears flowed, but they kept Kelly with her!

When it was time, Lynne walked downstairs and reminded Greg to head to bed. After he brushed his teeth, she tucked him into bed with a big hug and a tap on his little nose. "Sleep tight, little Greg. I'll see you early in the morning. It's going to be a busy day for you." She believed it would be so. She and Luke would do what was necessary to have his young life continue with a normal routine. They would find a way to mourn their daughter while surrounding their son with love.

When she walked back downstairs, Lynne found Luke in the kitchen with a beer in hand. She took his other hand and pulled him into the family room and onto the sofa in front of the TV. They scrolled through the channel guide, trying to find something to hold their interest and finally selected a rerun of "Christmas Vacation" with the hope that it would help lighten their feelings. It didn't work.

After a few minutes, Lynne turned off the TV, and looked at Luke.

"How will we get through tonight, let alone the next few days, the next month, the next year? I don't know how to live from minute to minute." Lynne didn't want to cry again but the tears that had defined the last months started again. The pain was overwhelming. She couldn't imagine how it would ever dissipate and their life could ever return to "normal." What could that "normal" mean going forward? For the past 3 months, with all the ups and downs, all the struggles that Kelly had miraculously survived, there was a glimmer of hope that she would become stronger and healthier as time went on. As terrible as the pain and agony of losing Kelly was, the loss of hope added a gripping despair to her heart.

As she looked at Luke's face, Lynne could see the same overwhelming pain that she felt. She had no idea how to heal his pain, what words to use, what could possibly bring comfort to her husband.

Then Luke looked at Lynne. "I'm hoping that going to work every day will help me. Do you think you would be ready to go back to work soon? It might help if you are on a regular schedule."

"I'm not sure that I'm ready for that. Facing everyone at the school would be so hard now, let alone getting back into the teaching. I would need to try to act as if everything was ok. I know that time will come but it's not now."

"Well, let's try to get some sleep. My plan is to get up tomorrow morning and try to get back into my work routine." Luke stood up and held out his hand to Lynne. They walked slowly up the steps to their bedroom.

It was a restless night for them both and Lynne was awake before her alarm went off. Luke was already out of bed and dressed as she went in to wake up Greg. Within an hour both Greg and Luke were out the door and Lynne was faced with that terrible moment of, "Ok, what do I do now?"

She also faced the physical reminder of her loss as her breasts felt full. On another day it would have been time to use the electric pump. Instead she took one of the pills that the doctor had prescribed to dry her milk and crawled back into bed. She wanted the release that sleep could bring but instead her thoughts trailed back through everything that happened.

"Did we do enough to prevent our daughter's death? We knew she wasn't ready to come home but we listened to the doctor and hoped for the best. Were there other things we could have said or done? What about that last office visit with Dr. Mark? Why didn't he see what was happening? Should we have taken her to the Emergency Room when she seemed to get worse later that day? I can't believe they gave me the wrong ratios for mixing her formula! How could the Nutritionist have given me instructions that were incorrect, with too much sodium? If she had stayed in the hospital longer, would this have happened? Would anything have resulted in a different outcome? What could God's purpose be for allowing this to happen?"

Chapter 27

Lora's Story May 1993

TRUST ME

And so, it finally became obvious to Lora that Rick would never take the steps to end the nightmare they had been living. There was no baby to propel him to make a decision. He would continue to live his life in limbo until someone decided for him. Would she file for divorce? Would "the other" become tired of waiting for him? She had come to believe that this was an indication of his selfishness, his focus on himself and his own needs. His unwillingness to decide wasn't a reflection of his love for two women. If he had really loved either of them, Lora felt he would have stopped the agony they both were living with. He would have allowed, would have forced, one of them to move on with her life.

She finally understood that she would have to do something if anything would ever change. She decided to take a cruise to gain some perspective and then come home and act. Wise Helen, her dear friend, offered, no insisted, that she would go with her.

Before Lora left, she found another in the series of notes he had been leaving for her.

"Cutie, I think we have a lot to talk about. I love you and I believe you still love me. Be careful. I'll see you when you get home. I'll take care of Elrond for sure. I love you!"

She read the note and laughed. He was definitely out of touch with reality!

She and Helen had selected a cruise out of Miami with stops at San Juan, St. Thomas, St. Maarten, and a party island.

She felt better as soon as she walked on board the ship. The sun, the smell of the ocean, the beach music, and her first boat drink made her smile, a real smile, and she started to giggle.

The ship pulled away from the dock and moved slowly down the channel towards the ocean, the city of Miami sparkling in the background. And then there was Wayne. After dinner the first night, she and Helen went to a lounge for a singles welcome party. Lora was excited, having fun, and felt for the first time in a long time that she looked good. It seemed the time away had already helped her. They selected a small table in an open booth and ordered drinks. A live band had begun to play, and the guests had started to arrive. After several minutes, a man walked up to Helen and asked her to dance. Helen agreed and Lora sat and waited until they returned to the table and both sat down.

"Hi, I'm Wayne." He looked good, with dark blond hair and that look of confidence that some men had, the look that had always been attractive to Lora.

Wayne and Helen continued their conversation, not paying any attention to Lora. She couldn't hear what they were saying but watched him lean closer to Helen and saw Helen respond with a smile. Lora sat quietly, and finished her drink as she began to feel increasingly uncomfortable. Helen and Wayne had started to connect and didn't need her help. She decided to go back to the room and go to bed. It had been a long travel day and she was tired, as much from months of stress as from the events of the day. The gentle rocking of a cruise ship was always soothing to her and she believed she would sleep well that night for the first time since the drama began.

As she leaned towards Helen, to tell her she would see her later in their room, Lora heard Helen say, "Why don't you ask my friend to dance?"

Wayne smiled as he stood and grabbed Lora's hand. He pulled her onto the dance floor with him. She began to move to the music and smiled at him. When they finished the first song, Lora turned to go back to the table. He pulled her back onto the dance floor as the band began to play a slower song and drew her closer into his arms. He grinned and sang as he swayed to the music in exaggerated movements. She laughed and he held her even more tightly, his head resting on the top of her head.

"I like how you feel. Come back to my room with me for a smash of Baileys."

"Are you crazy?! I don't even know you!" she laughed.

"That's ok. You'll like me! Trust me!"

"He's right," she thought. "I will like him, but I won't go back to his room with him."

When the song ended, they went back to the table and started talking with Helen. He was from Canada, here with a friend, Rolland, who had won a trip. Wayne had cruised before and said he looked forward to all the fun the week promised. He chatted on about plans for shore excursions and all there was to do on the ship. After about 20 minutes of conversation, Helen decided she would go back to the room, but Lora decided she wasn't so tired after all.

Instead, she and Wayne went up on deck, to the back of the ship to look at the stars. A full moon spilled bright light across the ocean. They sat in a couple of deck chairs and talked about their lives. He was divorced, with a young daughter, three years old. He shared a photo of a smiling blond child sitting on a small scooter. He said he had an awful relationship with his ex-wife, but he loved his daughter very much.

Lora told him some of her story. "You still love him," Wayne observed but she denied it. The sharing of her story brought back some of the feelings she had tried to escape, and she decided to go back to her room. No amount of persuasion changed her mind.

"Trust me! You'll have a wonderful end to your evening if you come back to my room with me!"

She smiled, touched his hand, and left him sitting on the deck.

The next morning Lora and Helen went up on deck to the pool area at about 10:00. They put their towels on a couple of beach chairs and sat down on the side of the pool. Lora scanned the pool, looking for Wayne but she wasn't even sure she would recognize him. When they met him, she'd already had several glasses of wine at dinner and more at the singles party. Some of the evening was a blur to her. Then she saw him, across the pool, talking to another woman, and her heart sank. He looked up and waved. She waved back but looked away, thinking that she should get up and leave. Before she could move, he was there, sitting next to her.

"I've been looking for you! Where were you?" She remembered the Canadian accent that sounded so attractive to her.

He introduced his friend, Rolland, to Lora and Helen. They were joined by Louie and Bobby, two men from Connecticut who appeared to entertain Helen for the rest of the day. Before dinner, Wayne tried to have them all seated at the same table but wasn't successful, so they met after dinner and the party continued.

They moved from lounge to lounge and tried to sample as many spots as they could in one night. Pittsburgh and Lora's real life seemed unreal, impossible, intolerable. She refused to think about it. When Helen left to go back to the room, Wayne and Lora went up to the back of the ship again.

This time they began kissing and his hands moved over her body, caressing, rubbing, squeezing.

She continued to say, "I don't even know you!"

And he continued to say, "That's ok. Trust me!"

She wanted to feel desired again. She wanted to excite and be excited. She wanted to trust him. But she was still cautious and afraid, and he didn't push beyond what she was comfortable with. She left and walked slowly back to her room, singing and swaying to the music that drifted from a nearby lounge. There was a real smile on her face.

The next morning, he knocked on their door at 7:00 a.m.

"Wake up, sleepy heads! The day is waiting for you! I'm waiting for you!"

Lora opened the door and he stuck his head into the room. She pushed him back into the hallway and stepped out with him.

"I'll be up soon. Meet me on deck 10, by the pool."

"How does he know where we are?" Helen looked at her when she realized who had knocked.

"Oh, I guess I told him."

"Lora, I know you like him but be careful."

Lora didn't listen to Helen any more than she had listened to the message attached to the Swedish fish. She met Wayne by the pool and then they selected and carried their breakfasts to seats on deck, overlooking the water. They spent the day at sea, watching the ocean go by. They arrived in San Juan in the late afternoon and had dinner at a small café on a side street and then had drinks at the Hard Rock Café. If she had been able to look at the photos they snapped, she would have seen what Helen was concerned about.

"Lora, you're acting like you're married to him."

"Well, not exactly. Not yet," Lora responded.

The next day Lora and Helen had a snorkel scheduled on St. Thomas but not till the afternoon. Rolland was on a morning tour and Helen walked away with Louie and Bobby after breakfast.

Lora and Wayne went to his cabin and he undressed her.

"Wow! You have a great body for a 40-year-old woman." They had sex that was amazing to Lora and then decided to shower together which would not be an easy thing to accomplish in a cruise ship shower.

"Wait," he said when she started to run the water. "I'll be right back." He pulled on a pair of shorts and walked out the cabin door with the ice bucket. When he returned a few minutes later, he put the now full bucket on the vanity in the bathroom and pulled her into the shower with him.

"You've never done this before?!!!" he said in mock surprise at her reaction to the chunk of ice that he placed in his mouth and began rubbing over her body. As he taught her how to tease his body with the ice, she started to suspect that that there was a lot of life she hadn't experienced.

That night after dinner, they all met in their favorite bar and planned another evening of cocktails and dancing, with some gambling thrown in just to be sure they didn't miss anything the ship had to offer. She went to Wayne's room with him while he changed into shorts and a t-shirt. When they went back to the bar they couldn't find Helen. They looked at a few of the spots that were quickly becoming the group's favorites but couldn't find Helen or Louie. Bobby wasn't sure where they went or when they were coming back.

"How sad!" Lora and Wayne laughed. "We'll just need to find something to do to keep us busy!" Later, they found Helen having champagne with Louie and Bobby and continued their rounds of the ship's lounges. Wise Helen never said where she was when they couldn't find her. She never asked where Lora and Wayne had been.

And so the night, and the next day, and the next day continued with incredible feelings and intense experiences that were new to Lora.

On Wednesday, they arrived at St. Maarten. Helen, Wayne and Lora had become a trio. They did the Explorer Cruise that featured unlimited rum punch. Wayne found the bottle of rum and added a significant amount to the punch. He passed out on the bus on the way back to the cruise ship. Lora and Helen had great difficulty waking him to leave the bus.

Finally it was the last day and Lora could feel her reality reaching out to her again. She tried to ignore that reality. She didn't want to face the decisions she knew she had to make. She wanted to hide here, with Wayne, and play and drink and immerse herself in the Caribbean for the rest of her days. She called Wayne at 7:00 a.m. in the morning and they met on deck. Then they had sex in Lora's cabin and took a shower with another bucket of ice.

Reality continued to knock at her brain and there were brief moments when Lora lost focus on the fun. She had also begun to feel a sore throat, probably the result of little sleep and exposure to foreign viruses. She ignored her throat as well and rolled through a final day at sea with Wayne. She numbed her throat with boat drinks and wine so she could continue to party and explore the man who had introduced her to so much. They decided to skip dinner because of drinking and partying by the pool.

Later when Lora went back to the cabin to change her swimsuit, she found Helen passed out on her bed. Lora changed clothes quickly, into shorts and a t-shirt, and met Wayne in the Trolley Bar at 9:30 p.m.. They had another quick drink and immediately began searching for a spot for one more chance to have sex. Rolland was in Wayne's room packing. Helen was asleep in her and Lora's room.

Wayne grabbed Lora's hand and pulled her into an elevator.

"I have an idea!" He sang and swayed as he pushed her against the wall in the elevator and began to rub against her.

They walked onto a deck where lifeboats were covered and suspended above the railing. Wayne started jumping, trying to touch the cover on the lifeboat.

"What are you thinking?!!" Lora laughed.

"Watch me" Wayne started pulling a small table and chair towards the railing as he continued to look up at the lifeboat.

"Excuse me, sir!" A crew member had emerged from the nearby door and walked towards them. "If you are considering what I think you are, you need to move on."

"Are you kidding me?! It's our last night on this ship! We need…!" But Lora pulled him towards the front of the ship before he could finish his thought.

"Just come and sleep with me. Helen is passed out on her bed. At least we can hold each other till morning comes."

They went to Lora's room and slid into her bed, beneath the blanket. Within a few moments there were sounds coming from Lora's bed and Helen jumped up, yelling, "Oh, my God! What are you doing?" She grabbed her robe and ran out of the room.

"Wayne, we need to leave. Helen can't be out in her robe."

They opened the door and found Helen sitting on a chair close to the elevator. "Helen, I'm sorry. We weren't going to…. But we're out now. Please go back to the room."

By 2:00 a.m. they were snuggled together in a stairwell, determined to stay awake all night and not waste the final moments of the cruise. Lora looked at Wayne's face and tried to memorize his Canadian accent and the way he said, "Trust me!" After one last, lingering kiss they finally parted at about 4:00 a.m. so she could go back to her room to pack the remaining few items into her carry-on bag.

Saturday morning was officially here, and it meant goodbyes and back to her life. Wayne called their room at 5:30 a.m.. He was already dressed and going up on deck. Lora dressed quickly and went up to meet him and watch the ship dock. Then they sat in a lounge, waiting for the ship to clear immigration. She clutched his hand and desperately wished she could continue the fantasy days she had been living. As Wayne walked out of the lounge with his friend, her last words to him were, "Please come to Pittsburgh." But she didn't believe she would ever see him again.

When Lora and Helen were finally on their bus, headed to the airport, she knew she was in trouble with her throat. All the alcohol from the previous day and night had worn off and it hurt so badly she knew she would need to find a doctor when she got home.

Several hours later, Helen dropped her off at her home. When she walked through the front door, he was there, sitting with Elrond in front of the TV and holding a glass of wine.

"Hi, Cutie! How was your cruise? I made dinner and I have some champagne. He moved to hug her, but she stepped aside.

She was unimpressed and too sick to focus on him. "I'm sorry you went to that trouble. I'm sick and not interested in dinner or champagne or you."

She dropped her bag, grabbed her keys, and headed for the urgent care office. She needed to feel better soon so she could begin her tomorrows. Where would she find the courage and strength to take the next steps?

Chapter 28

Shelly's Story
February to April 1985
THE NOTE

The next morning Shelly couldn't move. She lay there motionless as tears ran down her face. "I'll never get away from him," she thought. She got up and walked into the bathroom and into the shower. Her movements were robotic at this point. She was numb until she saw her reflection in the mirror while she dried herself. That little spark fired up inside her again. "If there's any hope at all, Lord, please give me a sign. Anything at all, just something so I know you're here with me."

She put on a pair of sweats and reluctantly went into the living room. She looked at the clock and was surprised to see it was 11:30 a.m. already. Todd was gone, "Thank God," she thought. The thought of seeing him sickened her. She turned on the TV and sat quietly, just her and the four walls, enjoying the peace as the hours ticked by.

Suddenly Todd burst through the door with a dozen roses. "Hey, baby, glad to see you're finally up. Look what I brought you," he said with a big smile on his face.

"How nice," Shelly said, looking up at him stone faced.

"Ah, come on, babe! You're not going to hold that little thing from last night against me, are you?"

Shelly was afraid to say anything. Todd sat down next to her taking her hands into his. "Look, babe, you know how I get. I just want to be sure you realize that I'm the only one you need in your life. Besides, who else would want you? I mean, look at you! I'm actually doing you a favor by loving you. That's just the way it is, babe," he said as he lifted her chin and caught her gaze. "Besides," he said, "I talked to Marty and he didn't say anything at all about you and Alissa, just that they had enjoyed us being there last night. See that, it all works out."

Shelly gave him half a smile and said, "I guess."

"Come on now, let's go out for pizza, get yourself ready" Todd said as he pulled her up off the couch, slapping her on the backside.

Shelly went into the bedroom to change clothes and get ready. She yelled from the room, "I'll be ready in a minute. Just putting on my lipstick"

Todd yelled, "Ok, baby. Make yourself pretty."

Shelly pulled a tube of lipstick from her purse and saw a piece of paper rolled around it. She closed the bathroom door thinking to herself, "What's this?"

As she opened it up she saw, "I don't know what you're going through but whatever it is, I can help you. Here's my number. (717) 555 -0169. Call me any time. I promise I won't say a word. Alissa"

A chill rushed through Shelly's body. "This is it," she thought. "This is the sign I needed. Thank you! Thank you! Thank you, God! I knew you wouldn't give up on me!" Her mind instantly started to think about her next step. "But I can't give Todd a clue that anything is happening."

She went out into the living room and kissed Todd hard on the lips. "Now, that's my girl," he said.

Shelly smiled as she thought to herself, "Yeah, you keep thinking that!"

They went to dinner that night and Shelly played her role flawlessly, trying to keep the trust she had worked so hard to gain. Shelly continued this act for days, then weeks, never mentioning home or family. Even as the mental, emotional, and physical abuse continued, Todd unknowingly began to be manipulated by Shelly. "He's playing my game now," she thought, "and it's working!" She never saw Todd so happy and content.

A couple of weeks later Todd came home one night and asked, "Hey, Babe, do you want to head over to Marty and Alissa's tomorrow night?"

"Sure," Shelly responded with excitement in her voice.

"Marty asked if we were doing anything and I said, 'Not that I know of.' So I told him I'd ask you."

"That sounds like fun! We should bring something this time, though. I hate going empty handed," Shelly said. "I think pies for dessert would be good."

"Ok, make me a list and I'll run to the store and get what we need," Todd said. He still didn't allow Shelly out in public very often. He continued to hold the reins tightly, but Shelly could see him lightening up a little.

"Here's what we'll need," Shelly said and handed him a list.

"Ok, Babe. I'll be back soon," Todd said.

"Ok, love you!" Shelly said as he walked out the door.

"Oh my gosh! Oh my gosh! You've got to plan this carefully! Think, Shelly, think!" she said to herself as she paced the floor. "This may be the only shot you have at this, especially since you're still not allowed to make any phone calls to anyone. Heck, there still isn't even a phone in this apartment and the closest one is a couple of miles down the road, at the Speedy Mart. That's ok," Shelly thought. "You can do this."

She started to plan how she would explain everything to Alissa. "First," she thought, "we'll need time alone, so Todd doesn't suspect anything, especially after the way he treated me the last time we got home from Marty and Alissa's. I've started to gain his trust, maybe just a little, but it's enough for now."

Shelly planned everything in her mind, careful not to write anything down, so there wouldn't be any trace. Before too long before Todd came home.

"Hey, Babe, I'm back," Todd announced as he walked through the door.

"Ok. I'll be right out." Shelly collected her thoughts as she walked towards the kitchen.

"I'm heading to the shower," Todd yelled.

Shelly yelled back, "Ok." She felt relieved he didn't hover over her while she baked, asking questions and giving orders. Shelly baked her pies, deep in thought. "What would it feel like to not walk on egg shells anymore? Not having someone watching my every move, just waiting to attack? It would be incredible!"

Shelly couldn't really remember what it felt like to be free. "WANTING TO BE FREE should never be part of a relationship, at least not part of a loving one. Those words are associated with being a prisoner, someone held against their will." That's exactly what she was, a prisoner in his world.

Shelly was very nervous and scared. She couldn't help but think, "If this doesn't work out, I may never know what it is to be free again." She continued going over and over in her mind how she would explain everything to Alissa in the little time alone they would have together.

The next morning finally came. Shelly bounced out of the bed trying to feel a little bit of confidence in what the day would bring. She was very nervous, but she tried hard not to let Todd suspect what she felt. She busied herself cleaning throughout the day until the time finally came for her to get ready to go.

"Oh, please, God, let this happen!" she prayed while looking at her reflection in the mirror. She stood there, staring at her image. It had been so long since she really saw herself. "It's going to work," she thought, looking herself in the eye. "God has got your back. All you have to do is execute the plan!"

Todd came through the door, "Are you ready, Babe?" His voice startled her at first.

"Uh, yeah! Almost done," Shelly replied.

"Well, don't you look nice!" Todd said sarcastically as she walked into the living room a few minutes later.

Shelly ignored his comment. He continued, "If I didn't know better, I would think you were planning something special."

Shelly responded reluctantly, "Well, I don't get out very much so to me it is kind of a celebration."

"What's that supposed to mean?" Todd said sharply.

Shelly thought quickly, turned, wrapped her arms around his neck. Looking up into his eyes, she began to implement her plan. "Oh, Baby, you know you're the only one for me. I did all this for you because I just love you that much. Where would I be without you?"

She kissed him tenderly. She could feel his body soften from the stiff stature he had just a minute ago.

Todd said softly, "That's all I ever wanted to hear you say."

Shelly smiled still looking him in the eye. "I know, Baby," she said with a smile. Shelly could feel a knot in her throat. In a strange way she still felt sorry for him. How sad it would be to live in his mindset.

"STOP!" Shelly screamed in her head. "You can't fix him! Stay focused!"

The car ride to Marty and Alissa's was quiet with the exception of some small talk about things they passed along the way. When they pulled into their driveway, Shelly looked at the two white doors at the entrance and thought, "Are those the doors to my freedom?" She smiled to herself, feeling both hope and anxiety.

Marty met them at the door with Rusty. "Hi there," Shelly said carrying her pie.

"What have you got there?" Marty asked.

"That's her masterpiece. It should be famous." Todd said laughing.

"Stop it!" Shelly said. "My pumpkin pie is truly like no other!" They all laughed as they headed up the steps.

Marty said, "Well, I for one can't wait to have some!"

Alissa met them at the door to the apartment. "Hello, hello!" she said smiling as she took the pie from Shelly. "Wow, does that smell good!"

"Thank you," Shelly said smiling.

"Dinner will be ready in a few," Alissa said.

"Thank God," Marty said laughing. "You know she wouldn't even let me have a single bite!"

Marty, Todd, and Rusty went into the living room. Shelly followed Alissa to the kitchen. Once the guys could no longer see them, Shelly grabbed both of her hands and whispered, "Thank you so much for the note in my purse! You'll never know how much hope a piece of paper brought to me!"

Alissa hugged her and said, "I am so glad you saw it! I thought you might need someone to talk to."

"If you only knew!" Shelly said.

"Why haven't you called me?" Alissa asked.

"Because we don't have a phone."

"What?!" Alissa asked. "Are you kidding me!"

"No! And that's just the beginning!" Shelly said.

"Wow!" Alissa said.

And, as if on cue, Todd walked into the kitchen followed by Marty. "Just grabbing a few beers, girls."

"Cool!" Alissa said. Shelly just smiled, hoping Todd didn't hear a word of what she had said.

"Well, since we're all in here, let's get dinner on the table." Alissa said. They carried the food into the dining room where there they ate, talking and laughing. Shelly was grateful that no one brought up anything about her family or her background. That would have caused Todd to get up and leave and she couldn't have that happen.

After dinner Alissa and Shelly headed to the kitchen while Marty and Todd headed to the living room. They stood at the kitchen sink, one washed, the other dried the dishes.

Shelly whispered, "Alissa, I really need to talk to you."

Alissa replied, "Do you think it's safe? I mean, Todd is always lurking around somewhere."

"I know," said Shelly. "But this can't wait."

"As soon as they take Rusty out for a walk, we'll have alone time, at least I hope so," said Alissa. They finished up the dishes and, as if he knew their plan, Rusty rang the bell on the door to go out.

"Looks like your turn, hun," Alissa said to Marty as she smiled at Shelly.

"Yeah, I guess. You got him the last two times. Come on, Todd," Marty said as he hooked the leash onto Rusty's collar. "Time for a walk."

Shelly was never so glad to hear a bell ring. "Thank God," she thought.

As soon as the guys walked out the door Alissa plopped down on the couch next to Shelly. "Ok, let's hear it. What's up?" Alissa said.

Shelly explained to Alissa what she had been going through with Todd. Alissa sat and listened, looking at her with wide eyes.

At one point, Alissa interrupted Shelly mid-sentence, "Why don't you just leave?" she asked.

"That's just it, Alissa. I can't, "Shelly said. "It's not that easy. I'm deathly afraid. I haven't been able to speak to anyone other than Todd for so long. I live in his world. I'm always looking over my shoulder waiting for him to say or do something. He's even threatened my family! I really feel he's capable of anything, but I can't be his prisoner any longer!"

"Oh my God! That's for sure," Alissa said.

"I've decided to devise a plan, but I haven't gotten very far. I know I need to gain his trust and so far it's working. That's as far as I've gotten with my plan. All I know is that I cannot fight back, or even mention my family at all anymore. He gets so full of rage. He becomes someone unrecognizable."

Shelly tried desperately to explain everything in the little bit of time she had before the guys came back in. She knew it was imperative that she get Alissa on board to help her with her plan.

"So, can I count on you for some help?" Shelly asked. "I know I can't do this alone."

"Of course, anything," Alissa said. "Where do we begin?"

Chapter 29

Lynne's Story February 1997

COMFORT

Lynne looked out the back window and watched Luke walk into their shed. She figured it was another attempt at some mindless activity to keep him from focusing on what he would otherwise be feeling. He spent a lot of time in their backyard now. He seemed to draw comfort from being outside, connecting with nature. When he was in the house, he was very quiet and didn't talk much to Lynne though he still attempted to connect to Greg.

It was now 2 weeks since the funeral. Somehow one day had passed, and then the next and the next. Lynne knew she and Luke were each trying desperately, in their own ways, to rationalize their loss. They both needed to find a way of understanding why this had happened and to begin the healing process. They had supported each other through the frightening days after Kelly was born but now neither was able to significantly help the other. They were no longer talking about their feelings and Lynne often felt totally alone. She felt sad that their quests for understanding and healing were taking them in different directions.

Lynne always had a strong belief in God. While Luke turned to nature, she turned to her religion to help her find acceptance. She looked for a reason. She looked for comfort. She needed the belief that she would connect with Kelly again someday.

Her mind continually rolled from idea to idea. There had to be a meaning for the heartache she knew would continue for the rest of her life. Thinking about what Rose had told them about Kelly's lungs, she wondered, "Could it be that God wanted to protect us from a lifetime of worrying about a sickly child? Was it an act of compassion and love from our heavenly Father?"

Her thoughts turned back to Luke and she watched the back yard for a few minutes longer, thinking, "Why won't he spend more time with Greg and with me? I wish we could have more of a normal life. I miss our life the way it was before this tragedy."

She knew it would never be the same and, at some level, she knew it was too soon to expect any feeling of normalcy. So she turned away from the window, with no anger inside but with very conflicted feelings. She longed for a life without sorrow, if not yet with happiness. But that life without sorrow would mean that Kelly had begun to slip into the past and she never wanted that to happen.

Not long after, Luke walked back into the house. He went to the refrigerator and started looking through drawers. "I think I'm going to head to the mountains this weekend." He spoke casually without looking directly at Lynne.

She started to say, "How could you think about leaving us now, even for the weekend??! It's too soon!" But she didn't say those words. She loved Luke and didn't want to prevent him from finding his relief. At the same time, she couldn't understand how he could leave them when they were all struggling to find healing. Why didn't he turn to her and their family life? She wasn't sure how she felt. Was there some resentment and also a touch of anger towards him? And so, she said nothing.

Lynne turned away and walked into their family room where Greg sat and watched his favorite TV show. She sat down next to him and started to chat about what was on the screen. She didn't look up but could feel Luke standing silently in the doorway. After a few minutes he turned and walked back outside. Lynne knew they loved each other but she had become increasingly concerned about her feelings.

She was afraid they were drifting apart. They were drawing comfort from people, places, and things beyond each other.

Lynne continued to sit with Greg without really seeing what was on the TV screen. The next day would be Friday and she dreaded the thought of filling her time over the weekend. What would she do with all the hours that slowly turned into days, days that seemed so long, nights that had become so lonely? She was still on her extended leave from work. Though there were quick contacts to check on her, very few people came to spend time. She understood that it was uncomfortable for many people who didn't know what to do or say.

Luke left early in the morning, perhaps to work for a while, perhaps directly to the mountains. Lynne didn't know what his plans were and wouldn't ask. She lay there, pretending to be asleep while he quietly slipped from their bed and out of the room. She heard him using the bathroom down the hall. Apparently, he wanted to avoid a conversation as much as she did.

A little later, Lynne watched as Greg walked down the driveway and joined his friends at the bus stop. Fridays had always been fun family days, sometimes a drive to the mountains together, sometimes snuggled around a fire in the back yard, sometimes out to dinner with friends. On this Friday she walked back into the house and climbed into bed. Maybe a few hours of sleep would help her. She stretched out and tried to enjoy the peaceful moments in the quiet house.

Then she knew, "How stupid am I? Why would I ever hope to enjoy quiet moments in this house again? I need to get out of here!"

She pulled on a pair of jeans and t-shirt, grabbed her keys, and headed to the garage. Her favorite mall and favorite store were only a few minutes from home. She was soon parked there. She pulled out a cart and started through the aisles. She didn't have a shopping list with her, but she knew there was a sale going on and there were always things they needed for their home or for Greg. And it was never too soon to tuck away birthday or Christmas gifts. Beyond the clothing and houseware sections, there were also food and cosmetic sections in this store. She wasn't sure what was in the pantry or refrigerator, but she could always use snacks for lunches and after-school. She could shop for it all right here!

Walking into the Ladies section, Lynne saw a top that could work well with jeans or business casual pants when she went back to work. She didn't feel like trying it on but put it into the cart. If it didn't work, she could return it. Then she walked to the bathroom section. She had been wanting to buy new towels for their bathrooms and the price was significantly reduced today. She chose different colors so she had what would work for each of their bathrooms. In the entertainment section she found a movie she knew Greg had been wanting. Spring items were starting to appear on the shelves, and she couldn't resist a wind chime that would be perfect for their front porch. After loading up in the food section, she went back to look at shower curtains. She had been wanting a new curtain for the main bathroom and didn't want to pass on the chance to get it for a great price. There were two that she loved. Should she take the geometric pattern or the beach and palm tree pattern? Lynne stood looking for a while, trying to decide on which would look best.

"Well, since I can't decide," she thought, "I think I'll just have to take both!"

And so, the pattern continued. Luke leaving sometime on Friday to head for the mountains with an occasional invitation for Greg and Lynne to accompany him. Lynne continuing to shop at her favorite mall. The shopping provided only temporary comfort, so it had to be repeated frequently.

The comments and questions from him had started shortly after the weekends at the mountains and the shopping had started. Luke and Lynne shared a credit card and he paid the monthly bill from their joint account. The dollar amounts she charged continued to increase week after week.

At first the questions and comments were gentle, "Lynne, what are you buying? I need you to be careful about how much you are charging. Our bill is high this month."

"Well, instead of taking medication for depression, I have found that the shopping gets me out of the house and takes my mind off of things."

Still, over time, the questions and comments began to sound like irritation. "Didn't we talk about this? What are you spending all the money on? You need to slow down!"

Lynne listened and verbally agreed but began feeling increasing irritation herself. She was a professional and "their" money was a lot of "her" money. She only bought things they needed. They were all necessary things. She and Luke had always been so busy with careers that there had been little time to purchase improvements and enhancements to their home. She felt some small pleasure as she brought home a surprise for Greg, badly needed new dishes that were a great bargain, or some new cosmetics to update her own look. And, it eliminated the need for medication.

So, Lynne refused to think about Luke's comments when he was in the mountains and he appeared oblivious to the enhancements she added to their home. It was only when the credit card statement arrived each month that she had to focus on what she had spent. The words between them became more and more agitated over her spending patterns.

"Again, Lynne! Look at this bill! You need to stop, S T O P, your spending!"

"Oh, but it's ok for you to take off for the mountains each weekend and leave us alone?! I don't check on what you spend or what you do when you're there! I don't try to stop you from doing the things that bring you comfort! I'm spending on things we need for our home or for Greg. It makes me feel good to see what I've done for the house and to make Greg happy and do you realize that I'm not relying on the medication that most people would need to survive?!"

"Do I need to take that card away from you?' Luke shouted. He obviously didn't really hear what Lynne had said.

Lynne jumped up and glared at him, "Who do you think you are in this relationship that you can talk to me like I'm a child?!"

Chapter 30

Lora's Story May 1993

TIME'S UP

Lora didn't bother to ask if Rick had decided or what he had decided. She went to work on the Monday following her return from the cruise and tried to start functioning like an HR Manager again. Early on the first Friday morning after her return, she met with a divorce attorney who gave her a lot of good information about the divorce process and she filed the papers.

After leaving the attorney's office, Lora called Rick and left a message asking him not to come home and not to call her. He had left on Monday morning and she hadn't seen or talked to him since. She assumed he was in Buffalo and he left the usual ongoing string of messages professing his love for her and asking for just a little more time but there was no live contact. By the time she got back to her office after her meeting with the attorney, Rick had already called her cell phone multiple times and her office number twice. He also called the office number while she was out to lunch and then again at mid-afternoon.

The messages were brief but there his voice sounded intense.

"Lora, pick up the phone!"

"Lora, you can't continue to ignore me! Pick up the phone!"

"Call me now!"

She finally answered the phone in her office and agreed that she would meet for dinner at a restaurant close to their (her) home. When she got there, she found him in the bar. They ordered a glass of wine in the bar and then went in for dinner.

When they were seated, Lora gave him the speech she had prepared. Many of the words were brave thoughts conceived in the office of Dr. Levy. But she delivered them with conviction, to the best of her ability, though she wasn't sure how she would live them.

"These months have been really hard for me, but the week apart has helped me to get some perspective on things. I can't believe how foolish I've been to tolerate all that I have over the past few months. As awful as these months have been, I've decided that I'd rather live alone than to continue to live as I have since January. It's time to end this farce and move on!"

He was silent.

"I now understand that I'm not special in your life. I'm just one in a crowd of many faces."

Still nothing from him. She flashed back to the classes they took years ago as they prepared for their marriage. They were asked to tell the other couples what they loved about their partner. Lora had gushed on about how wonderful he was in so many ways.

He had said, "We really enjoy each other's company. We have fun and enjoy traveling together." Or some other comments that had nothing to do about "her" as a person or why he loved "her." She realized now that hers could have been the face of any woman who agreed to live the way he chose and create few demands on him. How little she had understood about the way he would choose to live!

Lora continued, "I'll do whatever is reasonable to get your things out of my house, on my terms. But more importantly, I am going to do everything I can to get you out of my heart and head to spare myself any additional pain."

Lora smiled. "I'll miss you. And, by the way, I've frozen our joint assets till we resolve the terms of our divorce."

Finally, a reaction, anger. It was a new emotion for her to observe in him. He had always been laughing, pleasant, calm, in control. "You can't do that!"

"You're wrong. I have done it."

"I need access to those accounts!" He raised his voice and his eyes flashed with…., she wasn't sure what. Maybe it was anger, or fear, or shock at her courage.

"Why? What does "the other" need from us now?"

"Those accounts belong to me too!" It was a quiet upscale restaurant and others began to look in their direction.

"Do you know what?" she said quietly. "I don't really want to have dinner with you after all." She got up and walked out. He didn't follow.

They had a few scattered phone calls over the next week.

"I've seen an attorney," he said. "She told me it's illegal for you to keep me out of our house. I still have the right to live there. I don't want to battle with you but it's still my home. She suggested I try to work out something with you by the weekend. If not, she's going to get a court order to allow me back in."

Lora called her attorney who said, "Interesting! I've never heard of such a thing. Please ask your husband to have his attorney call and educate me about the process."

Lora didn't know where Rick stayed when he was in Pittsburgh, but she refused him access to their home. She did offer to pack his things and leave them on the front lawn. He declined that offer.

The limbo period continued for a few weeks. She had a sense that he had started to make plans and was ready to finally move out. But she began looking at their home, which was now over 15 years old and needed work. They had always been too busy, traveling, sailing, out to dinner, to the theater, off on a picnic, to do much work around the house. She started to think about being the person left with all the catch up work while he and "the other" moved on and enjoyed what had been "her" life.

Lora called him as soon as she made the decision. "You can come back to the house to stay when you're in Pittsburgh if you want. We can work out the details in our divorce settlement whenever that happens. But I've decided I don't want to live there any longer. I'm going to move as soon as I can."

"I'm surprised," Rick said. "You were so adamant that you wanted to stay in the house. But, whatever you want. I'll try to stop by one day this week for a key."

A phone call from "the other" followed the next day. "You are doing this deliberately, aren't you? How did you know that we were about to sign the lease for a condo together?! I'm packing to move to Pittsburgh!"

"The other" cried and shouted. "We are building our life together and it doesn't include living in your house!! Do what you want but he is not moving back there!"

"Interesting, but not my problem." Lora disconnected the call.

That night there was a knock at the door, and she opened it for him. Elrond was excited to see him, purring and meowing. Rick picked him up and cuddled while he scratched his head and behind his ears.

"There's a key for you on the end table," Lora said. I'm sorry if my decision has ruined your plans.

"No. My decisions have ruined so much more than my plans. Your decision is really... inconvenient for me but I'll handle it. I know you won't believe I have the nerve to ask this, but I just need a little more time."

She didn't reply as she walked to the door and motioned for him to leave. As she closed the door behind him, she heard him still asking, "Can you please find a way to give me just a little more time?"

Chapter 31

Shelly's Story, April 1985
NOW WHAT?

"You know where the apartment is that we live in, right?" Shelly asked.

"Yes," said Alissa. "But I think it's too risky for me to show up there."

"No, no, you're not going to come there. "You know the bottom road? It's called Ridge Road? It winds around the back of the apartment building, along the wood line. Right after the sharp bend in the road, is a big wide oak. It has a heart carved in it with S loves G."

"Yes, yes, I know just where that is," Alissa said.

"I'll meet you there tomorrow morning. Todd goes to work at 6:30 a.m., same as Marty. Once Marty leaves and is out of sight, you can head down that way. By the time you get there it will be around 7:00 a.m.. By that time Todd will be well on his way. I will leave the apartment at exactly 7:00 a.m.. I'll make my way down the hill and meet you at the oak tree. There's a place to pull off there where teenagers go parking."

"I know exactly where you mean," Alissa said.

"Great! It's a plan then?" Shelly asked.

"It's a plan," Alissa said as they hugged each other tightly.

"Oh, one more thing," Shelly said.

"Yeah, what's that?" Alissa asked.

"If I'm not there by 7:15 a.m., leave! We can't take the chance of Todd knowing you're involved in any way."

Alissa looked at Shelly with some apprehension in her eyes. "Will do. But what if you're just running late?"

"Don't worry," Shelly said. "I promise you. This is one time I won't be late."

"Do you want me to call your parents?" Alissa asked.

Shelly thought about it for a second and said, "No, just in case it doesn't work out."

"Ok," Alissa said. "My God, I've never been involved in anything like this!" There was a look of worried excitement on her face.

"I'm so sorry to get you caught up in this," Shelly said. "But I desperately need your help!"

"Oh, Shelly, please don't misunderstand me! I may be a little nervous but, if it means that you'll be free of him and his craziness, then I'm all in." The ladies hugged each other again as they heard the guys coming up the steps with Rusty.

"Well, we're back!" Marty yelled as they came through the door. "And we're ready for some of that famous pie!" They all started laughing.

Alissa got up and headed towards the kitchen with Shelly right behind her. Shelly stopped at Todd's side, kissed him on the cheek, and said in a very soft, sweet voice, "Hey, baby, I missed you!"

Todd reached over and squeezed her backside as he chuckled. "I missed you too!"

When Shelly got to the kitchen, she looked at Alissa with an expression on her face as if she were gagging. They both giggled. Alissa said to her, "I feel so bad for you. That's one game that I never want to have to play."

"Believe me, Alissa, I don't want to play it either. Unfortunately, I don't have a choice. It has to be this way for now if I have any hope at all of getting out of his grasp."

Shelly sliced the pie while Alissa placed it on small china plates adorned with roses. "These plates are beautiful," Shelly said.

"Thank you," Alissa replied. "I got these at a house auction."

"That's so neat! I've never been to one before."

"Maybe we can do that sometime. It's lots of fun."

"Sounds like it," Shelly said as she looked up at Alissa smiling. She had a sad, almost inevitable feeling in her heart that their friendship may not last if she ever got free. "How could it?" she thought. "Once I'm away from him, I'll never look back! I can't! No ties to anything he's a part of."

Shelly walked over, hugged Alissa, and said, "Please know that I really cherish the friendship we've made. You are the only good thing that will come out of this crazy time in my life. "

Alissa pulled back, looked Shelly in her eyes and said, "You are a beautiful person and a special friend. Don't worry! We'll always be connected in some way." Shelly wondered if Alissa knew what she had been thinking. They both had tears in their eyes as they smiled and hugged each other.

"Now, wipe your eyes," Alissa said. "We don't want to give Todd any reason to suspect anything."

They carried the pie into the living room and joined in the conversation with the guys. Marty took one bite of the pie and said, "That's one delicious pie, Shelly! It should be famous!"

"I agree," said Alissa. "Coming from Shelly I knew it would be delicious."

Shelly blushed, "Thank you, everyone! You're too kind." Shelly didn't know how to react to a compliment anymore. It had been so long since she'd received a sincere compliment.

After they finished the pie and the dishes were done, Todd said, "It's time to head out, Shelly. Get the coats."

"Ok," Shelly said as she walked towards the bedroom where Alissa had placed them.

Alissa followed behind her. When they both got into the room, Alissa said quietly but excitedly, "Ok, 7:00 a.m., right?"

"7:00 a.m.," Shelly said. "It's a date." The girls hugged and quickly carried the coats into the living room. Todd and Shelly said goodbye and headed home.

During the ride home, Shelly was quiet as she reflected on the time she had been with Todd. "You were so innocent," she thought. "Naïve and stupid is more like it. How dumb could you be, Shelly? If you hadn't been such an idiot, thinking you could change him, you wouldn't be in this position. What the hell was wrong with you, you dumb ass?" Shelly could hear her own thoughts criticizing herself.

"My God," her thoughts continued, "You have become the person he groomed you to be, the person he said you were all this time." Shelly knew she would never be the same person she was the day he took her on that picnic. She had changed forever. She used to see herself with so much zest for life, always kind, loving and happy. Now she felt dirty, crass, and worthless.

"Once I get away from him, who's going to want me? My family will never see me the same. My innocence is gone." Shelly turned her head and glanced over at Todd. She looked at him with a big smile on her face, still playing the game but inside she wanted him gone, erased from her life.

"Why are you looking at me like that?" he said.

As she continued to stare at him she thought, "Wouldn't it be great if I could just open his door and push him out on the road?"

"Hello," Todd said.

Shelly brought herself back into the moment and said, "Oh, sweetie, I'm just thinking how lucky I am to have you in my life." She was really good at playing this game. "Why'd you decide to go this way?"

"Oh, I just felt like a change, I guess," Todd responded.

Todd had decided to take the back way home which took them along Ridge Road. Although it was dark, Shelly could see the large oak as they made the bend and it gave her the chills. It seemed surreal to her that she could be meeting Alissa there the next morning. The oak looked so much bigger than she remembered. In the lights from the car she could see the heart carved in the bark. Her mind drifted as she thought, "I wonder who S and G are. Whoever they are, I hope they are in love and happy. Love, real love. I can't even imagine what that feels like. Will I ever know it?"

The anxious feeling in Shelly's stomach continued to grow. Was it just worry or was it a sign about what would happen tomorrow? She just didn't know.

They got to their apartment. "Well, here we are. Home sweet home." Todd said.

"Yep, home sweet home."

When they got into the apartment, to Shelly's delight, Todd said, "I'm just heading to bed, Babe. I'm beat."

Shelly tried not to sound too excited and said, "Ok, you do look a little tired."

He kissed her on the forehead. "Don't stay up too late watching tv. I like to feel you next to me, sleeping in bed."

"Of course, I'll be in shortly." She knew she wouldn't be able to sleep a wink, thinking about the next morning.

The alarm went off at 5:30 a.m. Shelly was already awake. She'd had little to no sleep, tossing and turning, going over and over her plan for the next morning. She lay there, keeping her eyes closed, pretending to sleep, hoping Todd hadn't notice her restlessness through the night. She could hear Todd moving through the apartment as he did every morning, only this morning he stopped at the bed and stared at her for a few moments. She could feel the intensity of his gaze and she opened her eyes.

"Good morning," she said as she stretched. "How are you this morning?"

Todd sat down next to her. "I'm good," he said softly. He reached over and placed his hand on her cheek. "You know I love you, right?" he said in the same soft tone.

"Of course. Why are you looking at me that way" she asked.

Todd had his eyes locked on hers. He just sat there and stared. His eyes had a strange look to them. It wasn't the typical way he would look at her with control or rage. It was different, soft, almost loving. Instead of making Shelly feel good, it gave her the creeps.

He kissed her on the forehead and said, "I'll see you tonight. Love you."

"Love you too," Shelly said as she smiled, touching his hand as he slid it off her cheek.

Todd walked out the door and Shelly could hear it close behind him. She lay there for a few minutes, just in case he had forgotten something and came back for it. She finally looked at the clock and it was 6:30 a.m.. "Oh, God, I've got to get moving," she thought.

She kept dropping everything she touched, her clothes, her makeup, her purse. She knew she was nervous, but she started to believe it was a sign. As she walked through the apartment, she stopped and just froze in place as she thought, "My God, wonder if this doesn't work? This is too easy! Something is bound to go wrong." She looked at the clock again. It was 6:50 a.m..

"What do I do?! What do I do?! Oh, God, Shelly, calm down and think!" It was then she could see light shining, just a little, from the parking lot onto the window-pane. Shelly's heart dropped. "My God, he's back! But he can't be! He's supposed to be at work. I didn't hear his car pulling in."

Their apartment sat below the parking lot. Only the lights from the cars were visible, not the actual vehicles. But she always heard that familiar roar of his car. This time she hadn't heard it. "Stop being so paranoid, Shelly! Just stick with the plan!" she thought.

Her gut told her something different. Shelly started to sweat profusely. Her stomach started to churn. Flashes of hot and cold ran through her body. With one hand on the doorknob to leave the apartment, she turned and looked at the clock – 6:55 a.m..

"Oh God, I still have a few more minutes before Alissa will leave." She ran to the bathroom and, just as she settled on the toilet, she heard the dead bolt on the apartment door. She froze.

"Hey babe, you still in bed?" It was Todd. "I decided to take the day off and spend it with my favorite girl."

"Oh my God, it's him!" she thought. "He did come back!"

"In here," she yelled as she quietly pulled the bathroom door closed. "What a surprise," she said, trying to sound excited. "I'll be out in a minute."

Shelly hurried to take her coat off and shoved it and her purse under the bathroom sink. She also wiped off the little bit of lipstick she had on. She tried to calm herself and walked to the living room. "Wow! I can't believe you're home!"

"You've been such a good girl, I thought I'd surprise you," he said as a smile spread across his face.

"This is definitely a surprise," Shelly said as she thought of Alissa waiting at the big oak. She looked at the clock, 7:10 a.m. Her chance was slipping away. It was as if the feeling of hope and freedom had been sucked from her. She felt defeated. All she could feel for Todd at that moment was anger, resentment, and contempt.

"It's such a nice day. I thought we'd take a ride up to the mountains."

"That's the last thing I want to do," Shelly thought. But she said, "Whatever you want!" trying to sound happy.

She knew the look on her face would show the opposite, so she began folding the towels that lay on the table. She tried not to think about the fact that, if she had gotten out, she would be on her way home by now. One part of her asked, "Why did I have such stupid, stupid nerves?" Another part of her was thankful she hadn't walked out the door right into Todd's path.

Now what?

Chapter 32

Lynne's Story, February 1997
JUSTICE?

Lynne continued to find it difficult to get back into a normal routine, but she knew she had to keep trying. Greg needed to feel love and stability. She believed she needed the extended leave of absence from work to focus on healing her family. But she still didn't know how, didn't know where to begin to fill the void. Even the most normal activities felt strange and unreal to her. Most nights brought only restless sleep, most mornings fragments of dreams of tiny smiles, squeaky cries, and anguished fears.

Lynne's mornings began as always with getting Greg to the bus stop on time, down the driveway and across the street. One of the most difficult parts of those mornings was when she would come face to face with Jessie who was having a healthy pregnancy and was close to her delivery date. Like most people in their neighborhood, Jessie knew about Kelly's death but appeared to forget or to be insensitive to Lynne's feelings. Lynne began to call her the "mean lady" in her thoughts.

This morning was no exception. Lynne tried to smile as she approached Jessie and her 7 year old daughter.

"Hi, Jessie! How are you doing today?"

"Oh, I'm feeling ok. But I'm getting so big with this baby that I can hardly walk! Who could ever imagine that a second pregnancy could be so difficult?" Jessie giggled and rubbed her stomach.

Lynne felt a stab and thought to herself, "How can this woman be saying these things to me? She knows about Kelly! She knows what I went through! It's not like she's a stranger."

Lynne took a breath, fighting against tears and anger as she said, "I hope you realize how blessed you are to be having this healthy pregnancy. Surely you realize how hard this is for me."

"Well, this is what I'm experiencing right now. Holding back my thoughts won't take away any of the pain you've been experiencing! I'm sorry if it's difficult for you but this is my life and you should try to move on with your life!" Jessie didn't sound sorry.

Lynne wanted to scream, almost wanted to slap a pregnant woman, but luckily the bus came around the corner and she was able to walk away. She knew that she would go to a different bus stop in the future so that she wouldn't have to come face to face with Jessie. She wondered how this woman could be so oblivious to the pain she caused, or perhaps so uncaring. Surely anyone would realize the impact of those words on another woman who had just lost her baby.

On most mornings, Lynne continued to go back to bed after the bus left with Greg. Sleeping through part of the morning shortened the length of the day that she would have to endure. Though the days slowly slipped by, Lynne felt that her family still needed help. She had avoided the need to use medication, which she felt was a good thing, but sleeping and shopping could only bring temporary relief from the pain. Shopping didn't heal the pain, didn't help her to see a way to find happiness again without Kelly in their lives.

So one day Lynne contacted the office at their church and was given the name of a grief counselor. She made an appointment for the three of them to see him. Surprisingly, Luke agreed to go with no resistance. Lynne believed it was an indication of his own ongoing pain, and his desire to help his family heal in whatever way he could, short of giving up his weekend trips to the mountains. She was glad she had taken the step to find a counselor and was hopeful he would help provide her family with the tools they needed to get through each day.

The first visit with the psychologist, Dr. Sales, was a quick one. He appeared to be middle age, with slightly graying hair, and had been told he was highly recommended by other members of their church. He met with Lynne, Luke, and Greg to understand their reason for coming to him. He seemed to be a good listener and even appeared to become a little teary eyed as Lynne told their story.

"I think I can help you find the tools to move forward," he said. "I have 5 children myself and can't imagine losing any of them. I'm glad you came to me. Let's schedule another visit for next week. We'll continue to use the family meeting format."

Lynne left that meeting feeling optimistic. The following week, the three of them were back at Dr. Sales' office.

"Hi, everyone. How did this past week go for you?"

Lynne tried to sound a little upbeat for Greg's sake. She said, "We're managing, trying to keep on schedule. Luke went to work, Greg went to school. I did some shopping."

"It's good to keep busy," Dr. Sales said.

"And I try not to think too much," Lynne continued. "Greg's getting into basketball now. We've been going to games. We're helping him to get together with friends."

Lynne and Dr. Sales did most of the talking about activities during the previous week. The 50 minute session seemed to drag on with few suggestions or comments from Dr. Sales. He didn't probe about their feelings or offer ideas about how to move forward. He was a good listener but didn't seem to offer much help.

When the three of them were back in the car, Luke said to Lynne, "What was that all about? How is that supposed to help us? I thought he would help us build some coping skills."

"Well, maybe we just don't understand how it's supposed to work. Let's see what happens next time. What do you think, Greg? Did Dr. Sales make you feel better tonight?

"Not really," Greg said. "I know what I did last week."

The next family appointment was very much the same as the last one. Lynne did most of the talking about what she did that week. Luke added a little about the events of his week. Greg looked bored. Dr. Sales listened again but spoke very little. It was another long session, until he smiled and said, "I'll see you next week."

Lynne desperately wanted help and didn't know where else to turn. She knew that therapy could change lives, could even save lives, but she started to think that maybe the family meeting format wasn't right for them. She didn't want to talk about her restless sleep and haunting dreams in front of Greg or Luke. She didn't want to explore Luke's frequent absences and her repeated shopping trips in front of them. At some level she still wasn't sure that she really wanted to heal. The pain kept Kelly from slipping into the past. She was the only one who could keep that from happening.

Lynne could only guess about the struggles to heal that Luke experienced. She could only imagine the things he needed to talk about though she believed they would be similar to hers. He didn't talk to her about his pain. He didn't ask about her pain. He withdrew to trees, wildlife, open air, where she hoped he found comfort. He didn't explore his feelings with Dr. Sales. Undoubtedly they both believed their adult feelings were not appropriate to be explored in front of Greg.

Over the next few days, they all thought about it, talked about it, and finally decided not to return to Dr. Sales. Lynne and Luke agreed that it wasn't the help they thought they would get. She knew from talking with friends that it could take multiple tries to connect with the right therapist. Maybe Dr. Sales wasn't the right person for them. Maybe it wasn't the right format. Maybe they should continue to look elsewhere. Maybe there was no way to stop the pain. Maybe there was no way to regain the feeling of a family connected, a husband and wife connected, that had bonded them as they anticipated the birth of Kelly.

In addition to the overwhelming sense of loss, another strong emotion started to emerge…. anger!!! So, instead of

Lynne spending time looking for a different therapist, she started thinking about another option. She started doing research for an attorney who could help them bring a medical malpractice suit against the doctors who worked for the hospital where Kelly had lived for 95 days. Was there an attorney who could help them get justice for their daughter?

Chapter 33

Lora's Story June to Nov 1993
FRIENDS OR MORE?

Lora was geared for action now. Action held the pain at bay. She focused on her search for a new home, and her job. She was sure rumors about her were on the grapevine. She had lost weight and some days she had been so distracted she was barely able to function. Her team members knew some of what had happened and stepped in to cover for her. Now she knew she had to refocus and do the job expected of her.

One day a business planning meeting focused on an exercise designed to help the managers of the group learn more about the strengths they each brought to the team. Lora felt good as she stood in front of the room to do her short presentation that was supposed to capture the essence of who she was professionally. Until recent days, she had lived her life as an optimist and chose as her theme, words from a figure who had always inspired her "If you can dream it, you can do it." (Walt Disney)

During the meeting, she also spent some time observing the manager named Mark who was also the topic of office rumors. Her interest in him had grown over the past few months. She knew him professionally, though their interactions had been limited. She didn't know much about his personal life until recently. She'd heard that he was in the middle of a nasty divorce and struggled with the separation from his wife and daughters. He was tall, slim, and slightly graying. He was about her age, she thought, and wrote a note to herself to check out his profile on the HR database.

Over the next few days she had meetings scheduled with each of the managers in her group. Her meeting with Mark was brief. He didn't look like it was a good day for him, and they agreed that they would schedule a more in-depth meeting in a few weeks. She was afraid she could be crossing the professional line but, as she started to leave his office, she said to him, "You may not have heard, but I'm in the middle of a fairly difficult divorce. I don't want to cross into your personal life, but I've heard you may be having some difficulty also. If you ever want to talk, I just happen to have lots of free time in my personal life."

He managed a weak smile. "I have heard, and I am also. Thanks for the offer."

Lora began to join the after-work activities that she had never known about previously, drinks at the small bar across the street, concerts at the arena nearby, parties at the homes of single co-workers. She was surprised to see that many of her married colleagues joined the gatherings. She had always maintained a social distance because of her role in Human Resources but she needed to connect, to begin having fun.

Gradually Mark began to appear at some of the events and they started to talk.

"I never knew this office had so much after work partying," she smiled as she sat in a large booth with Mark and a few other managers. "In my HR hat, I just have a few worries because there are both managers and employees here. I'm not sure that's smart."

"Oh, Lora, take off your HR hat. We're careful. You won't see the face of anyone here who's in a problem situation in the office." Jack was a very experienced, long term manager with the company. So she decided to try to relax and enjoy her connections with the group though she couldn't totally take off her HR hat when she was with them.

Lora and Mark continued to connect at the after-work gatherings. Over time, he began to share his story. He had been married for over 10 years and they had two young daughters.

"You may not know a lot about me, or maybe you know more than I realize because of your role. But I'm a fairly private person and don't share a lot," he said one night when they were alone at a table. "We moved here from Denver when I took the job as Manager of my department here. It was a huge move with 2 young children, but the money and advancement were more than I could turn down. My wife is a nurse and we knew she could find a job anywhere in the country."

"I knew some of the basics but not anything about your wife or kids."

"I really love my wife and my family life but I'm afraid it's over," Mark said looking down at the table. "This is humiliating for me." There was a long hesitation. "She's having an affair with one of the doctors she works with"

Laura reached out and touched his hand, "Oh, Mark, I'm so sorry! I understand what your pain may be like because of my own situation."

"She said she's always been honest with me so, once I found out, she's been telling me so much more than I want to know. I thought we always had a great sex life, but she's told me what she does with him and to him. She says she loves me but her experiences with him are so much more than she's ever experienced with me. She says she can't walk away from him." For a moment Lora's thoughts moved to an earlier night and she wondered whether ice was involved in his wife's experiences. She struggled to suppress the urge to smile which would have been really inappropriate while this man shared such personal information.

"You don't need to tell me all this, Mark. You've had some wine to drink. I don't want you to regret talking to me like this when tomorrow comes."

He ignored her and continued, "I've moved out and I'm living in an apartment now. I miss my daughters! I miss family dinners! I miss snuggling in bed with her! I'm a lonely man!" He squeezed her hand and raised his eyebrows. "Maybe we can bring some comfort to each other?"

He finally looked up at her as she asked in a shocked tone, "OMG! What are you suggesting?"

"I think you know what I'm suggesting." Lora laughed as though it was a joke though she wasn't sure it was. When he laughed also, she felt relieved. She really liked Mark. She liked his look and his sense of humor. But, despite the attraction she felt, she knew she couldn't cross the line that being his HR Manager placed between them.

"Ok, it's time for me to head out. See you tomorrow." She waved goodbye to the others and quickly headed across the street towards the parking garage. She was glad when she reached her car and drove away. Fun with this group was one thing. Even the thought of something more significant with a co-worker was something totally different. She finally allowed her thoughts to drift back to ice and smiled on the drive home.

A week passed before Lora decided to join the after-work crowd again. She had thought about Mark a lot. When she saw him in the office, she felt there was a secret connection between them. She sometimes went out of her way to walk past his office or made up a reason to meet face-to-face with him instead of talking by phone.

When the group began to head home, Lora and Mark decided to meet at a small Chinese restaurant, partway between her home and his apartment. Neither had been there before but Lora had heard that the food was very good, and she really liked the area where it was located. They were seated in a front room with huge windows that overlooked a small town street that was lined with ancient looking trees. They ordered multiple dishes to share and glasses of wine.

Mark was in a mellow mood tonight, probably impacted by the glasses of wine he had with the group. There was no talk of his wife or their divorce and Lora was careful to keep the conversation light.

"It's been a lot of fun getting to know you outside of your professional role. Our office is a little crazy at times but a good place to work and probably no crazier than any other branch office. At least you and the other managers have a great HR Manager to work with and keep you out of trouble!" Lora laughed.

"Or maybe an HR Manager who could entice me to get myself in trouble,…looking for a connection that isn't smart professionally! What do you think?" He was teasing, she knew, and the conversation was comfortable for her. The teasing and laughing continued throughout dinner. His comments were sometimes suggestive but felt like jokes and silliness.

When the waitress placed the check on the table, she grabbed it. "This one's on Rick!" she said as she pulled an American Express card from her purse. It was Rick's account and he would get the bill. "It's the least he can do!" Lora laughed as she added a very generous tip.

Drinks and/or dinner with Mark and sometimes the manager group became something Lora looked forward to. It was another Friday, late afternoon when she and Mark headed out alone for drinks and dinner at a new restaurant that was located on the side of the river a few miles from their office. Lora offered to drive, and Mark agreed. She tried to do her share of the driving and tonight was a good night to offer. She had never learned how to parallel park and she knew that there was off street parking at the restaurant.

They sat at a window table with a great view overlooking the river. They ordered wines and a variety of appetizers and small plates to share. It was only about 7:30 p.m. when they were done and headed back to the office and Mark's car. Within a few minutes, they pulled up in front of the office building and continued to chat for a few minutes. Lora was surprised when Mark leaned over and kissed her lightly. She was even more surprised when she felt excitement as he pulled her closer and the kiss intensified.

"Come to my apartment with me," he whispered.

Lora knew this was crazy but said, "Ok but I want to drive my own car. I'll follow you."

Within a few minutes she was driving behind him, out of the city. She knew the roads he took and kept thinking, "I should get off this road and head home." And then, "I could turn here, and he'll certainly understand." And then, "I can't do this. I'm his HR Manager!" But she kept following.

He pulled into the parking lot of an upscale looking group of buildings. As they walked towards the door he said, "I kept expecting you to stop following and head home."

She laughed, "I kept thinking I should turn and go home. But here I am!"

"Well, I'm glad you're here. Let's go have another glass of wine."

They went into his apartment and he poured two glasses of red wine. She perched on a stool in his kitchen, but he grabbed her hand and pulled her into the bedroom. The room was dark, but Lora could see a king size bed with crumpled sheets and blankets. Mark reached out and placed her glass with his on the dresser. And then he pulled her towards the bed as he began to kiss her. He slipped off her blazer and pulled her top over her head. There were no words from him, just an overwhelming sense of urgency. They were both undressed, and he was on top of her before she realized what had happened. He was significantly taller than her with a lean, firm body. He moaned as he touched, kissed, pulled, rubbed her face, her neck, her breasts and beyond. It was too soon when he entered her, but she didn't resist or ask him to slow down. It wasn't a forced or unwelcome joining, but neither was there the feeling of fun and adventure she had experienced with Wayne. This was a sad man, a man in pain, a man looking for a physical release. And she was his Human Resources Manager!

Lora thought he was asleep as they lay, entwined and resting. Finally, he raised his head and looked at her.

"I can't believe that just happened! Are you ok?" He touched her face and looked concerned. "It's been a while for me and I'm afraid I rushed you. I'm sorry if you weren't expecting…." He hesitated and waited for her response.

"Yes, I'm good!" She returned his gaze and smiled. "Am I the first person you've had sex with since your wife?"

Oops! She realized too late that it was the wrong question to ask. His expression hardened and he pulled away.

She reached out and touched his shoulder. "I'm sorry. I didn't mean to cause you pain. I just thought…. Sometimes it helps me to talk about my soon-to-be-ex. You don't have to answer that question. I think it's time for me to head home now."

They both dressed and he walked with her out of the building and to her car. It was a night that would be repeated many times over the next few months. Lora felt herself being drawn into thoughts of her future with this man a part of it. She didn't love him, yet, at least in the same way she loved Rick. But she did begin to look forward to weekends with him. He was funny and made her laugh. He helped to fill the lonely, empty hours. She did love the way they physically connected. They spent time in his apartment and he also came to the home she shared with Rick where they had sex on the bed she had shared with her husband. There were new experiences, new positions, new sensations she had never experienced before, even with Wayne.

Lora and Mark's time together expanded to include weekend picnics by a stream in a park north of the city. They used Rick's season football tickets to go to games. They found they both liked to cook and prepared new, interesting recipes. They also continued frequent Friday evening outings, sometimes alone, sometimes with colleagues. The small bar and restaurant across the street from the office building was the group's favorite spot. After being spotted by a co-worker having dinner at what Lora and Mark believed was an out-of-way restaurant, their involvement had become common knowledge around the office.

Still, they tried to hide their physical, and at some level emotional, connection even from other members of the management staff. It was very convenient to have their office across the street from the bar they frequented. There were times when they were at the bar with their colleagues and Lora could feel him trying to catch her eye. With a look and motion of his head towards the door, they would discretely leave and cross to the office building. The guard would roll his eyes as they signed in and showed their identification. Within minutes of entering his office, they would be on the floor, entwined and quickly moving to a climax unlike their usual in-depth exploration of physical sensations and reactions. Then they would quickly cross the street again and rejoin the group, wondering if anyone had noticed their absence.

In September they visited her favorite vacation spot, the most magical place on earth, and had sex on the floor, in the shower, on the sofa, and slept snuggled together. She thought he seemed to share and enjoy a feeling of connection, especially of course the physical connection.

Waking up in the same bed in their villa in that magical vacation spot, Mark said, "It feels so good to wake up with someone next to me!" Lora continued to see her therapist, Dr. Levy, and when she shared Mark's comment with him, the doctor asked, "Did he mean that it felt so good to wake up with YOU?" Lora chose to ignore the significance of that question.

Before she knew it, it was finally November. She was ready to close on the town home and wanted to move before Thanksgiving. Rick showed up the night before her appointment to sign the papers, still asking for a little more time.

"Tell them you're not ready. Let me fix this before you take this step. I just need a little more time."

But she was ready and the next day, she signed the papers. Then she went to her car and cried because she felt so alone. She had signed a lease for a new car several weeks earlier – her first new red car ever! She had a new town home to move into soon. And she went home, by herself, for one of the last times, to the home that had been theirs, and had just enough wine to make her go to sleep without thinking. As she drifted into wine induced nothingness she thought, "What have I done? What will life be like? Should I have given him more time?"

Chapter 34

Shelly's Story, April 1985

FLIGHT

Suddenly Shelly felt Todd's presence next to her. He pulled her face up by her chin. "You didn't hear a word I just said, did you?" he asked.

"Sure I did," she said quickly.

"You know," Todd said, starting to raise his voice. "What the fuck is your problem?" He pushed her down into the chair.

Shelly started to speak quickly, "I'm so sorry, Todd! I didn't sleep too well last night. I must be tired. I wasn't ignoring you. I promise."

"Well, then, snap out of it and get your ass moving, girl! I didn't take the day off to waste it!" he said in a raised, agitated voice.

"I'm moving! I'm moving!" Shelly said as she walked towards the bedroom to grab her coat and purse. She suddenly remembered they were under the bathroom sink. She retrieved them and quickly walked back out to the living room.

"Ok, I'm ready."

"About time!" Todd said.

Shelly put her head down and followed Todd to the car. She didn't care where they were going. All she could think about was her family and Alissa. But in some weird way she was relieved. Relieved, because she knew that once Todd found out she was gone, all hell would break loose. He would never just let her walk away without retaliation of some sort.

They drove for what seemed like forever. As they started up the mountain, Shelly recognized where they were. They were headed to Secret Springs, a ski lodge at the knob of the hill.

"I knew it," Shelly thought. Todd's brother owned part of the lodge. "We came here to do a run for his brother. So, this is what it's all about. It has nothing to do with spending the day with me. He's such an asshole!"

Shelly didn't dare ask why they were there. She knew it would infuriate him if she questioned him. The sadness she had been feeling started to turn to anger and frustration. "I missed my chance to go home for this?!!" she thought. She sat there in the passenger seat staring at him and then her anger began to turn to pity. There was still that part of her that felt sorry for him.

They pulled into the parking lot. "Wait here, babe, I'll be right back," he said.

"Sure," Shelly said. As he walked into the lodge she thought to herself, "What's going to happen to him when I'm gone? I'm truly all he has. Stop, Shelly! You can't fix him!"

She struggled to turn her conflicted thoughts away from Todd and tried to focus on the day. It was cold for April and it had started to snow just a little. She could see each flake as it landed on the window, each pure white, unique and incredibly beautiful.

"Amazing," she thought. "They land so gracefully but their beauty is only there for a minute, and then it's gone, melted away." Her heart ached as her thoughts continued, "That was me, so beautiful inside, so full of life. But it all melted away. He stole it and that part of me is no longer. I'll never be that pure ever again."

The car door opened, jarring her mind back to the present Todd climbed into the car, "See, it didn't take that long. I'm starving, how about we stop at that barbeque place you like so much?" It was dinner time and they had been gone most of the day.

"Sure," Shelly said. Halfway down the mountain was Skip's Country Barbeque. Shelly liked to stop there for the conversation as much as the food. Skip and his wife, Roxanne, took the time to talk to their customers and make them feel welcome. That was something Shelly craved even more than the barbeque chicken.

They pulled up to the front of the building. The place was small but had a nice area for dining. It had cute little round tables, with red and white checked tablecloths. Shelly and Todd ordered their food and took a seat at the corner table. Shelly sat across from Todd and didn't say a word. They sat there in silence and stared out the window.

Suddenly a car pulled up that looked familiar to Shelly. When the driver and his passenger got out of the car, Shelly couldn't believe it and she smiled. "It's Marty and Alissa," she said to Todd.

"Oh, yeah?" Todd said, stretching his neck to see. "I'll be darned! Talk about timing!"

When Alissa walked in the door, Shelly jumped from her seat and hugged her so tightly she almost knocked her over. "Hi!" Alissa said. "I never imagined we'd see you here."

"I know!" Shelly said, sounding giddy.

"Why don't you go ahead and order and then come to our table to sit with us?" Todd said.

Once Marty and Alissa got back to the table Shelly tried to think of how she could have a moment to speak privately to Alissa. She came up with a plan.

"Hey, Alissa, I need to hit the ladies room. Do you want to come with me?"

Alissa looked at her with a knowing smile and said, "Of course!"

Once they were in the bathroom, the girls locked the door. Alissa grabbed Shelly's hands and asked, "What the heck happened this morning?"

"I was ready to walk out. I even had my hand on the doorknob." Shelly explained to Alissa what had happened that morning.

When she finished Alissa asked, "Ok, now what?"

"I don't know. I haven't gotten that far. I had no idea I would see you today," Shelly said.

"I know. What a crazy coincidence!"

"Alissa," Shelly said. "There is no such thing as coincidence! At least that's what my high school teacher, Miss Mara, once said."

The both looked at each other wide eyed. Then Alissa said, "Stop! You're giving me the heebie-jeebies! So, are we going to try again?"

"Yes!" Shelly answered, louder than she meant to.

"Alright, same plan? But when?"

"I think tomorrow will be good," Shelly said. "I can't imagine him taking two days off in a row.

"Alright! Tomorrow it is!"

"Wait," Shelly said. "I don't think it's safe for you to drive me all the way home." She scribbled a phone number on a small piece of paper. "Here's my cousin Leslie's phone number. Give her a call. Believe me, she'll be glad to hear from you. But tell her to keep it on the down low, so my family doesn't find out, just in case."

"Right!" Alissa said. "But I could take you all the way home."

"No, trust me. Once we're halfway there, I'll jump into her car and you can be home way before Marty walks through the door. No one will be the wiser. Tell Leslie to meet us at St. John's church along Aurora road. She'll know exactly where you mean. By then I'll be halfway home. Halfway home! I feel like Dorothy on the Wizard of Oz."

"Yeah, too bad you can't just tap your heels together." Alissa said.

"I know, right? Anyway,' Shelly continued. "Are we good then?"

"Yes," Alissa said. "I'll wait till 7:15 a.m., just like last time."

They both held their hands up with fingers crossed, hugged each other, and walked back to the table.

"Finally," Todd said. "Took you long enough."

Shelly just looked at him and put her head down. The rest of the meal continued without incident. By the time they left Todd had started to laugh and his mood seemed happy.

That night Shelly couldn't sleep again. She relived the past few years with Todd and the things she had been through. "Whoever would have thought that she, Shelly Ziegler, would be in this position?" She lay there thinking, "I wonder if Alissa has called Leslie by now?" She looked at the clock. It was midnight. "I'm sure she has." Shelly laughed to herself as she pictured Leslie doing cartwheels because she was so excited. They used to do them all the time together as kids.

Shelly finally dozed off. Before long, the alarm went off, causing her to sit straight up in bed. Todd rolled over and looked at her. "Jumpy, aren't we?" Even half asleep he sounded sarcastic.

"Yeah, must have been dreaming."

"That had to be some dream!"

"I guess," said Shelly as she lay back down. She listened to Todd going through his daily routine, although it seemed to drag on this morning. Shelly felt anxious and nervous. She trembled so much she thought her teeth were going to start chattering.

Todd finally came in, kissed her on the forehead, and said, "Love ya. See you later."

Shelly thought, "Not if I can help it!" But she answered very calmly, "Yep, love ya. See you later."

The door closed behind him. That was Shelly's signal to set her plan in motion. This time, even though her body trembled inside, she moved about the apartment with purpose and determination. She tried not to think about the what ifs.

Then it was 7:00 a.m.. She couldn't wait any longer. "Here we go," she said out loud as she opened the door. As she stepped outside, she could hear the main door upstairs opening and she felt the hair stand up on the back of her neck. She turned to look at the apartment door. It had already closed and locked behind her. She started to panic.

"Fight or flight," she thought, looking out the glass door at the back of the apartment building. The sun was shining, just a little bit. "FLIGHT!" she thought. She grabbed her purse tightly in her arms and pushed open the back door. When the cool air hit her face, and she passed though the sunshine, all she could think was, "This is what freedom feels like!"

She ran as fast as she could, down the hill and across the wood line. Then she saw it, the big oak, and Alissa didn't disappoint her. She was parked on the side of the road, with the car running and ready to go. As Shelly ran towards her, she could see the biggest smile cross Alissa's face.

Alissa pushed open the passenger door, "Get in! Get in!" she yelled.

Shelly jumped into the car and closed the door behind her, "Go! Go!" she yelled.

As they sped down the road, Alissa screamed, "We did it! We did it!"

Shelly laughed out loud and said as she caught her breath, "We're not out of the woods yet! Drive fast but not fast enough to get us a ticket."

"Why? That might actually be a good thing," Alissa said.

"No, we don't need anything slowing us down and tying you to the whole breaking away from Todd thing. Alissa, you have no idea how dangerous he can be."

"I believe you," Alissa said.

"Did you talk to Leslie?" Shelly asked.

"Yes. And I gave her an ETA, so she'll be there on time. I also gave her a little information about what's been going on so she's not completely in the dark."

"Oh, she'll be there! I can't believe I'm moving down the road and Todd isn't the one driving me." Shelly looked over at Alissa and started to cry. All her pent-up feelings finally had come to the surface.

Alissa reached over and patted Shelly's hands that were shaking uncontrollably. "I will never forget what you have done for me," Shelly said.

"Oh, Shelly, I'm so glad I could be here for you," Alissa said smiling.

As they continued on Ridge Road, Shelly fidgeted in her seat, constantly looking over her shoulder to be sure they weren't being followed. Todd was nowhere in sight. "Thank,

God!" she thought. But by no means did that comfort her or take away any of the fear and anxiety she felt.

They finally reached Aurora Road and Shelly knew it wouldn't be long before they arrived at St. John's church where Leslie would be waiting. So many emotions ran through her mind. She was sad, happy, excited and scared, all at the same time.

"I hope she's going to be there," Alissa said.

"I feel sure she will. She's never let me down before. We should be coming up on it any minute now."

"I can see the steeple," Alissa said, with excitement in her voice.

"Me too!" answered Shelly. "This feels too much like a dream. I think you're going to have to pinch me."

"Oh, it's real, my friend," exclaimed Alissa. "You're going home!"

At that moment they pulled into St. John's parking lot. Shelly quickly turned to look at Alissa. "I don't know when I'll get to see you again. I have a feeling things are going to get a lot crazier before the dust settles."

Alissa answered with a smile on her face, "You have my number. It will all work out, I promise. I'm a firm believer in people walking into our lives for a reason. You need to focus on mending your life. Everything else will fall into place."

Shelly's eyes filled with tears. "You're amazing and wise! Thank you so much for helping me find my way back home and for being such a wonderful friend."

Shelly and Alissa hugged each other, both in tears. Suddenly a knock on the car window startled them. It was Leslie. Shelly jumped out of the car and wrapped her arms around Leslie's neck.

"Hey, girl, I had begun to wonder if I would ever see you again," Leslie said.

"I wasn't quite sure either but, you know me, I never give up on something worth fighting for."

Alissa got out of the car and Shelly introduced her to Leslie. "It's so wonderful to meet you. Thank you so much for helping Shelly get back to us!"

"I'm so glad I could help," said Alissa. "Thank you for being here to meet us. I was so happy to be able to help her get away from that horrible excuse for a man. You two better be on your way. We have no idea if Todd has found out you're gone yet."

Shelly hugged Alissa again and whispered in her ear, "I will never forget you!"

They said their good-byes and got in their cars. As they pulled out of the parking lot, Shelly watched Alissa's car driving away. Once her car made the bend, she could no longer see it and tears rolled down Shelly's face. This time as she wiped them away, it felt as if she wiped away another chapter of the nightmare she had lived for too long. Alissa was the spark that helped ignite the fire in her. She was the strength and help Shelly needed to get this far.

"I hope someday I can thank her for all she has done for me," Shelly said.

Leslie reached over and squeezed Shelly's hand and said, "Just getting yourself home and starting over is the best way to thank her."

"I guess," Shelly said. But she felt as if she owed Alissa so much more.

"So, what do you think? Straight home or should we stop at the police station first?" Leslie asked.

"I don't know! I just want to get home but I'm so afraid of what he's going to do."

"Then we'll stop at the police station first. I'm not sure what they'll be able to do but at least they'll be aware of what happened to you. They're close to your house so, if Todd shows up, it won't take them long to get there."

"True," Shelly said. "Todd is so crazy! I'm so excited to see my parents but so scared of what's to come. I can't even begin to tell you how twisted his mind works."

"Oh, I can only imagine!"

"Believe me, no, you can't" Shelly said adamantly.

"My God, Shelly, what has he done to you?"

Chapter 35
Lynne's Story, March 1997
HOPE

Lynne's search led her to a renowned medical malpractice attorney in the city and Luke agreed to meet with him. Friends who were medical professionals encouraged them to pursue action, so they scheduled an appointment to meet with Mr. Connors.

On the day of their appointment, they sat down with him and began to tell him their ugly, ugly story of faulty decisions and actions that had resulted in the death of their daughter. Lynne was in tears as she and Luke described what had happened and the impact on all of them. They explained to Mr. Connors how they had continued to express their concern about Kelly coming home too soon. She had still been under 4 pounds when her doctors insisted that she go home! She had started to show some different behaviors that caused them to really worry. There was also the nurse who had tried to tell the doctors that Kelly wasn't ready to go home and the inaccurate directions from the Nutritionist about the formula! Mr. Connors listened carefully and took notes as they spoke.

"I feel sure we have a case here," he said. "I recommend that we pursue it."

Mr. Connors then explained the process. The law firm would request the paperwork from the facility where Kelly had been. A nurse employed by the law firm would help review and organize the documents prior to sending them to an independent neonatologist. It would take months before they would hear anything. As Lynne and Luke left the meeting, they felt optimistic about the investigation. Hopefully it would show that the doctors at the hospital had misjudged Kelly's readiness to go home. In the meantime their anger would have to simmer with no resolution.

A few days later Lynne talked with a friend whose husband worked at another local hospital. He was the head neonatologist there. From her friend she learned that all the local hospitals in the city had convened emergency meetings following Kelly's death to discuss their policies for when to send a premature baby home. The outcome of those meetings was that the policies had changed. Premature babies could no longer be sent home until they weighed more than 5 pounds. This change in local policies regarding when to release premature babies from hospital care had to prove that their procedures were flawed. Lynne and Luke felt the hospitals' actions acknowledged the terrible mistake that had been made with their baby and probably others. This knowledge added to their simmering anger and their feeling of hopelessness. They needed to find justice for their daughter.

Their quest for justice for Kelly seemed to be reconnecting Lynne and Luke in some ways. They were spending some time together as they talked about their efforts to be sure that Kelly's brief life had not been in vain. They believed they would not only show that Kelly had died because of a faulty policy, their action could also prevent the same outcome for other premature babies. Kelly's death would shield other families from the agony their family had been living. They were a family joined for a purpose.

Their physical connection, however, still needed work. Luke was interested and willing, but Lynne still had reservations when it came to more than cuddling. Luke was gone many weekends to their camp and on weekdays he was often very tired from his job, so there wasn't a nightly effort. Lynne was relieved because the thought of trying to be romantic and to experience physical and emotional pleasure was still beyond her comprehension.

So, many nights they would lay and cuddle and snuggle, and Lynne would be relieved when Luke would fall asleep and she would hear the sound of a gentle snoring. On nights when he appeared to be more interested in a physical connection, Lynne would try her best to relax and feel the urge to respond to him, but she couldn't and eventually he would turn away from her. She didn't want to continue to refuse his advances because she knew it was important for them to stay strong and to move forward. She loved her husband, but she wasn't ready to resume their sexual connection.

One Friday evening when Luke was home and Greg was invited to a sleep over, Luke suggested that they have a quiet evening alone with good food and some wine. He went to a local Italian bistro and brought home Lynne's favorite pasta dish, Caesar salad, and Crème Brûlée for dessert. He opened a bottle of red wine and poured two glasses as Lynne placed dishes and silverware on the table.

"Let's think good thoughts tonight," Luke said as they sat across from each other at the dining room table. "You look beautiful tonight, as always. It's been a long time since we've just enjoyed each other."

"It feels a little silly for the two of us to be sitting at this table alone," Lynne said. "Maybe we should move into the family room with our food. That would feel more like us."

"Yeah, you're right! I just wanted to set the right mood. But, this isn't us."

They picked up their food and glasses and moved to the sofa in front of the TV. They debated news channels vs. a sitcom and selected the sitcom. Luke was unusually chatty, and Lynne laughed at some of his stories about his work week.

After they finished the food, Luke said he would find something else to watch while Lynne took the empty plates to the kitchen. He filled their wine glasses and then, as Lynne returned from the kitchen, she saw he had selected a romance type movie with what she knew had some erotic scenes. She had really enjoyed their dinner but felt concerned as they sat on their sofa and started to watch the movie. As the story line developed, he reached out and pulled her closer to him, then slid his arm around her and rubbed her shoulder. And then he stood, dropped his jeans and was on top of her, gentle but intense. Lynne knew she couldn't resist this time.

"I need this," he whispered. "I've missed you! It's been way too long!" He pulled at her sweater and began to touch her in the ways she hadn't experienced for many months.

She wanted to scream, "No, no! I'm not ready! I can't do this!" But she didn't scream. Instead she tried to mimic the responses she used to display and the emotions she used to feel. She tried to find the movements, the sounds, the ways she would touch and encourage him. She tried to remember the words she once whispered.

It was over quickly, release for him, but only sadness for her. He quickly lifted his head to look at her and saw the tears streaming down her cheeks.

"I don't imagine those are tears of joy?" he said with a half-smile as he pulled away from her, grabbed his clothes and walked out of the room. A few minutes later she heard the door to the patio and back yard open. He had retreated to the outdoors, his sanctuary place. She knew he didn't understand but she didn't follow to try to explain.

Lynne felt no one could understand the depth of her pain, her longing for her tiny baby. As much as she wanted and needed to find a way to return to a normal life for Greg's sake, and for Luke, at some level she continued to resist a return to a normal life. She didn't want a normal life without Kelly. With each day, Kelly slid further into the past. Kelly saw the beginning of this Winter but wouldn't see the flowering of Spring. Kelly's experience of life was so brief! Had she experienced joy? Had she experienced love? In 100 years would anyone even know that she had been here and been loved? How many lives would she have touched if not for the mistakes of the doctor? What holes would there be in the unfolding of events in their family, their neighborhood, perhaps their country, or even the Earth?

The laughter of friends and family was still incomprehensible, almost hurtful to Lynne. It made her want to scream, "No, no, you can't be happy when my Kelly isn't here to share the laughter! You can't forget that we miss her!"

Luke came to bed very late that night and Lynne was able to pretend she was asleep. She didn't want to talk about her feelings about the events of the night and she was afraid to hear his reaction. When Lynne heard him get up and start moving early Saturday morning, she knew that meant he was headed to camp. He was dressed and headed towards the door of their bedroom when she asked, "When will you be back?"

Luke paused but didn't look back at her. "Umm, I'm not sure. Maybe the better question is.... When will you be back?"

Chapter 36

Lora's Story December 1993 to January 1994

MOVING FORWARD

Lora was excited that she had decided to buy the townhouse. She was glad she had realized she didn't want to live in the home where she lived what she believed were both the most incredibly wonderful and the darkest days of her life. She and Rick were still officially married since he refused to sign the divorce documents, but the time would come when she would be able to finalize the divorce without his agreement.

Somehow, it had become the next day, and then the next day, and then the next day since the "revelation." Amazingly, a month, then 3 months, then 6 months, then 10 months, had passed since she had learned about "the other". She often wondered how she had lived those first days, that first month.

But, finally, the closing was done and the next day it was time to walk into "her" townhouse. Mark wanted to be there with her for those first moments of ownership. He hadn't seen it previously and quickly ran through the empty rooms. The townhouse had 3 bedrooms on 3 levels including a balcony off the dining room and a one car garage.

"I like it. I like it. But when does the bed come?'

Lora laughed. "It's being delivered tomorrow. And then the furniture I'm taking from my old house will be here the next day. So, before the end of the week, Elrond and I will be living here!" She was excited and so ready for the move. At that moment, the excitement overshadowed any feelings she still had about her pending divorce.

Mark said, "Let's pop the champagne. I brought glasses."

They sipped the champagne as they moved from room to room, gabbing about what furniture would go where in each of the rooms and what she still might need. Lora had brought blankets and pillows and placed them on the floor in the master bedroom. She told herself it was just in case she and Elrond decided to sleep there that first night.

Mark, not unexpectedly, had other ideas. He plopped down on the blankets and pulled Lora down next to him. Lora's relationship with him had become familiar in many ways but the physical connection still felt new and very exciting. She held her breath as he began pulling at buttons and zippers and removing their clothing. His mouth was on hers, his tongue slipped through her lips, as he rubbed and squeezed. She could feel his excitement grow in anticipation of the pleasures yet to come. Later, after Mark left, she and Elrond curled up in the crumpled blankets and both fell asleep. She was too exhausted to make the drive to the lonely bed in her former home.

It was Christmas Eve a month later and Lora was still unsure about where her friendship, or relationship, with Mark might be headed but she liked the feelings she experienced with him. She liked the man, his looks, his sense of humor, his intelligence, his sexual appetite. He also helped to make the transition from a home with Rick to a home of her own an easier process. Though there were still hard, sad days, Mark helped to fill the hours and keep the pain away. He enabled her to focus on fun instead of loss.

She and Elrond were alone on this Christmas Eve. She organized gifts for the next day when her family would all gather at her parents' home for a mammoth gift exchange and dinner. This was the first Christmas Eve in her entire life that she would spend alone. Christmas Eve with Rick had always meant a Seven Fishes dinner at his grandparents' home and then late night snuggles with glasses of champagne. She felt sad but not panicked about this evening alone. That probably meant progress in her separation from her prior life. Or, perhaps, it meant that Mark continued to distract her from her pain.

It was about 7:00 p.m., when there was a knock at her door. Lora got up and peeked through the blinds towards the front street. She saw Rick's car parked in front of her townhouse which undoubtedly meant it was him who just knocked at her door. She hadn't realized that he knew the location of her home. She slowly opened the door to see him holding a gift bag with a huge smile on his face.

"Can I come in, please?"

"How did you find me?' By now, Elrond was perched on the back of a chair close to the door and meowed loudly. He obviously was excited to hear Rick's voice.

"I couldn't let you move without knowing where you were going, and I found some of your paperwork. I was here to check out this neighborhood before your closing. I still care about you. I had to know you would be ok."

She wanted to laugh but didn't and opened the door wider to allow him to come in. "How did you get away on this important evening? Surely you're being missed!"

Rick ignored the question and the comment as he held the gift bag towards her. "Please open. I think you'll love it."

The bag was very, very heavy. She pulled out the box and opened it. Inside was a limited-edition miniature replica of Mickey Mouse and Goofy riding the Disney World teacup attraction. The ceramic teacup holding the two characters sat on a slab of marble. It was a perfect gift for a Disney fanatic.

"I love it! But I can't accept it. I didn't buy a gift for you and didn't expect one from you. Please take it with you." She was surprised to see tears in his eyes as he stood up and walked out the door without the gift.

Lora and Mark had no plans to be together on Christmas Eve or Christmas Day. She didn't ask questions but assumed it would be family time for him with his daughters. She could see him struggle as the holiday approached. They had been seated at the same table at a company holiday luncheon that included some Christmas themed music. She could see the pain on Mark's face as he listed to music that undoubtedly brought back so many memories of days with his wife and daughters. Eventually, he left the table and didn't return. Lora felt deflated that his connection to her hadn't brought significant healing into his life.

A few days later Lora was at his apartment with him while he experimented with a new recipe. He liked to eat, liked to cook, and was very skilled in the kitchen. His mood was lighter again now and they gabbed, laughed, and sipped wine while he worked on the dinner.

"So, what are we going to do for New Year's Eve?" Lora asked. "Do we want to go out somewhere fun or just play at my house or your apartment? I'll buy a bottle of Dom Perignon, my favorite champagne, for us to drink wherever."

"Um, we haven't talked about New Year's Eve, have we? I'm not sure that I want to do anything. I may just stay here by myself." Mark said quietly and didn't look at her.

"So, I'm not welcome to join you if you don't want to go out?! Is that where we are in this relationship? It's the most festive night of the year and I'd really like to be with you!" Lora couldn't believe that he would not have planned to spend New Year's Eve with her.

"I think you're getting ahead of me. We're friends, yes. And we enjoy each other physically, of course, but I can't say we're in a relationship at this point."

"So, you're ok to pull me into your bed or to climb into mine multiple times a week but we're not in a relationship. Is that really what I'm hearing?!"

She had come to know the look that crossed his face. The look that surfaced when he thought his private thoughts about his wife, his family, their life together. He had just shut Lora out and was unwilling to explain his feelings about her or discuss her comments. He turned to the stove without responding.

"Nothing to say? You know, I don't think I really feel like eating dinner this evening. I'm out of here. I've obviously misjudged." Lora grabbed her jacket, purse, and headed for the door. This time he didn't follow to walk her to her car. She headed to a drive-through restaurant, not willing to have another empty stomach because of a man!

Lora didn't see Mark over the next several days. When she was at work, she avoided the area of his office and didn't see him approach her office. Part of her still hoped that he would re-think New Year's Eve and they would spend the night together. She knew that, because of his separation from his daughters, his pain was much different than hers. But she also knew that they had connected physically and, she believed, emotionally. How could he possibly not consider it a relationship?!

So after another sad and lonely holiday night, Lora was back at work on January 2 and headed straight to Mark's office immediately after she had logged in and checked email. It was a corporate culture with an open-door policy, so it was extremely rare to see a manager's door closed. She wasn't sure what might be on the grapevine about Mark and her but what was about to happen would certainly add to it. She walked into his office and closed the door.

"That's not a good idea," Mark said as he looked up. His face was cold and not welcoming.

"I don't really care if it's a good idea. I have some things to say to you and they are better spoken in private."

He didn't reply.

"You pushed for this physical relationship when I knew it was a really bad idea professionally. I believed we were colleagues and friends before anything else. I have shared with you my fears and pain and I have tried to provide comfort to you, even when you were unwilling or unable to talk about your pain. A friend would have been with me on New Year's Eve. A friend would have understood what a terrible night that would be for me to be alone. A compassionate human would view even a friendship as a relationship. We are not friends!"

Heads were down when she walked out of his office. Later that day as Lora walked through the office she thought she heard someone whisper, "Did you hear what happened this morning between that one and Mark?"

Chapter 37

Shelly's Story, April 1985

YOU'RE HER!

"Let's just say the Shelly you knew after graduation no longer exists. She is dead now and I'm left to pick up the pieces and try to make something out of what remains. But I'm determined to find my way. I think everything happens for a reason. I haven't figured out what reason there could be for all I've been through, but there's got to be one."

"It better be a good one," Leslie said.

"I'm sure you have so many questions but, for now, if you don't mind, I'm just not ready to relive it all," Shelly said.

"No problem," Leslie said. "Alissa filled me in a little bit. Just know that I'm here if you need me."

"You have given me the world, coming to meet us today. I couldn't have done it without you."

Shelly saw the familiar buildings as they got closer to home. It seemed like forever since she had seen them. Some things had changed, just like she had but, for the most part, it looked like home.

"We should be at the police station in about 10 minutes," Leslie said.

"Ok," said Shelly. She was a little less worried about being followed now that she was in Leslie's car. The closer they got, the more Shelly's hands started to tremble. Her stomach was in knots and she could feel herself becoming flushed.

They finally pulled into the police station. Shelly was so scared to tell her story for fear no one would believe her. "It's one crazy story!" she thought. "But the facts are the facts as they say. And the facts don't lie."

They parked the car and walked towards the door. Shelly's legs felt weak and shaky. Once inside they were greeted by an officer who sat at a desk behind a glass window.

"May I help you?" he said.

"Yes, thank you," Shelly answered quietly. "My name is Shelly Ziegler. My boyfriend Todd kidnapped me in July 1983, and I was able to escape today. I wanted to come here because I'm afraid of what he might do when he finds I'm gone."

The police officer looked up from his tablet with a surprised look on his face. "You're her!" he said.

"Her?" Shelly asked.

"Yes. The girl who went missing. Your mom and dad were adamant that you didn't leave on your own."

"That's true. I didn't." Shelly said.

"Just wait here for a minute while I go get my sergeant."

A few minutes later, the offer returned with his sergeant.

"Hello, Miss Ziegler, I'm Sergeant Tanner Cook, and I have followed your case from the beginning.

"Hi, and please call me Shelly"

Once in his office the Sergeant said, "The first question I need to ask is, are you alright?"

"Well, that's a matter of opinion. Physically I'm good. Emotionally, not so much. I know there are some scars that will never heal."

"I'm sorry to hear that. However, you need to know you are safe now and there is help out there for you and your family. Have you seen your parents yet?"

"No, not yet," Shelly said. 'They have no idea I've escaped."

"Would you like to give them a call?"

"Yes. I would love that."

'Ok, how about if I get some information and then we can make that call."

"Well, actually, could I just go home instead of having them coming here?"

"Are you sure?'

"Yes," she said.

"Ok. That can be arranged. I'll have an officer go with you if that will make you feel safer."

"That would be great. Thank you, So, what all do you need to know?" she asked.

"Just start from the beginning."

And so she began to relive the horror that had been her life for almost 2 years. The sergeant didn't say much. He just took notes and filled out paperwork. Leslie sat next to Shelly and held her hand for support.

An hour or so later, when they had finished the sergeant said, "You know, Shelly. We're going to have to arrest him."

Shelly started to panic. "Oh, I don't want to press charges! I just want to move on with my life and start the healing process. I don't want to see him again. I just want it to be over."

"I'm sorry, Shelly. But, if we don't arrest him, he will be out there doing it to someone else or coming back after you. And the fact is, he broke the law."

"But, he said if I ever left him, he would kill himself."

"Then that would be his decision and not the result of anything you have done."

Shelly wondered how she could still have pity for him, even after all he'd done. She sat there with her head down and tear-filled eyes. "Will I have to go to court?" she asked.

"Most likely, yes."

"So, you're saying this is far from over."

The sergeant replied, "I'm afraid so but that doesn't mean the healing process can't begin. Look, you are sitting here in front of me today. That's a big step forward. Now let's sign these few papers and get you on your way." Shelly signed the papers.

"Thank you," the sergeant said. "There's one more thing you need to be sure to do."

"And that is?" Shelly asked.

"When the courthouse opens in the morning, I want you to go and file for a PFA."

"PFA?" Shelly asked.

"Yes. Protection from Abuse Order. He will not be allowed to come within 100 yards of you."

"But I thought you said he would be arrested," Shelly said.

"He will be but this is one more layer of protection for you. If he comes anywhere near you, he will be in contempt of court and it will be one more reason for his arrest."

"Ok, I'll go up as soon as they open tomorrow morning."

"Great," the sergeant said. "Now, let's get you home."

As they drove towards Shelly's home, she was flooded with emotions. "Wonder what mom and dad are doing? Are they even going to be there? What do I say? Do I just walk in and say 'Hey, mom, I'm home?' "

The hurt her parents had been feeling had to be devastating. "Will they be mad at me and ask me to just leave?"

Chapter 38

Lynne's Story, August 1997
ISOLATION

Lynne couldn't comprehend how almost a year had passed since Kelly had been born. How had she possibly moved through day after day of a life without her daughter? How had she found a way to eat, to sleep, to drive her car, to hug her son, with arms that continued to ache, and a mind filled with sounds of squeaky cries and visions of a panicked drive to the hospital?

One day the phone rang, and it was the nurse who worked for the malpractice attorney. Lynne had been anticipating the call because it had been about 6 months since they had initially met with Attorney Connors. At that meeting they had decided to move forward and prepare to bring a case against the hospital where Kelly had been for over 3 months. Lynne felt her heart start to pound when she heard who it was. She knew the nurse would give her significant information.

"Mrs. Murray, I'm very sorry! I know this will not be the information you're hoping to hear but the independent neonatologist doctor based in Philadelphia, has determined that there is no cause for you to pursue a case against the hospital." Lynne stopped breathing for a moment as she struggled to understand what she had just heard.

The nurse continued to talk, and Lynne tried to focus on her words. "He stated that, on the day that Kelly died, the medical determination was that she could have continued to grow and thrive, or she could have passed. As a result of this determination, Attorney Connors feels there is no logical reason to pursue a case. Of course, you have the right to seek another opinion from another attorney. Do you have any questions?"

Lynne was so shocked by what the nurse said that she couldn't think of any questions, but she did have things to say.

"I'm shocked that the attorney feels there is no case here! When I think back to what some of the medical staff said to my husband and me…. Some of the nurses told us that Kelly wasn't ready to go home. We also learned that the formula ratios the nutritionist gave us were incorrect. This meant that we gave Kelly too much sodium. And the day we took her to the doctor, we were told she was fine despite the fact that she wasn't eating and looked puffy! Where is the justice for my daughter?!!"

Lynne hung up the phone without waiting for a response and began to scream. "No, no, no! How can this be happening!?"

All the emotions Lynne had tried to work through resurfaced in their darkness, their agony, their despair. There would be no justice for Kelly! Multiple people had made terrible mistakes and Kelly had died. It wasn't her or Luke's fault! They had relied on the doctors and the doctors were wrong in their assessment of Kelly's condition!

Lynne couldn't begin to comprehend how she would move forward. The simmering anger, the need for the acknowledgement of the flawed protocol that had sent her daughter home, the disbelief that a doctor on-call could allow batteries to be dead in his beeper, had carried her through the last months. The ache in her arms suddenly overwhelmed her. Lynne could feel the tiny hand that had grasped her finger. She could hear the tiny squeaks that Kelly made when she cried.

Lynne ran up the steps and pulled Kelly's sleeper from the drawer in her dresser, the sleeper Kelly had worn the last time she slept through the night at home, the sleeper Lynne had pulled from the dirty clothes hamper, the sleeper that still smelled of Kelly. She held the sleeper to her face and breathed deeply to connect with her daughter, still not believing the message the nurse had delivered. There would be nothing they could do to help make sense of this tragic loss.

Then her thoughts turned to her family and their life together. "Luke has been back to work for months now. He has a schedule and demands on his time. Greg will be going back to school shortly and has already reconnected with school friends. I am scheduled to go back to work in the Fall and I don't know how to face that life."

Lynne sat there and relived everything that had happened to bring them to this moment. Their hope for justice was gone. That hope had helped them to move forward through the difficult days. How would they go on now? But then, her thoughts turned to Greg. She still needed to talk with Luke about the phone call but first came Greg.

So, after lunch Lynne dropped Greg off at his friend Sam's house. Sam's family had been very supportive over the past months. Greg was frequently invited to their home and was included in many of their plans and events. Lynne believed it was good for Greg. She knew that every event, every experience, would have an impact on him, on them all, and the rest of their lives. She couldn't totally sense what Greg thought about Kelly, but he smiled frequently, did his chores, and was always ready to join friends for whatever was planned. She hoped these were good signs. She hoped the love that surrounded him was enough to shield him as his family struggled to heal from such a devastating loss. She hoped that, though the death of his sister would always be a sad memory, he would thrive, find a happy life for himself, and remember Kelly's brief life with love.

Lynne arranged to pick Greg up after dinner that evening and turned to drive home. At the turn into their neighborhood, Lynne continued straight and headed towards the mall. She knew she would have to deliver the message to Luke that there would be no justice for Kelly. She dreaded that moment but, for now, there were things at the mall that could distract her and make her feel better. She pulled into a spot in front of her favorite store and smiled a little as she thought about what she might buy to take her mind off of the message the nurse had shared.

Two hours later Lynne headed back to her car with multiple bags in hand. As always, she hoped that the contents would help beautify her home, make Greg happy, and not upset Luke too much. Her smile started to fade as her thoughts turned back to her family and her upcoming conversation with Luke. She was glad that Greg was with a friend, glad that Luke could find his comfort at their camp almost every weekend. But she wasn't glad about the dynamics of her marriage at this point and the news from the attorney could be another blow to their relationship.

The quest for justice for their daughter had bonded Lynne and Luke with a common purpose. Beyond that quest, Lynne still often felt disconnected from Luke and alone, both physically as well as emotionally. Since the last sad physical connection, even the occasional cuddling and snuggling had subsided. The sense of isolation overwhelmed Lynne. They had lost laughter. They had lost adventures. They had lost romance. And now they had lost the justice they believed their daughter was owed. Could their love for Greg possibly be enough to sustain their marriage?

What would happen now? The feeling of hopelessness surfaced in her again. She was afraid of where this sad lonely road would take her. Could it be that, after all they had survived since Kelly's death, they ultimately would not survive as a family?

Chapter 39

Lora's Story February 1994

MEOW

It was 11:00 p.m. on a Saturday night and Lora sat alone in a very quiet house, her townhouse. There was no one to talk with, no one to cry with, no one to distract her from looking at her life. Her nightmare had become a reality. Last April she had signed the divorce papers, shortly after she came back from the cruise with Helen. By October she had vacationed with another man, flushed her wedding band down the toilet, and had also found the townhouse she wanted to purchase and began to pack. Her soon-to-be ex, had tried to talk her out of making the move on one of the occasional evenings when he decided to make an appearance at their home. He refused to sign the divorce papers, but she moved on and took step after step to separate from him. She had also begun to lash out at him in ways designed to cause him the greatest degree of embarrassment, if that was possible.

"Why didn't you tell me that our love making was only second rate?!! You were so much more experienced than me, with so many different women, even during our marriage. I never knew till you gave me the opportunity to be with another man. Why didn't you show me?!!"

Excitement about her new home had carried her through a few months. There were details to attend to and plans to make. She needed a mortgage, carpet cleaners, someone to paint. She needed phone, electric, and cable service. A new bed was a must, as were bed linens, bath towels, and a grill for her deck.

When she had finally made the move in November, the excitement continued. There were phone calls, best wishes, and there was Mark. She arranged furniture and clothing, set up her kitchen, and made dinner for some friends. The next few weeks were filled with Christmas shopping, holiday celebrations, and, for a while, there was the expectation of a significant relationship with Mark. Then, after the first two months, the silence began, the dreaded awful silence, and aloneness. It was a new year and people stopped thinking about the fact that she had moved into a new home. They went on with their own lives, often in ways that didn't include her.

Since the end of her intimate connection with Mark, there had also been a sporadic parade of faces from blind dates, dating services, personal ads, and bar pickups as she tried to find a way to avoid the solitary weekends. The blind dates she met were a diverse group of faces. There were men who wanted to impress their friends with her, men who wanted to have sex with her. There were men who wanted her to heal their pain and men who wanted to have fun with her. There were men who would cook for her and men who would send her flowers. There was no one who touched her soul or her heart. There was no one who could heal the emptiness within. She didn't know yet that she would have to heal it herself.

Friday had become the beginning of another weekend, often full of loneliness, fear, and panic. The weekdays were tolerable. She had an office to get to, people who needed her expertise. She had always found both challenge and satisfaction in her role as Human Resources Manager. But now, in the lobby of the office building, on Thursday evenings, she could feel Friday looming before her.

Her new home became a prison. And so, on Friday night, she would open a bottle of wine and drink just enough, two maybe three glasses to fall asleep on the couch in front of the TV. The wine and half a can of soup replaced the elaborately prepared dinners she had enjoyed with her husband. At 1:00 or 2:00 in the morning, she would awaken and climb the stairs to her new bed and an uneasy sleep. It was the beginning of a pattern.

She knew she should be concerned about the wine. It wasn't healthy to drink for a release from pain, but she couldn't face the weekend nights without it. She thought about her grandmother who had a stroke shortly before she died. When she was in the hospital, the only way Lora and her sister could get her to take some soup was to tell her they were giving her whisky. Her grandmother loved to take a drink, sometimes too many in her later years when both her husbands had died, and she was lonely. Dry, rich, full-bodied red wine had now become Lora's companion on lonely weekend nights. Some of her grandmother lived on in her.

Lora felt herself slipping deeper and deeper into despair, into a life without joy, without peace. As she sat alone in her new townhome, she tried to find answers to the questions that probably have confronted many humans since they first evolved on the planet Earth.

"Why should I get up and go to work on Monday?"

"Why should I force myself to take another bite of food when I haven't felt hunger for months?"

"Why should I struggle to prolong my existence on this planet? We're all going to the same place at the end of our lives."

"In a hundred years will it make any difference if I lived for 40 years or 80 years?"

"When our sun ceases to exist, will it make any difference that the planet Earth, with its millions of tiny life forms, was once here?"

"Are we any more than tiny insects, scurrying for some obscure purpose, undetectable by higher life forms?"

"How long can I feel this way before the questions without answers become more compelling than the instinct for survival that seems to be an innate part of all creatures?"

The instinct for survival didn't seem to be working in her. Instead, she started to fantasize about ways out of her life. She had heard that people facing certain death appear to lose all fear once they slip beyond a certain point. Had she slipped far enough to be able to step off a bridge or a building? She doubted that she could overcome her fear of heights. Could she point a gun at her head and pull the trigger? It was doubtful that she could find a gun or figure out how to use one. Could she swallow enough pills to slide into oblivion without even knowing it? Yes! If she could get the pills, that could be the way to go.

She started asking questions of those friends who might know how to help her secure the pills she needed. She put on a show about how much better she felt. She laughed at the thought that she could ever have contemplated leaving everything because of him! And she said, "I wouldn't even know what to take!" And she asked, "How do people even get the pills?" And she listened and she walked through drug stores and read labels on packages.

She lost more and more weight and her assistant at her office finally said, "You need to buy some new clothes! What you're wearing is falling off you!" For the first time in many months, she looked at herself in a mirror and didn't recognize herself, especially the look in her eyes.

On one visit to Doctor Levy she learned that her sisters had called him to share their concerns about the possibility that she might try to end her life. Their call resulted in a referral to a medical doctor who prescribed an anti-depressant for her. And so, she thought she had acquired the pills that could help her exit her life. She would take the entire bottle, she thought, and probably a bottle of wine, just to be sure. She experimented with just a couple of pills and lots of wine but couldn't feel anything more than the feeling she got from the wine alone. So she stopped experimenting. She didn't want to waste the pills. She wanted to be sure she could do the job when the time was right.

This had been another weekend evening with a new face and she finally got the guy to leave. "I thought we agreed that we were just going to start as friends," as Lora tried to push him from on top of her.

"I thought we agreed that we just wanted to have fun together! And what could be more fun?" as he tried to slip his hand under her t-shirt.

"No, I'm not ready to have a physical connection with you! And, actually, I'm sorry but I'm not ready to spend more time with you tonight. Please leave!"

Better to be alone than with this one. She felt lucky the face hadn't pushed for more. This face wasn't Wayne or Mark. She didn't feel the immediate connection she'd had with Wayne on that magical escape cruise or the common bond she'd experienced with Mark. She wanted to take her time with this face. The face wanted sex immediately.

So after another failed attempt at companionship, she was ready to give up. The thought of sliding into oblivion, of joining whatever there was to join with in the universe, felt very attractive tonight. She was tired of the struggle to continue. She didn't want to solve another issue at work, go to the grocery store, clean her home, or prepare another meal. She didn't even want to plan another cruise or open another bottle of wine. She wanted the life she had known but that life was destroyed forever. She wanted the man she believed she had married but that man had never existed.

Her vision of a solitary life, growing old with no children to love, and now no marriage, had become her reality. And so, finally and awfully, she was alone, not just in time and space, but psychologically and emotionally as well. She went to her bathroom and pulled out the bottle with the special pills in it. She carried it downstairs to the sofa, grabbed her glass of wine, and turned on the TV to nothing in particular. She sipped the wine. Yum! It was great, dry, full bodied, red wine, just as she liked.

She sat looking at the bottle of pills and the bottle of wine. She guessed it would be easy to swallow both and slip into the oblivion she imagined. It wouldn't bring comfort, but it would bring an end to the pain. She would join those who had lived before her. She would recycle into another component of the universe. She believed she had been here since the Big Bang in countless forms. Her time in this form was nothing more than a blink in the existence of the planet that was currently her home. Her sad reality was that nothing and no one would be significantly impacted if she exited the planet now.

And then she heard the soft "Meow" and her cat, Elrond, rubbed his face against the sofa, then jumped up and sprawled next to her. She had forgotten to give him his dinner. She hadn't played with him today. He loved to chase the mouse on the end of the string she would swing! He had lived his days with her since he was about 9 weeks old. She scratched his head and he purred. There was love there.

Could she decide to leave that little face?

Chapter 40

Shelly's Story, April 1985

HOME AT LAST

"Oh, God, I don't know what they'll say or do! All I know is I'll be so glad to be home! 'Home!' That word means so much to me now!"

As the cars traveled down the hill and around the bend, there it was, her house, her home. As she and Leslie opened the car doors and got out, Shelly's legs shook so obviously that the police officer ran up to her and asked, "Are you going to be alright, Shelly?"

"Yes, I think so," she said.

They all walked down the steps towards the front door. There was no sign of her parents. The front door was closed, and Shelly hoped it wasn't locked. Her hands were wet from sweat and they trembled as she reached for the doorknob and turned it. It was unlocked and she slowly pushed the door open and stepped into the house.

Shelly looked through the living room and saw that her mom was in the kitchen at the stove. Then her mom looked up, dropped a spoon from her hand, and froze in place. "Oh, my God, Shelly!"

"Hi, mom!" They ran towards each other and hugged tightly as the tears flowed from their eyes.

Suddenly the basement door opened quickly. "Sue, are you alright? I heard something drop..." Before he could finish, her dad stopped, stared, and rubbed his eyes. He couldn't believe what he saw.

"Shelly, is it really you?"

"Yes, dad, it's me. I'm finally home!"

"My God!" he said as he joined in the hugs.

The officer and Leslie approached Shelly and her parents. "Yes, welcome home finally" the officer said. Shelly's father shook the officer's hand and thanked him.

"Come on, sit," Shelly's mom said, motioning towards the living room.

As they all walked into the room, Sue couldn't stop touching Shelly's hair and hands as if in disbelief. When they sat down, the parents' questions started from Shelly's parents.

"How did you get out? Why didn't you call us? Where's Todd? Does he know you're gone?"

With the help of the officer and Leslie, Shelly answered their questions one by one. She knew Todd would find out soon and that really frightened her. But, for now, she enjoyed the love and happiness she had waited for so long.

Shelly's dad asked the officer, "Where do we go from here?'

The officer said, "I took Shelly's statement before we brought her home so that part is taken care of. However, I advised her to go to the courthouse in the morning and apply for a PFA, protection from abuse order. If you have any questions, or if you need us this evening, just give us a call. Everyone at the station is well aware of the situation and we would be here ASAP."

He turned to Shelly and said sternly, "Shelly, do not call him. Do not talk to him. If he shows up here, you need to stay inside and call us. Do not, for any reason, go outside! Understand?"

"Yes, sir," Shelly said.

"Promise me," the officer said.

"I promise," Shelly replied.

"You don't have to worry about that at all, officer," Shelly's dad said. "There's no way we would allow her out the door or to answer the phone. She's safe, now, with us and that's how we're going to keep it."

"Good to hear," the officer said. "I'm going to head out now. Remember, we are literally only minutes away. Just call."

Shelly stood and gave the officer a hug. "Thank you so much!" Sue, George, and Leslie thanked him also.

After the officer walked out the door, George locked and dead-bolted it.

"Well, you folks have a lot to catch up on," Leslie said. "Maybe I should give you time to reconnect."

"No, please stay," Shelly said as she grabbed for Leslie's hand. "Besides, dad has you locked in here now." They all laughed.

"Mom, are you alright?" Shelly asked.

"I'm perfectly fine," Sue answered. "I just never thought I'd see this day come. I mean, I prayed so hard."

Shelly hugged her mom. "I know, mom. I did too. I'm here now. Our prayers were answered."

"I'd better check on dinner. We're having spaghetti. I hope that's alright."

"Mom, that's more than alright. I can't wait."

Sue smiled, "Ok, girls, you have about a half hour before the sauce is ready. Shelly, your room is the way you left it. Go ahead and get settled in. I'll holler when dinner is ready."

"Thanks, mom," Shelly said with a smile. Then she and Leslie went up the stairs to her room. As they entered, Shelly felt like she stepped back in time. "Wow!" she said.

"Wow, is right!" said Leslie. "When your mom said it was the way you left it, she wasn't kidding."

Shelly's clothes were still on her chair, thrown over the back as she often did in the morning. Her journal lay on her bed along with the calligraphy pen she always used. She started to cry.

"I wish so much I could go back to that day and start over!"

"I'm sure you do," said Leslie.

"I'm not that innocent girl anymore. It's like I'm looking at someone else's stuff in someone else's room."

"Do you want to talk about it?" Leslie asked.

"No, I'm good. Not sure if I'll ever want to talk about it."

"You do realize the police will be talking to him, maybe even arresting him."

"I don't want that," Shelly said. "I just want to get on with my life. I won't press charges. Then there will be no trial and I won't have to relive it all."

"That may not be your choice, Shelly. You do understand that, right? I mean, he kidnapped you and held you against your will. God only knows what else he did."

"You're right. God and I only know, and I want to keep it that way. Why can't I just go back to school and pick up where I left off, like it never happened? I already lived that nightmare and I don't want to relive it ever again. I don't want to hear his name or see his face. If I don't then he doesn't exist."

"But he does exist, Shelly. As sure as I'm standing here, not only does he exist, but he thinks you're his property. He's not going to just walk away quietly. He will fight for what he believes is his."

"I know what he did was horrible, but he's sick, Leslie. He needs help. If you'd met his parents you'd know what I mean."

Suddenly they heard an awful sound, the rumbling noise Shelly was all too familiar with. "What is that?" Leslie asked.

"It's him!!!"

"Todd?" Leslie asked.

"Yes, Todd!"

Shelly and Leslie could hear Sue scream. "I think he's coming, George! "

"Call the cops!" George yelled as he ran to his room and loaded the shotgun. "All I can say is that he better not come down to this house."

"George, don't do something you'll regret!"

"Who said I would regret it?"

"I mean it, George. We have all gone through enough."

Shelly and Leslie watched from the upstairs window as Todd stopped his car and just sat there, staring at the house. Shelly opened the window when she saw Todd get out of his car. Despite what the police had told her, in some way, she felt she needed to protect him.

He started to scream, "Shelly, come out here right now!"

Shelly yelled back, "Todd, just get back in your car and leave!"

He continued screaming, "I'm not leaving without you!"

Shelly could hear her dad open the front door, "You want to bet?"

"Get back in here!" Sue screamed at George.

Todd continued to scream, "Shelly! Shelly!"

"Todd, just leave!" Shelly screamed.

And again, he yelled, "Shelly, I need you!"

Her heart pounded and all Shelly could think was, "Please leave, Todd!"

"Is he for real?" Leslie asked sarcastically.

"Unfortunately, yes," Shelly answered.

George screamed as he cocked his gun, "Leave now, Todd! If you take another step towards this house I cannot be accountable for my actions!"

It was then that Shelly could see the red and blue flashing lights coming down the road. She could hear a voice say, "Stay where you are, Todd! Don't move!"

Todd did as they said. They put him in handcuffs, read him his rights, and took him away.

Part of Shelly thought, "Thank God!" and another part of her felt sorry for Todd. If her dad had known everything Todd had done to her, she believed Todd would not be driving away with the police. She was so glad not to be in his clutches anymore but she knew he needed help and she cared about what happened to him. How strange that was! How could she feel sorry for him and worry about what would happen to him?

Chapter 41

Lynne's Story, August 1997
SEARCH FOR HEALING

Soon after she received the devastating news from the attorney, Lynne started to think about the possibility of adopting. Maybe there was a way to ease the never ending ache in her arms and find a new connection to Luke. Maybe Greg could still have the opportunity to grow up as the big brother. Maybe adoption could be right for them. Adoption could be what they needed to heal. Adoption could unite herself and Luke in a new quest that would end in happiness. The doctors were firm when they spoke about Lynne not being able to have any more biological children because of her history of developing pre-eclampsia. Adoption could be the only way to fill the void in their family and replace it with love for another child, another daughter.

Lynne didn't know if Luke would agree. She was terribly afraid he wouldn't. He had continued to withdraw into nature and shared little of his feelings with Lynne. She knew there were so many objections Luke could raise. There were so many possible complications with both domestic and international adoptions. The adoption process could also be expensive which she feared would be very problematic for Luke. They had always lived a comfortable life, but Luke was frugal with their dollars as demonstrated by their continual arguments about her shopping.

It was another Friday evening and Luke had just finished his packing to head to camp for the weekend. Greg was at a friend's house for a sleepover and Lynne sat alone in their family room. She felt anxious about the conversation she wanted to have but hoped that there could be a reason to be excited. She wondered if the timing was right tonight.

She hesitated and thought about the best words to use, until she saw that Luke was ready to walk out the door. Then she called, "Wait! Don't go!"

Luke paused in the doorway and looked back at Lynne with a question in his eyes. "What now?"

"Please don't go to camp this weekend. Let's all go together next weekend. We need to fix this family, Luke. We need to fix our marriage and our relationship. I love you and I believe you love me, but we haven't been connecting. I've heard stories of how the loss of a child can also be the loss of a marriage. I don't want that to happen to us!"

As always, Lynne was in tears. Luke hesitated for a moment and then walked over to the sofa where Lynne sat.

"Of course we love each other! What's this all about?"

"We need to talk. I've been thinking. I have a question for you but I'm nervous about asking it. I'm afraid you'll say no."

Luke sat down next to her. "Well, I don't even know what the question is. Why do you think I'll say no?"

"Remember when I went to the mall the other day. Remember when I came home with multiple bags and you weren't happy?"

"How could I forget?" but Luke smiled.

"Ok, here it goes..." Lynne took a deep breath and said quickly, "I've been thinking about the possibility of adopting a child." She watched his face closely and looked for any reaction.

"Hmm, let's talk about that a little bit. What are you thinking? Domestic? International?"

"I'm not really sure but we can do some research and figure out what's the best way to go. I just needed to know that you would agree to look into this before I started doing research. You know it could be costly."

"I think that's a great idea!" Luke said with no hesitation.

Lynne couldn't believe what she heard. Not even a question about the possible cost!

Luke put his arm around Lynne and pulled her close to him. For the first time since the extremely disappointing news from the attorney, Lynne was feeling hopeful. She could sense that Luke felt the same.

"As long as I know that I have your consent, I can start making phone calls." Lynne snuggled closer to Luke and she began to talk.

"I'd want the baby to be a girl," Lynne said. "I don't care from where. It would be nice if she was a newborn, but I'd be ok with a slightly older baby also. I don't think we should tell Greg until we have more information. It could take a long time. I wouldn't want to tell our family right away either. It probably won't happen by Christmas this year but possibly by the next Christmas we could have a baby girl!"

Luke stopped her chatter with a long kiss, and she wondered where the evening might lead. It could be the first step to healing in many ways. She returned the kiss and pressed against him. This time Lynne initiated the next move.

"How about giving me a little time and then let's meet in our bedroom?"

A few minutes later Luke took a deep breath as he walked into their bedroom and saw what waited for him. There was no need for either of them to force a response as the night began to happen for them.

The next day Lynne thought of a student she worked with whose mother was a doctor with connections to a children's home. She thought to herself, "This is a very strong connection. Maybe the doctor could make it happen."

Lynne looked up the phone number for the children's home. She called and spoke to a social worker. She told her their story and what had happened.

The social worker said, "We process families in groups. The next group of families will start in the Fall." However, in the next breath she said, "But, Lynne, you need time to grieve before you can think about adopting. You need to be sure you are adopting with love and the ability to focus on a new child in your life, not with a need to fill your own emptiness." With that sentence, Lynne knew that this was not the agency for them. They had already grieved and suffered in so many ways the social worker would never understand. How could she possibly know what they needed? Lynne knew what they needed was a reason to hope and they needed that hope in their lives now. They could give love and a home to a baby who needed a family at the same time they could begin to heal the brokenness within themselves.

After that Lynne really started to pray for a sign of what to do. Luke agreed with the idea of adopting because he believed it would be healing for them. They both knew you never could replace a child, but they needed someone else to love. Lynne's arms would actually physically ache when she thought about holding a baby. The only way Lynne believed she could ease that ache was to adopt a baby. It didn't matter to her whether she gave birth to a baby or adopted. She just knew her baby had to be a girl.

Over the next several months Lynne and Luke began to explore options. They were thinking about adopting from Russia because they believed the baby could look like them, with light hair and eyes. Their friend, Rose, gave them the phone number of a lady she worked with who had adopted a baby boy from Russia and suggested that Lynne should call her.

The woman was very helpful. She said her son was beautiful, but they were beginning to have some concerns about his behavior. He was being tested for attention deficit and non-attachment syndrome. As she talked about her fears and described the process of adopting from Russia, Lynne knew in her heart that it was not for her.

Russia required two trips, the first to meet the baby, and the second to bring the baby home. Lynne couldn't imagine meeting her baby, holding her baby, filling that ache in her arms, and then leaving her to come back to the U.S. for an undetermined period of time. So, they continued to search for other options. Where would their search lead them?

Chapter 42

Lora's Story March 1994

RECOVERY

Lora continued to see Dr. Levy. Each week he tried to help her chip away her fear. He tried to help her understand and cope with it. One of his techniques brought laughter with her tears.

"I want you to play two roles today. I want you to be the child in you who is so afraid, sitting in a chair to my right. Then I want you to be the adult you are, sitting in the chair to my left. Talk to that child."

She sat in the chair to his left. "What's the matter? How can I help you?"

She sat in the chair to his right. "I'm so afraid. I'm so alone. I don't know how to be ok by myself." "How silly," she thought, but she started to cry and sob.

And she moved to the chair on his left. "It's ok. I'm with you. I'll take care of you. Don't be afraid. You'll be ok."

Then back to the chair on his right, "But I AM afraid. I think I've been afraid to be alone since my mother died and I was left with no one. No one talked to me about losing her. No one hugged me anymore. I always felt alone. I didn't feel loved by anyone. I didn't feel safe again until I connected with Rick."

She moved back to the chair on his left. "It's natural to feel afraid when your life has become so difficult. But, you survived the days after your mother left. YOU survived! You worked three jobs to make it through college; you found the way to pay for an apartment and food; you found a good job that led to a great career; and you're now working on your master's degree. He didn't do those things for you! You did them for yourself! I am here with you. I will help you survive this time also. You don't need him!"

With Dr. Levy's ongoing help, Lora slowly found the strength she needed to continue. She felt so fortunate that she had connected with the right therapist. She believed he was literally a life saver for her. He helped her to plan a new life for herself. They talked about what she cared about and what she enjoyed. She had always loved animals, so she trained to become a docent at the local zoo. She attended all of her master's classes and started getting "A's" again on projects and exams. She went to a concert with friends from work. She volunteered to lead fundraising events for local charities. She discovered that her loneliness was often a self-imposed disease and she now worked to reject that choice.

Lora felt like she was back in grade school again. Week after week, she reported to Dr. Levy on what she had done the prior week, how she had worked her plan. She had always been a high achiever in school, and she didn't want to fail at her weekly assignments. She found that all the hard work had an impact. Lora began to find moments of peace though the moments of panic, the agony of loneliness, the inability to envision a happy life, still surfaced at times. During the moments of peace, her inner core tried to find a way out of the psychological mess she had been in. She had always been a reader and turned to reading to help herself. And so, she began to collect thoughts about change.

- Find the opportunity in the problem you're facing! You can't control what's happening. But you do have the ability to decide how you will react to what happens to you
- Life isn't about waiting for the storm to pass. It's about learning to dance in the rain (Vivian Greene)
- Don't try to hang onto the past because you're afraid of the future. Move into the future with courage,

optimism, and a smile. The smile will send a positive message to your brain.

- The only thing you know for sure is that tomorrow will be different than yesterday.
- Thinking about terrible things will make you feel terrible. So don't think about them any longer!
- Don't assume you know what will happen. You have no idea how this frightening change will impact your life long-term. You may look back on these awful days as leading to the best day of your life.
- Sometimes the path to a better future will lead you through days that feel like your life is a failure.
- During the next months, you'll need to decide if you will run against the wind or ride it. Don't find a battle you know you won't win. Choose to ride the wind and move forward!
- "Mankind faces a crossroads. One path leads to despair and utter hopelessness, the other to total extinction. Let us pray that we have the wisdom to choose correctly." (Woody Allen)
- Some people say that crying can be healing. But I think you'll find it's really smiling that's healing. Choose to smile and to laugh!
- "The best way to predict the future is to invent it." (Abraham Lincoln) Make a plan and create your own future! Taking action will relieve feelings of fear, anxiety, depressions, and uncertainty.

At times Lora told herself that Rick was not the most wonderful person in the world. He was selfish, self-centered, arrogant, insensitive and emotionally closed. At times she thought she could never love anyone else as much. But she knew she could never go back to that prior life and she mainly just wanted the pain to go away.

Then she reminded herself to think of her mother and be strong. Her mother had died at age 38 when Lora was only 13 years old. She never had these years to live. Lora had the opportunity to go out and make a whole new life for herself as if she were just born today. Would her mom have wanted that opportunity, even under these circumstances? Lora felt sure she would have. So, she told herself to live these years for her mother and forget about Rick. Look at the sun and the stars for her mother. Breathe the air for her mother.

Her recovery started to happen in ways Lora didn't even realize. Her townhome had somehow transformed from her prison to her refuge. She found more reasons to smile. Sometimes she looked forward to a weekend. She thought about taking another cruise. Maybe Wise Helen would want to join her. If not, maybe she would just go alone. Her meetings with Doctor Levy gradually reduced from twice a week, to once a week, and he talked about further reducing to once a month. Lora didn't want to give up her time with him and didn't like that idea.

During one of their meetings Doctor Levy's eyes widened and he smiled when she said, "No plans for this weekend. I'm just planning some quiet days at home with Elrond. I'm in the middle of a great book and I've had a crazy week at work."

One day the phone rang and when she answered...

"Hi! It's me. Will you meet me for dinner?" She recognized the voice and the tone that had once captured her love and commitment.

"Um, I don't think so. What do you want? Are you ready to sign the divorce papers?"

"It's important. Tomorrow will work if you can't make it tonight. Come on, let's have a glass of wine at the Riverside Café and talk. I'll pick you up in 20 minutes."

Lora was uncomfortable with that tone in Rick's voice. It was the tone he used when he walked into a room full of strangers and began to make connections. She could imagine the smile on his face and the gleam in his eyes.

But still she agreed. "Do not come to this house! But I'll meet you there soon."

Lora hadn't seen Rick for a long time, and she paused to watch him for a few minutes before he saw her. His movements were familiar but strange to her. He had his look of confidence back, none of the teary, agonized look on his face. He sipped his wine and looked around the bar.

Then Rick saw her and waved. She walked towards him, towards the smile, the gleam, the tone. They no longer had the same impact on her. She even felt uncomfortable looking at him as she moved to join him at the outdoor bar that overlooked the river. This time it was her who avoided eye contact. She felt almost embarrassed that this man had been the focus of such wonderful and such dark passion in her life.

"I like your look," Rick said as she slid into the seat next to him. She had on blue jeans with a glittery t-shirt and flip flop sandals. He had never been a blue jeans man and she hadn't worn jeans for years, until recently as she redesigned herself.

"Thanks. It's comfortable. I'd forgotten how to be a blue jeans lady. I like the feel."

"I ordered a glass of wine for you while I waited. Does a red Zinfandel still suit your taste?" Again, the smile, the gleam, the tone as Rick slid the glass towards her.

"Yum! Yes. I still love red wine." Lora smiled back. Lots had changed but the dry, full bodied, red wine was still a match for her.

"How are you?" he asked.

"I'm good now," she answered slowly, still not looking directly at him. "It's always crazy at work. I've done some more traveling. I'm almost done with my master's program. Things are…" She hesitated and thought about the recent parade of faces. "Things are busy. How have you been?"

"Busy too. Travelling a lot but I've really needed to talk with you."

"If you want to conclude this marriage, you just need to talk to your attorney and then we can work on the details of the settlement. I'm sure you'd like access to our joint funds again," Lora said.

"No, that's not it by any means! I think we should try to keep our marriage together!" He tried the smile that had always drawn her into his vision. But now she knew how many others he had undoubtedly captivated with that smile.

This time her eyes flashed as she looked at him. She wanted to scream. She wanted to laugh. He really didn't know her, did he? He probably had never known her, had he? He would not have spent much of his time trying to know, trying to understand a prop!

She wondered briefly what had happened with "the other" that moved him to try to reverse the events of the past 14 months but then decided the wondering wasn't worth her time. Maybe he required a change of props for the next move in his life and figured she knew the role. He undoubtedly would assume she could step back in with little effort from either of them, right?

"Can you really believe that it's possible for us to resume our marriage?"

Chapter 43

Shelly's Story, December 1996

FULFILLING THE PROMISE

It wasn't until after Shelly began to receive extensive therapy that she learned that what she was experiencing was called Stockholm Syndrome. This syndrome occurs when a person in captivity sympathizes with their captor. It explained why she was worried about him. Despite all the awful things Todd had done to her she still cared about him!

Though Shelly didn't want to have Todd charged with kidnapping, the police moved forward. She had known from the day she escaped that she didn't want to relive the last 21 months in front of a jury or a courtroom full of people. She didn't want to tell her story and answer the questions that would follow. She didn't want to explain why she couldn't leave with her family when they found her. She didn't want newspapers to share the details of her mental and physical abuse with the public. The terrors of her time with Todd already haunted her thoughts and nightmares. She believed a public display would make it worse. So she agreed to a quickly scheduled hearing in the judge's chambers. Unbelievably, Todd was ultimately only given 6 months' probation under his brother's watch and was ordered to never have contact with Shelly or anyone connected to her. She later learned that the judge, unfortunately, had ties to Todd's brother. The judge's son had purchased cocaine from him many times and Todd used that information to his advantage.

Shelly didn't pursue any further contact with Alissa. Todd never found out that Alissa helped Shelly get away and Shelly never had contact with her again. Though she would always be so grateful to her, Shelly in no way wanted to risk crossing paths with Todd again. It wasn't until after Todd was sentenced that Shelly realized one really important detail. She shared it with no one until it was almost too late.

"Oh, my God, what am I going to do? This is the third month that I haven't had my period." Shelly knew she had missed the two prior months but hoped it was due to stress. "I've got to find out for sure," she thought.

Shelly went to the drug store and bought a pregnancy test. She was scared to see the results but took the test as soon as she got home. Her hands trembled and her clothes were damp from her sweat as she waited for the results. Minutes seemed like hours but then the result was in front of her, "Positive." Shelly stood there in horror, staring at it as if it was a flashing neon light.

"Oh, my God, now what? This can't be right!" But she knew deep down that it was right. It explained the missed periods and the morning nausea. "What am I going to do?" Shelly sat on the floor, crying and shaking all over.

Back and forth, as she weighed out options, she said to herself, "I'm Catholic. I can't abort this pregnancy. But, if I have the baby, Todd will have to be notified and I will forever be tied to him. But, it's a baby, Shelly. Yes, it is, his baby."

Shelly kept her pregnancy a secret. A few days later, she lay on her bed in emotional agony. "My, God, what do I do?" she asked as tears rolled down her face. She lay there in silence then she prayed.

"Dear God, I come to you with such a heavy heart. I know this is his baby, and if I have it, Todd will be forever in my life. I just can't do that, Lord. What kind of life would a child have with Todd as a father? Giving it up for adoption isn't an option. I know it sounds selfish but I can't carry a child for 9 months and then give it up for someone else to raise."

Shelly continued to lay in silence with her eyes closed. She continued to pray, "Dear Lord, I have made my decision. If I abort this pregnancy, I promise you and myself, that I will never give birth to a child of my own. I will find a child to adopt who is either unwanted or unable to be cared for. And I will love that child with all my heart and soul. Please forgive me! This is a very difficult decision, but I believe it is the right one."

And so, she moved forward with an abortion. Shelly and her parents traveled to Cincinnati to have it done so no one in her hometown would know anything about it. The hurt and pain of what she planned to do was unbearable, so she chose not to feel. Once again, Shelly used the ability she had learned throughout her time with Todd. She escaped her body and made herself not feel anything. When it was over, she and her parents traveled back home and not one word was ever spoken about the baby or the abortion. Just the way Shelly hoped it would be, it was over now, or was it? Would she ever be able to put this experience of emptiness behind her?

Shelly moved forward with her life, continuing with therapy, while dealing with terrible nightmares and flashbacks. She tried not to allow herself to think about Todd. She just focused on healing and finishing art school. She went on to become a successful artist. She owned a studio and gallery, sold her artwork to many, and shared her talents. However, in her private life, something was missing. As time passed, relationships came and went. It continued to be very difficult for Shelly to trust and form a loving, long-term relationship. Her friends encouraged her to go out but most of her evenings were filled with quiet nights at home alone.

One evening, she sat sketching while she watched TV and enjoyed a wine cooler. 20/20 came on with a feature story about baby girls in China. They were given up due to the One Child Policy. They needed homes, but more importantly, they needed love. Shelly put down her tablet. She watched and listened to what was said. Tears filled her eyes as she heard detail after detail about the mothers of these girls. For one reason or another they had to give their daughters up and never knew what happened to them.

Shelly felt a connection to those mothers. She could relate to what they were going through. There was a sudden feeling of warmth throughout her body that she had only felt one other time, the day she realized a life was growing inside her.

Suddenly Shelly thought of the promise she had made to herself and God. "Could this be it?"

Chapter 44

Lynne's Story September 1997
THE SIGN

It was a Sunday in late summer when Lynne and Greg went to an 11:30 a.m. service at their church. During the Mass, there was a baptism taking place. Lynne didn't have even one tissue with her, and tears streamed down her face as she looked at the lucky couple having their baby baptized and thought, "Why couldn't it be me on that altar with Kelly?"

She prayed for God to send her a sign about where and how to adopt. She and Luke had decided that it had to be an international adoption because of the long wait times for a domestic adoption. They had been told that it could take up to 5 years for a domestic adoption and they would have difficulty because of their ages. She understood that international adoption would have difficulties also. There were multiple options to research, Russia, China, Korea, Romania, Guatemala, and so much to consider. What was the process? What would the cost be and how would Luke react? Would they travel to the country to adopt and how many times? At times the research felt overwhelming but better to be overwhelmed with hope than desperate with heartbreak.

After the service, she and Greg walked towards the back of the church. She looked to the right of the vestibule and saw a young couple standing with a beautiful baby girl. The first thing she noticed was the baby's black hair and she thought to herself, "I wonder if that's an Asian baby." The baby wiggled and stretched to look around and Lynne saw her beautiful almond eyes. She was definitely Asian.

Lynne said to Greg, "I have to go talk to those people."

He gave her a strange look and said, "But, mom, you don't know them."

She felt goose bumps from head to toe as she said to him, "I'll explain to you later."

As they approached the couple with the baby, Lynne started to cry. The woman looked at her and said, "Are you ok?"

Lynne said, "Your daughter is beautiful." She introduced herself and Greg and said, "My husband and I have been thinking about adoption."

"Well, my name is Karen. This is my husband, Joe, and our new baby daughter, Kim. We just brought her home from China a few days ago and we are so happy!"

Lynne said, "I need to tell you that I just prayed for God to send me a sign about what we should do about adopting. And then I saw you. Are you my sign?"

Karen looked at Lynne in disbelief and said, "I am your sign! We've never been to this church before. We still have jet lag and had called around to find a church with a later Mass. After Mass I said to my husband that I felt like we should wait here. And here you are!"

Karen and Lynne hugged, and Lynne said, "Do you mind sharing your story?"

After listening to their story, Lynne asked for the name of the agency they used. Karen said it was called Adoptions from the Heart and the social worker's name was Debbie Cohen. She also wrote down the phone number and gave it to Lynne.

On her way home from church, Lynne kept replaying her conversation with Karen and knew she would call that number. She tried think of where she could go to make the call in private. She didn't want anyone to hear or distract her. She wanted to get some facts before she talked with Luke. She didn't want him to say no. She needed to have the answers to questions he might have. She believed that this had to be what they were supposed to do. It was such a concrete sign.

Lynne decided the best place to make the call was on the basement steps. She had the light on and the piece of paper with Debbie Cohen's phone number. She situated herself on the steps and felt so nervous.

She kept saying to herself, "You know she's not going to be there. It's Sunday."

She dialed the number and, as expected, heard a recorded message with the office hours. Just hearing the woman's voice gave her a lot of hope. After she listened to the message, Lynne left her name, phone number, and a little bit of information about meeting the family in church.

Lynne went upstairs and 5 minutes later the phone rang. She grabbed the phone and ran back to the basement steps because she had a feeling it might be Debbie. She sat down and answered the phone.

"Hi! This is Debbie Cohen from Adoptions from the Heart. I just listened to your message on the answering machine." Lynne immediately liked the sound of her voice. She sounded warm and friendly.

"I had to call you today because I met a family in church who had just come home from China a few days ago. Their names are Karen and Joe and they had their beautiful daughter, Kim, with them."

Debbie said, "That would be the Sables. They came home last week." It felt like such a close-knit operation that she would know who Lynne was talking about.

Lynne shared her story and what they had recently been through, the overwhelming heartbreak, the search for healing, and now finding new hope in the thought of adopting. Lynne told her that Luke was open to adoption from another country. Debbie then explained about the information meetings that met monthly at various locations throughout the Pittsburgh area. There was one that grabbed Lynne's attention. It was at a church that wasn't far from their home. It was scheduled for the end of October.

Lynne still felt nervous, but the feeling started to turn into excitement as she felt her hope turn into a real possibility. She tried to digest everything that Debbie said so she could present it to Luke in a way that would make him as excited about it as she was. She made a mental note of the dates but knew that she wouldn't forget the date of the meeting because it was so important. She didn't want the conversation to end. She felt that the more she spoke with Debbie the more real it became.

Finally, as they were ready to hang up, Debbie said to her, "Lynne, can you be ready to bring home your daughter in about a year from now?"

Chapter 45

Lora's Story, August 1994 to April 1996

COULD THIS BE REAL?

"Ok. Lora, now tell me, do you really believe he's from another planet, another part of the universe? Do you remember the Swedish fish? If he looks like a human, he probably is a human!"

"Well, Helen, I definitely think it's possible! He's different from other men I've met. He tells me things about the stars, about the Earth, about life here and in other parts of the universe."

It was late summer now and she had been living in her townhouse for over 8 months. There were so many new memories being created, new experiences with a lifeform named Jim. No more wondering what Mark might be thinking or feeling. No more Friday nights on the sofa by herself with a bottle of red wine. Or, usually worse, no more "first dates" with guys connected through dating services or well-meaning friends and the usual outcome either a push for too much too soon or boredom.

Jim was not boring. He told her he came from another planet, in another part of the universe, and she believed him. They had met about 2 months ago and her life already felt so different. She had been taking a golf class as part of her Doctor Levy homework. She didn't know any of the other students in the class but on the first day of class she thought she could feel a man watching her and smiling when she looked his way.

"Is he smiling at me?" she wondered. Apparently he was and months of fun together followed.

Still, beyond the fun, a terrible emotion had started to surface for Lora, fear. She liked this alien life form, though she had come to believe he was actually an Earthling, or at least part Earthling. She had so much fun with him, but she didn't believe she could handle a serious relationship with him. Her marriage had been a disaster and left her feeling angry, embarrassed, naïve, the stupid wife. Then she had jumped into a physical and emotional connection with Mark though she knew it was not the smart thing to do. Adding to her fear now, beyond Jim's horoscope sign (the same as Rick's), was the fact that he admitted that he'd had a relationship with another woman as his marriage failed. The other relationship wasn't the cause of the failed marriage, but his horoscope sign and his fidelity history made Lora very uncomfortable.

Lora continued to think about Jim and how her involvement with him was growing. She had initially opted in for the fun, the sex, and the adventures. She had promised herself there would be nothing more, no emotional involvement. But, despite her efforts, her feelings for him were growing. Maybe it was now time to end the relationship, to give up the fun, to ensure that there was no strong emotional involvement. The awful events of the past few years, had helped her to a place of strength and confidence in herself. She knew it was time to be honest with Jim.

A few days later they were out walking together through her neighborhood on a cool evening. Lora became quiet as she started thinking about what to say to him.

"What are you thinking about?" Jim waved his hand in front of her face. "Are you in there?"

"I'm here but I've been thinking about all the time we spend together and I'm getting really concerned."

"Why? Have I done something? Aren't we having a good time together?"

"Of course we are." Lora paused for a few seconds then continued, not looking at him. "That's the problem. We are spending soooo much time together. We have so much fun! Our sexual connection is incredible!"

"And so, the problem is…?" Jim laughed.

Lora took a deep breath. Her heart pounded and she was nervous about where the conversation would lead. "I'm feeling like I could love you but I'm afraid it would only lead to hurt. If I let myself love you and I don't believe in you, my life would be terrible. And, if I let myself believe in you and I'm wrong, it would be much worse than terrible. I'm not sure that I could survive that again."

"I understand your fear," Jim said. "For the 17 years of my marriage, love meant a battle for me. I don't ever want to live that again. So, I'm not ready for love either, but I'm not ready to give up our connection. I'm not pushing for anything more than what we already share. We both agree on fun with no love. Is that too much for you?"

There was a long pause before Lora responded. "No, it's not too much. I'm really glad we had this conversation! Let's stay friends who enjoy each other in every way! We can continue with all the fun without using, or feeling, the "love" word." Lora felt relieved but, at some level that she wouldn't even acknowledge, she also felt a sadness.

The next evening, when Lora was home alone, she started thinking about the "love" word again. She was afraid they both might love each other already and were just afraid to acknowledge it. They both agreed they had never been connected to anyone else with such incredible chemistry in every way – intellectual, physical, love of adventure, perhaps emotional, though they were afraid of that aspect. She had begun to have fantasies of a life with him, but she knew she couldn't give in to it and certainly wouldn't admit it to him.

Their lives moved on with no further discussion of the frightening word, only a continued focus on fun together. Lora found he was a better sailor than Rick and they spent hours on a boat at a local park with a beautiful lake. She joined Jim on a European trip he already had planned with friends. They did a Caribbean cruise together and, after the cruise, he joined her on her annual pilgrimage to the magical Florida destination. She started learning to ski which was one of his passions. They prepared interesting foods and sipped the red wines they both enjoyed. They went to theater productions of musicals and comedies. They sat in local bars listening to their favorite bands. They snuggled before their TVs and slept entwined with each other.

One Friday evening they sat on the sofa in Jim's apartment, and started to discuss what they wanted to do for the weekend. Suddenly Jim paused and looked at Lora.

"This is crazy! Who's going to say it first?"

"Say what?" But Lora thought she knew what he meant.

"Ok. I'll go first. I love you! I want you to be part of my life!"

"Oh my God!" Lora said. "This is still so frightening! But I love you too!"

It was months later when Lora and Jim were driving to her townhouse after buying groceries for another special dinner. They had started to talk about having him move into her townhouse with her and possibly, if all went well, even getting married in the future. Beyond the happiness they found with each other, the trust they felt for each other had grown. They had gradually shared more and more about their prior lives, more and more about anger and sorrow, more and more about pain and betrayal. On this day, Lora started to share her feelings about her quest for a child that may have led her husband to reveal his relationship with "the other."

"It's taken me a while to orient my brain to the fact that there will be no child for me," she said quietly. "Life has become so much fun again because of you and that has helped. I love the feelings and the adventures. I can envision the future that we've talked about sharing. But, sometimes, I still wonder how I will feel looking back on my life when I'm 60 or 70 or maybe even 80."

"Well, you really don't need to orient yourself to that fact if you don't want to," Jim replied. "I'll adopt a baby with you!"

Lora's world stopped as she turned to search his face for a sign. "Could this be real?"

Chapter 46

Gotcha Day

It was an annual event now; something they would repeat again and again as long as any of them drew breath. It was a pilgrimage through time, as memories took them back to the day that tiny bundles forever changed each of their lives. It had also become a celebration of family and friendship as the bonds that joined them became multi-dimensional and grew beyond the links that their daughters provided.

Ten years ago these families, these women, had been strangers. Ten years ago, small bundles were handed from caregivers to arms that waited to give love, guidance, belonging. Ten years ago the prayers of the unknown women in China were answered. Today, after years of laughter, celebrations, shared fears and dreams, they were an integral part of each other's lives. They were more than friends and sometimes closer than family.

This Gotcha Day was the tenth to be celebrated. Gotcha Day was the name given to the celebration of the day each of these families met their daughters for the first time. To these families Gotcha Day was as significant as birthdays. None of the mothers had been there to see the first breaths drawn by their daughters. Neither of the fathers had been there to grasp tiny hands as they began to explore life. So they memorialized and celebrated the moment when their lives became entwined with their daughters.

They were going to begin with dinner at a Chinese restaurant. Then they were all going to Lynne's home for cake, champagne toasts, and remembrances. The girls would play together while the parents talked and teased and laughed.

Each of these women had walked different paths that had converged in China when they met their daughters for the first time. They had lived through fear, heartbreak, uncertainty, and tragedy to feel the joy they experienced as they looked into their daughters' Asian eyes for the first time. At that moment they had become part of the mass exodus of Chinese girls from their home country in the late 1990's and the early 2000's. Each story, and the love for each girl, is unique, special, and very personal. Still, when the history books tell the story, their families will be among the thousands of anonymous families that were formed because of the hardship in China. The pain of thousands of birth mothers had become the genesis of thousands of other families.